2023:V

W9-AEY-602

# Dog Gone, Back Soon

**Also by Nick Trout**

**Tell Me Where It Hurts**
**Love Is the Best Medicine**
**Ever By My Side**
**The Patron Saint of Lost Dogs**

# Dog Gone, Back Soon

## NICK TROUT

**Doubleday Large Print
Home Library Edition**

New York

Hyperion
Hachette Book Group
237 Park Avenue
New York, NY 10017

Hyperion is a division of Hachette Book Group, Inc.

The publisher is not responsible for websites (or their content) that are not owned by the publisher.

Printed in the United States of America

ISBN 978-1-61129-240-4

**For Whitney**

**Yet, taught by time, my heart has learned to glow for other's good, and melt at other's woe.**

**Homer**

# ≪ CONTENTS ≫

# Tuesday

"Pick up, pick up, pick up. No, no, no! Amy, it's me—me as in Cyrus—calling to say . . . just wanted to say sorry, for this evening I mean. Okay, I can come across as too . . . inquisitive, but in my defense, a question is not an accusation, you know?" I take a deep breath, let it out in a long sigh, and realize too late that now I seem impatient. "Look, I'm sorry. Maybe we can try—"

The high-pitched beep in my ear tells me time's up. Damn. I hang up, indicate right, and pull the old Silverado into the parking lot of my new home, The Bedside Manor for Sick Animals. I slump forward over the steering wheel, driving my head into the horn. Just like the missing sun visor and broken reverse gear, the horn on Dad's jalopy must be an optional extra because nothing happens.

"What have I done?"

Yes, I say this out loud and to no one in particular—a question leveled at two particular facets of my new reality. It's January in northern Vermont—ten below—and I've given up everything (and I mean everything) to rescue a decrepit, if not derelict, building that aspires to be a veterinary practice. Rather than an inviting, brightly lit animal hospital, the place lies in shadows, looking haunted, a mugger's paradise or somewhere to score a drug that requires no prescription. Bad enough, but I've just spent the last ninety minutes blowing the best chance I've had in years of connecting with a woman I can't stop thinking about.

I get out and catch a snowman (correction—snowwoman) emerging from an idling car across the lot. It's her ruddy cheeks, flowing pink scarf, black Stetson, and puffy white ski jacket that create the illusion.

"That was quick," she shouts.

"I beg your pardon."

"I only called a few minutes ago. Margot. We spoke on the phone. Doc Lewis, right?"

"No," I say, "I'm Dr. Mills. Doc Lewis is the other vet at the practice. Can I help?"

If she's confusing me with my seventy-three-year-old partner-in-crime then she's clearly not from Eden Falls. Everybody knows everybody in this town.

I look past her as a second figure emerges from her car, the vehicle's interior light spilling over a tall, rangy character in a gray hooded sweatshirt.

"It's Tallulah," says Margot, and then, across the empty lot, she screams, "Gabe, the Unabomber impersonation has been done to death." And then, in a normal voice, "My son, Gabe," before another drill-sergeant cry of "Don't just stand there! Help Tallulah out of the car."

Gabe does as he's told, pulling the hood back to reveal steel-rimmed glasses and a fuzzy 'fro of red hair. When he opens the car's back door, I glimpse what appears to be a large marine mammal. My double take has me rushing over to assist a half second too late to prevent the creature from sliding off the seat and flopping down hard on the rutted ice and snow.

Turns out, despite her pleading, seal-pup eyes and layers of blubber, Tallulah is actually an enormous English mastiff. She doesn't seem to have the use of her legs, making her a formidable dead weight.

"Let's get her up and inside. You got a towel or a blanket that we can use as a sling?"

Margot doesn't hesitate. Ignoring the biting cold, she unzips her coat (to reveal a particularly festive reindeer appliqué sweater) and slips it under Tallulah's belly like an enormous white cummerbund.

"How much does she weigh?" I ask, unlocking the front door and finding a light.

"One ninety-three," says Gabe, coming around to help lift.

**The greatest weight ever recorded for a dog was an English mastiff—343 pounds.**

"What was that?" asks Margot.

I don't bother explaining how I find solace in mumbling obscure facts and trivia during stressful situations but instead reply, "Would you mind calling Doc Lewis?

Let him know I'm here and he can go back to bed."

If Margot nods or replies, I don't see or hear it, as Gabe and I grunt, strain, and stagger our way through the front door and on to the work space in the back. Tallulah is as nimble as a Zeppelin-sized float at the Macy's Thanksgiving Day Parade, her legs making drunken, halfhearted attempts at walking.

"It's my fault," says Gabe, breathless as his dog crumples to the floor in the center of the room. "Theobromine toxicity. She ate a whole tray of chocolate brownies I baked."

I consider the teenage kid pushing his glasses back onto the bridge of his nose. Theobromine is the ingredient in chocolate that is toxic to dogs. How many high school students would know this fact?

"When was this?"

Gabe consults his wristwatch. "Fifty-two minutes ago. We called our regular vets, Healthy Paws in Patton, and paged the doctor on call, but no one called us back. That's why we drove over here."

I decide not to mention that about an hour ago Amy had spotted the entire veterinary staff of Healthy Paws, loud and loose-tongued, on the far side of the noisy bar she had suggested for our ill-fated first date. I guess that explains why Gabe didn't get a call back.

"He's not picking up," says Margot, sans Stetson, letting me see where Gabe gets his hair color and texture. "My little girl's going to be okay, yeah?"

I grab my stethoscope and get down on the floor with her "little girl." Tallulah's out of it, neck outstretched, head flat to the floor, eyes closed, jowls wet and droopy like a sad, sloppy frown.

I listen to her heart—thirty beats per minute—really slow, even for a dog of this magnitude.

"Has she vomited?" I ask.

"No," says Margot. She checks in with Gabe, who seems to deliberate before shaking his head in agreement.

I lift up a heavy eyelid. Tallulah's left eye is unfocused, eerily black because her pupils are almost fully dilated.

"Could you pass me that thermometer? On the counter."

Gabe obliges, but I catch the nervous tremor in his hand.

"This is your fault, Gabe," says Margot. "You and that girlfriend of yours."

"She's not my girlfriend," Gabe protests, but the blush in his cheeks begs to differ.

Margot folds her arms across her chest. "Okay, so what happened to this . . . friend . . . who happens to be a girl? Funny how she had to rush off."

"I told you, this has nothing to do with her."

"I even cooked a cobbler for supper. Why bother with brownies at this time of night?"

Still holding on to the thermometer, I realize where I've seen Gabe. Or rather, someone who looks like him. Remove the glasses and he's Art Garfunkel in **Catch-22**. (Hey, I happen to love classic movies, but if you prefer pop culture, leave the glasses on and go with **Napoleon Dynamite**).

Gabe ignores the question. "We need to make her throw up, right, Dr. Mills? I read online how that's one of the first things you do for chocolate poisoning."

I check Tallulah's temperature—97.2°F— way too low.

**The most expensive dog ever sold**

**was a red Tibetan mastiff named Big Splash, the price tag: $1.5 million.**

I study Margot and Gabe. For all the similarities in their features, two distinct and separate facial expressions capture my attention: concern on hers, guilt on his.

Getting to my feet, I say, "This was a store-bought brownie mix?"

Gabe nods. "But I added chocolate chips," he says. "Lots of them."

"What's a lot?"

"Couldn't have been more than six ounces, half a bag," says Margot. "That's all we had in the pantry."

Six ounces of chocolate ingested by a 193-pound dog.

"And the chips were what, semisweet chocolate?"

"That's right," says Margot. "Hershey's."

The expression in Gabe's eyes has transitioned from shame through remorse to beseeching.

Tallulah's clumsiness, low body temperature, slow heart rate, and dilated pupils tell me Gabe may have been making brownies, but they were almost certainly laced with something more interesting to a teenage boy than chocolate chips.

I hear the chime of the old shopkeeper's bell that sits over the front door, and Dr. Fielding Lewis appears. It's after eleven at night, but he's still sporting one of his trademark silk bow ties—wisteria and blue plaid.

"Ah, I see the good Dr. Mills is already on the case. What's going on?"

"Sorry, Lewis. Ms. . . ."

"Stiles," says Margot. "Margot Stiles. And this is my son, Gabe."

Gabe manages a sheepish nod.

"Ms. Stiles did try to call you back and tell you not to come," I say, "but since you're here, maybe you could give me a hand. Where do we keep the activated charcoal? Tallulah has an acute case of semisweet chocolate poisoning."

Lewis considers the collapsed dog on the floor before eyeing me with overt skepticism. He reaches down, feels for Tallulah's femoral pulse, inspects her pupils, and claps in her ear. Tallulah doesn't even flinch.

"You quite sure of your diagnosis?" says Lewis, pulling a large plastic syringe from a drawer, filling it half-full of water, and ladling in enough black powder to make a gruesome-looking slurry. "Only, to me, it looks much more like . . ."

"Baking chocolate," I say, too loudly, snatching the syringe from him. "Yes, you would think . . . but Tallulah's clinical signs are practically pathognomonic."

"Patho-what?" says Margot, visibly suspicious of our contrived banter.

"Pathognomonic," says Gabe, deflecting her skepticism. "It means characteristic of a particular disease."

"Very good, young man," says Lewis. "You have a bright son, Ms. Stiles."

Margot appears to vacillate, caught between accepting the diagnosis and the compliment about her son. "Yes, well, if he'd stop playing on that computer of his and pay more attention to what's going on in the real world around him, perhaps my poor dog wouldn't be in this state. She is going to be okay, isn't she?"

"Definitely," I say, almost too quickly and in unison with Lewis saying, "Of course." The two of us share a moment of understanding of what we are keeping to ourselves. Time to clear the air.

"Lewis, would you mind taking some basic information from Ms. Stiles so we can start a file for Tallulah? Gabe and I will set about getting her warmed up and starting some IV fluids."

Lewis looks like he actually does mind until I catch his eye and jerk my head in the direction of the waiting room, urging him to get Margot away from her son so we can have a word in private.

"Here," I say, handing Gabe a tower of clean towels and blankets. "Wrap her up in these while I grab an IV catheter and a bag of warm fluids."

Gabe does as he's told, creating an inviting nest, leaving Tallulah's forlorn face poking out like she's wearing a babushka. He kneels down on the floor next to her, closes his eyes, presses his pimply temple into the vast wrinkly dome of her forehead, and whispers, "I'm sorry."

Let me be clear, I don't do pep talks or shoulder squeezes with virtual strangers. For the past fourteen years I relished working as a veterinary pathologist. The only patients I examined were deceased. This line of work nicely avoided awkward, emotionally fraught confrontations with the pet-owning public, which was fine with me, until just over a week ago when I took over my late father's practice, Bedside Manor (yes, I appreciate the irony in this ridiculous name).

"If you must know," I say, squatting down and gesturing to the unresponsive brindle blob on the floor, "your dog is on the verge of a coma caused by the ingestion of tetrahy-drocannabinol. It seems pretty clear the canine ganja high is not a pleasurable experience."

Gabe can't meet my eyes. Interesting. It's definitely a little easier to do preachy over touchy-feely. So long as he doesn't think I'm offering fatherly advice.

"How did you know?" he whispers.

I smile. He's petrified. I could let him suffer a little longer but instead say, "Look, I'm not going to tell your mom, so relax." Gabe reaches out, pats Tallulah, and this rouses her enough to open her lids. Her eyes roll up, revealing waning crescent moons around the edges, the little-girl-lost effect noticeably compounding Gabe's sense of shame.

"For what it's worth, fatal marijuana ingestion is pretty much unheard of in dogs. And I knew because her signs were all wrong. Chocolate toxicity makes dogs hyper, nervous, with a racing pulse. Tallulah's clearly stoned. She's the one who got baked this evening. Here, let me show you how to raise a vein so I can place this catheter."

Gabe seems eager to be involved, to physically help out, and as we get her hooked up to fluids he talks about a recipe for pot brownies he found online. Clearly his use of the word **epic** differs from mine.

"Mom'll kill me if she finds out. I'll be without a computer for like . . . a **week**."

I flick some air bubbles in the line with my finger just like in the movies. Gabe makes an Internet-free seven days sound like a sentence on death row.

"I swear I'd never harm her. She won't have any permanent damage, will she?"

I look over at Tallulah, resting comfortably, and think about Gabe's question.

**Mastiffs rank number eight in the list of—how best to put this?—most intellectually challenged breeds of dog.**

"No," I say, keeping the "not so as you'd notice" to myself.

"Thanks, Doc, for everything. You know . . . for keeping this . . . between us. I owe you."

"Sure, but don't worry about it."

Gabe presses his glasses into the bridge of his nose again. It's like a nervous tic.

"Where are you from, Doc? Your accent?"

I can't tell if he's making conversation or snooping.

"Here, originally, but I've spent the past twenty-five years in and around the Carolinas."

Gabe gets to his feet, visibly deliberates, and then asks, "You married? Dating? Got a significant other?"

Definitely snooping. Don't tell me he's trying to set me up with the snowwoman.

"Let's keep our focus on the patient," I say, nodding to the sleepy beached whale.

The kid regards me with a vapid expression worthy of his frizzy-haired doppelganger when his mom walks back into the work area with Lewis in tow.

"How we doing?" she asks.

"Good," I say, as Lewis hands over the new file he's put together. "We've got Tallulah set up for the night. Pretty sure she'll be able to go home tomorrow."

Margot eases herself down, pinches both of Tallulah's doughy cheeks, and plants a drawn-out kiss on the dog's snout like the creepy aunt children try to avoid at family gatherings.

"Most expensive brownies of all time." Margot waves for a hand up. "Gabe, what do you say to the doctors?"

Gabe assists his mom before stepping over to Lewis, deferentially bowing from the neck. Then, pointing to the manila folder in my hand, he says to me, "You ever want to go paperless, let me know."

Margot lights up. "Maybe we can barter on the bill? My son's a genius with computers."

Lewis seems intrigued by the offer.

"Thanks, Ms. Stiles," I say, "but I'm pretty sure we won't be computerizing our record keeping anytime soon."

I hope that sounded like a polite refusal rather than a desperate need for actual cash.

Lewis reads her disappointment and swoops in. "We can sort out the bill tomorrow," he says, ushering them toward the front door. "Have a good night. Give us a call in the morning."

Neither of us speaks until the chime of the shopkeeper's bell confirms that they've gone.

"Baking chocolate?" Lewis says with a bemused smile.

It's nearly midnight, and this old man with his steely thatch of hair is not only wide awake, he's actually enjoying himself.

"I know. Lucky for me, marijuana poisoning was one of the few intoxicants I recall from my days as a vet student. In dogs, not people. I mean, I never—"

"Of course, Cyrus," says Lewis, stepping in. "Have to say, I'm impressed by your . . . your . . ."

"What?"

He searches for the word. "Benevolence," he utters, looking pleased with himself.

If this is a compliment, I ignore it. My motive was simple—figure out the problem and solve it. And also avoid an embarrassing scene.

"Smart kid, but obviously not smart enough," says Lewis. "Mom wouldn't stop going on about his addiction to computers. Let's hope that's the least of her worries. Now, to more pressing issues. You all set with your license to practice?"

"Yes, sir." If the "sir" sounds too formal, blame my time in the south. For the last three days, I was back in Charleston making sure I'm not going to get arrested for impersonating a veterinarian.

"Excellent. You get back in time?"

He's referring to my much awaited but postponed first date with Amy, one of the waitresses from the Miss Eden Falls diner in the center of town. Not much gets past Lewis. The phrase **an elephant never forgets** refers to the way these pachyderms pass on a genetic memory of directions and locality, including their loved ones' final resting place. Lewis may lack total recall, but he's clearly watching my every move.

"Yep," I say curtly, hoping he'll back off.

"How did it go?"

No such luck.

"Not well."

Lewis folds his arms across his chest, eases back in his stance, obviously awaiting details.

"Look, I'm out of practice at this dating game. Amy got this phone call that she simply **had** to take, so I'm twiddling my thumbs for a full twelve minutes and then she's all cagey about who it was and—"

"Well, knowing Amy it must have been

important. She apologized for taking the call?"

"Yeah."

"But she wouldn't tell you who she was talking to?"

"She wouldn't answer any of my questions."

Lewis leans forward. "**Questions**, plural? Not a good idea."

"That's what I said. 'Maybe this wasn't such a good idea.' And Amy said, 'Tonight or coming home to Eden Falls?' That was just before she stormed off."

"Let me guess, you replied, 'Both'?"

I hang my head in shame and then feel my left bicep squeezed by his trademark lobster claw grip and meet the slate gray eyes of this little old man.

"Take it from someone who's been married for fifty years," says Lewis, "women are not attracted to insecure, pushy men."

As if to emphasize his point, my right bicep gets the vise grip as well.

"Call her. Apologize." He waits a beat before adding, "Besides, isn't all this about second chances?"

How does Lewis do it, the way he manages to angle his head up, unblinking, to peek inside you?

"I saw what happened to you last week," he says. "Coming home, taking this place on. Something hibernating in your life woke up, right?"

I say nothing. Blame guilt or a craving for redemption, but I walked away from my old life as a respected pathologist (okay, there was the matter of a suspended license and huge legal bills) and committed to saving the late Bobby Cobb's floundering, debt-ridden practice. For fifteen years, after the death of my mother, I willfully never saw or spoke to my father again. Last week, Bedside Manor taught me what a fool I'd been. It's his legacy, all that's left of him, and I woke up because I caught a glimpse of something worth fighting for.

One last double-barreled squeeze and Lewis turns his attention to taking another rectal temperature on Tallulah. Our patient barely notices.

"Ninety-nine. Much better. Nice to upstage Healthy Paws," he says. "It's not often we get new clients from over in Patton."

Patton lies across the valley, and with a population five times the size of Eden Falls, it can sustain a mall, movie theater, and chain restaurants, making it a metropolis compared to our little town.

"Amy and I were out that way," I say. "The Yardarm. She saw them, the vets from Healthy Paws. Out celebrating I guess. The bar was packed and I couldn't make them out, except some guy with an annoying, distinctive laugh."

Lewis offers a sage nod. "Let me guess, braying donkey meets croupy pig?"

"That's the one."

"He's their office manager. And that laugh may be his most charming feature. According to Doris, he's declared war on Bedside Manor."

Doris is the Bedside Manor's only other employee—a chain-smoking, beehive-wearing, geriatric receptionist who makes it her business to know everything about everybody. I am not surprised to hear her gossip network extends out to Patton.

"Come on. War?"

"This is serious, Cyrus. Round these parts Doris provides better intelligence than a CIA drone. Healthy Paws was convinced you'd either default or sell the practice to them. Apparently our little trick with the free clinic last weekend has set them on edge."

Before I left for Charleston, we opened up the practice to the public, trying to attract new business with the promise of a free examination for their pets. To be honest, the accompanying free booze and munchies were probably the bigger attractions. Somehow we clawed back enough bad debt to temporarily stave off closure by the odious Mr. Critchley of Green State Bank.

"Look at this place. Sometimes I wonder if my father used the word **manor** instead of **clinic** or **hospital** to avoid false advertising. We're not in the same league."

Lewis steps into my personal space again, and I try not to flinch. "Sure, we lack their bells and whistles. But they're still worried about the competition."

"That's ridiculous."

"Not at all. Think about it, Healthy Paws is a national chain. Doris's source swears their doctors are jealous of the way we get to practice veterinary medicine. And I mean the scary type of jealous."

A scary type of jealous? Is that how I acted when Amy insisted she had to take her phone call ten minutes into our date, going all wide-eyed and animated on me, feigning her apology as she giggled with the caller on the other end of the line?

I come back with a dubious nasal huff.

"I'm not kidding," says Lewis. "Healthy Paws eats up struggling practices for breakfast. Their unofficial catch-phrase is 'If we can't have you, nobody else can.'"

What have I done? Gone for three days and now I've got a rival for Amy's affection as well as a rival for our business. As it is I'm hopelessly romantically challenged and Bedside Manor's already received last rites.

I take a deep breath, mustering renewed resolve. "Well, like you said, Lewis, this is about second chances. Yes, I'm out of my league, comfort zone, and probably, my mind, but if you're willing to fight then so am I. I mean how bad can this be? Surely a little competition will do us good?"

Lewis looks up at me with his piercing eyes, his tightening crow's feet adding to my unease. "Listen to me. This makes handling the bank look easy. Pay up and at least the bank leaves you alone. This is different. This is about professional reputation. This is about quality of service. Healthy Paws employees play dirty, and they'd love to expose our flaws and our antiquated ways. They'll try to highlight every weakness because for Healthy Paws this is personal. This is about humiliation. I wish it was just about competition, but I'm telling you, they don't want to compete. They want to wipe us out. They want to bring Bedside Manor to its knees."

# Wednesday

« **2** »

Living in the apartment over the practice, my childhood home, feels like a blessing and a curse. Great commute in the morning but no possibility of truly escaping from work. Given this new development, maybe that's not a bad thing. If the rival practice thinks Bedside Manor is going to roll over and pee like a submissive dog, it's very much mistaken. And that's why I jog down the flight of stairs and step into the waiting room like the president stepping off Air Force One, a distinct pep to my stride.

It's my first morning of appointments since getting back to Eden Falls, and what's this? A Christmas miracle—the waiting room is full.

"Good morning, Doris. Don't suppose there are any urgent messages for me?"

From behind the reception desk, the mocking arch of her penciled-in eyebrows is all the answer I need. Damn. Still nothing from Amy.

"A word in your ear, Dr. Mills," says Doris, the summons enforced by a nicotine-stained index finger insisting I come closer.

"Looks like a full house," I say under my breath, trying to contain my delight. "Guess the word must be out."

Doris eases back her chin and narrows her eyes as though she can't decide whether to pity me or stamp on me. For the record, Doris's loyalty still lies with my father, the late Doc Cobb, and she harbors a grudge for the son who was never there for him. I'm not sure I'll ever be forgiven (or if I deserve to be), but I sense there are moments, however brief, when she almost approves of what I'm trying to do to save this place. This might not be one of them.

"You seen this crew?" Doris asks. "Take a closer look."

Her eyebrows jump with a "well, go on then" ferocity, and I do as I'm told. It seems everyone on two legs, four legs, and no legs—a yellow python drapes over the shoulders of a teenage boy with what looks like brass knuckles tattooed into his neck—is staring at me, and to some extent, I see what she means. Dog collars and leashes have been replaced by lengths of frayed rope; cats are restrained not by carriers but by nylon shopping bags or ratty, partially unzipped ski jackets.

"Could have told you that free clinic last Saturday was a bad idea," says Doris. "All it did was bring back the low-rent pet owners we've already sent to collections. You won't get a dime out of this lot."

An imaginary itch at the back of my neck gets the better of me. I hate public speaking, but I think this is the time to air an unpleasant truth.

I turn to address a blank but attentive crowd. "Ladies and gentlemen, um . . . thank you all for coming in this morning, but I need to draw your attention to this particular notice."

I point to my handwritten poster pinned to the wall.

PAYMENT IN FULL IS EXPECTED FOR SERVICES RENDERED.

"Hate to be so, um . . . so direct, but this is not a free animal clinic."

The room swells with moans and curses. I even catch a "told you" as pets perk up and people stand before shuffling out through the chiming front door as though they clearly came to the wrong place. In seconds, what was a packed waiting room has been pared down to just two people and two dogs. There's a straight-backed, stern-looking woman with an excitable, even squirrelly boxer by her side and a middle-aged man with a poodle. The man locks eyes with me, mulling me over. His face is beyond gaunt, his skin more translucent than ashen. The collar of his shirt gapes widely, accentuating the size of his head on a pipe-cleaner neck. And there's his black, almost woolly dog, aside from a few tan-colored whiskers around his snout. This scruffy specimen must be the biggest version of the poodle breed, the standard (as opposed to toy or miniature). He wears no leash, standing perfectly still, staring straight up at his master, oblivious to his surroundings as if bracing for a command.

"Here's the file for your first case," says Doris, handing over a wafer-thin folder.

I open it and notice there's no previous history—a new client with an address in the neighboring town of Patton. Interesting.

"Ms. Sauer and . . . Sox," I announce, noticing how all four paws of the tap-dancing fawn boxer are a brilliant white. "If you'll please follow me."

I lead the way to my examination room. The standard poodle never flinches, never blinks, so intent is his devotion to the sickly-looking man.

"I'm here 'cause I can't stand that other vet practice, Healthy Paws," says Ms. Sauer, "especially that . . . well, I won't say the word . . . but that . . . that Dr. Honey."

Ms. Sauer almost dry heaves as she says the name. She's a short woman with pinched features, twitching predatory eyes, and barely any lips on which to hang a pale pink halo of lipstick. Though her voice is shrill, her words are music to my ears. In my past life as a veterinary pathologist, I managed to avoid any and all banal banter with the pet-owning public. Now that I'm a **real** veterinarian, Lewis insists I be warm, straightforward, and engaging. What he's really saying is stop being so cold, unnecessarily scientific, and downright hostile. Well, when it comes to Ms. Sauer, I'm all in, for here's a woman not only stroking my ego by asking for a second opinion, but bent on despising my professional rivals. I can hardly wait to hear more about this reprobate Dr. Honey.

"Here are his records." Ms. Sauer hands over a thick file of photocopied notes. "Sox is only a year old, and aside from vaccines and worming and what have you, these are pretty much all about his lump."

I look over at Sox. There's a lot of snuffling and throaty gargling going on as he snorts and sniffs his way around the room like he's rooting for truffles. That's when I notice his most conspicuous feature—his tail. He actually has one—not a nubbin, not a docked stump—a full-fledged wagging tail.

"Nice to see a boxer with a tail," I say, taking her notes.

"We got her from Nova Scotia. They don't allow docking."

I'm barely listening because I'm transfixed by the medical records, financial statements, and, of all things, a wad of coupons. The workup for what has been described as a red, raised, one- by one-centimeter hairless skin lump over Sox's right shoulder is both exhaustive and, from what I can tell, extremely costly. Ms. Sauer's MasterCard has been soaking up some serious dollars, and some of these tests appear to be, well, questionable, if not unnecessary. Why did Sox need his urine analyzed? What did a test for Lyme disease have to do with a skin problem? For now I'll try to give Dr. Honey the benefit of the doubt—and assume she was just being thorough, not gratuitous.

The glossy flyers find me less charitable. There's an offer for fifty dollars off all ultrasounds and X-rays, and one for free grooming or a soothing doggy massage if you get your dog spayed and vaccinated at Healthy Paws. Soothing doggy massage? When did choices in animal health-care start to feel like shopping for deals on groceries? Apparently, a lot has changed since I graduated from veterinary school.

"So this mysterious lump, how long has it been around?"

"About a month," says Ms. Sauer. "She

did all these tests, like the computer told her to, and we're still no further along."

"She being Dr. Honey?"

"Yes."

"And she . . . she . . . um, uses a computer to communicate?"

"No, course not," she snaps. "The place is paperless, computerized. Dr. Honey types into her laptop thingy and up pops a list of the tests and procedures needed to diagnose and cure the problem. Pretty fancy, only it didn't work so good with Sox."

I lean back and purse my lips, totally perplexed. "Let me get this straight. Healthy Paws has a computer program that tells its doctors what to do?" I stop short of saying, "And how to think?"

"Exactly," affirms a wide-eyed Ms. Sauer, as Sox grumbles over what appears to be a toenail clipping under a counter, thankfully just out of reach of his ropey pink tongue. "Oh, they'll tell you it ensures 'optimal patient care.'" Out come the air quotation marks. "But I'm thinking it's just a fancy way of getting every penny out of you that they possibly can."

My eyes drift to the corkboard hanging on the green wall behind her. It's home to a collage of family photos, but it's the picture at its heart that has my focus. It's one of me as a boy sitting on my mother's lap, my father, Robert, smiling, his eyes half-closed, by our side. It's the only tangible memory I have of the three of us together as a family, and I wonder what the man who left me this ailing practice would have made of this brave new world of veterinary medicine. Bobby Cobb was your classic, old-school animal doctor, cut from the same cloth as Lewis. He lived to fix sick animals. Ask the right questions, get your hands on the animal, trust your five senses, use your brain, your experience, your gut instinct, and don't cut corners. Making money was never part of the formula. Connecting with the patient and the owner was all that mattered. No wonder Cobb was revered as a local deity while his business was going belly-up. How do I find a happy medium?

"Um, so how long ago did you notice the lump?" I ask, shaking out of my reverie, attempting to channel my late father.

Ms. Sauer stiffens. "You already asked that. Like I said, 'bout a month."

"Right. Got it. Getting bigger, smaller?"

Ms. Sauer shrugs. "Staying about the same."

**Come on, Cyrus, keep going.** Maybe the Healthy Paws computer program isn't such a bad idea, especially if it gives you ideas for what to say next.

"Does it bother him? Does he try to scratch it, rub it, lick it?"

"No, he couldn't care less."

**What else? What else?** And then, with haste, as though time is running out, "Oh yeah, and this lump, is it the only one he's got?"

My excitement at mustering a pertinent question only makes Ms. Sauer regard me with even more suspicion. Or is that regret?

"So far as I can tell," she says, becoming impatient. "Look, Doc Honey stuck a needle into it and had it sent off to be reviewed by some fancy pathologist. Even they couldn't tell me what it was."

I could let her know that every so often a sample will simply not yield an answer despite your best efforts, but instead I shake my head, purse my lips, and join her in a moment of eye-rolling astonishment and disgust.

"Now Doc Honey wants to put poor Sox under the knife and lop it off, even though she and her damned computer can't tell me what it is. She says it could be a bug bite, it could be cancer, but surgery is the only way to know for sure."

**Hmm, boxers are the number one breed of dog for skin tumors, by far.**

"What was that?"

"Oh, nothing, just thinking how skin cancer may be common in boxers but unusual in such a young dog." Though not impossible, I keep to myself. "Okay, let's take a look."

Sox leans into me, happy to deposit a dollop of stringy drool near the crotch of my chinos as I check out the strawberry-colored bald bump on the point of his shoulder. My fingers pinch and squeeze his mysterious lesion while my brain churns with the possibilities. Presumably the Healthy Paws computer wanted to test for Lyme disease in case the bump was caused by a tick bite. But what about a brown recluse spider bite? What about a cyst or an in-growing hair follicle? What if the program has a glitch or the computer goes rogue?

"I'd like to try sticking a needle into the

lump, aspirate some cells, and take a look at it myself."

"What makes you so sure you'd do any better? And more importantly, how much will all this cost?"

Lewis warned me about the folks around these parts, suggesting they respond best to a no-nonsense honest approach that I, with my southern sensibilities, find perilously close to rudeness.

"Well, I'm pretty good with a microscope." She eases back in her stance, head canting to one side as her lower jaw slides forward to show me the entire lower arcade of her incisors. Did she learn this trick from Sox? I can't tell whether she finds me defiant or arrogant. Tactic number two—when all else fails, appeal to the pocketbook. "Tell you what, if I don't get a diagnosis, I won't charge for trying."

Even with that generous offer Ms. Sauer still deliberates, but she eventually consents. A few minutes later, armed with a glass slide smeared with cellular debris from Sox's lump, I head on back into the work area to find Lewis, coffee mug in hand, leaning into the counter with a copy of the day's **Eden Falls Gazette**.

"Morning, Cyrus. Good to see your mastiff looks better." Lewis raises his cup in the direction of Tallulah, who stands at the front of her run, tail wagging, eager for attention or perhaps a jumbo-sized bag of Cheetos. "What you got there?"

Lewis notices me dipping my slide into a series of small glass vats containing blue and crimson stains and waving it in the air like a Fourth of July sparkler. I need it to dry before I slip it under the microscope lens and unmask its secret.

"A second opinion," I say, taking a seat in front of the scope. "Disgruntled client from our mortal enemies at Healthy Paws. What d'you make of that clairvoyant computer program they've got over there?"

Lewis turns the page and takes a sip. "Ridiculous. You can't apply a set formula to fit every pet ailment." He meets my eye and winks. "Besides, takes all the fun out of it, right?"

"Maybe, but it probably makes good business sense," I say. "Maximal billing disguised as good medicine."

Lewis puts his mug down, closes the paper, and comes over to where I'm sitting. Again, he squeezes my shoulder with his best Vulcan death grip. I'm beginning to appreciate how the pain is proportional to the gravity of what he's about to impart. "The day I run a test or offer a pill simply to make money is the day I hang up my stethoscope. Let's you and I focus on good medicine, and the bills will get paid."

He's right. And then it hits me. "That's it. That's what we'll do. What you and my father have always done. We'll set ourselves apart by promoting our old-fashioned approach to veterinary medicine."

Lewis's fuzzy-gray-caterpillar eyebrows knit together as one. "Not sure we want to highlight the old-fashioned. Sounds antiquated, out of date, ready for the boneyard."

"No, no. I'm talking about our style: the way we practice and the services we offer. Think classic, vintage, and timeless. Think friendly, warm, and homey."

Lewis looks even more skeptical.

"Did you just say homey?"

"Okay, well at least you're friendly. But bottom line, it's personalized, not computerized."

Lewis concedes a nod. "Hey, maybe you should see if Tallulah's owner, Panama Red, can hack into their program and shut it down. Then we'll see whether the Healthy Paws vets can actually think for themselves."

I assume he's joking. At least I hope he is.

"Anyway, best get going. If you're free later this morning, I'd appreciate your opinion on one of my house calls."

"Of course," I say, slipping the prepared slide under the clips on the stage of the microscope, letting my fingers twitch and flutter with the focus adjustment knobs, cozying my cornea up to the eyepiece.

"Excellent," I hear over my shoulder. "Ask Doris for the directions." My reply is no more than a perfunctory grunt. I'm distracted by what Sox's sample is telling me, written in a familiar language of foamy cytoplasm and juicy round nuclei. My aspirate is good, plenty of decent cells—what I don't see is just as important as what I do.

"Sorry to keep you waiting, Ms. Sauer, but I have good news." I'm smiling as I return to the exam room, energized, relishing this opportunity to one-up Healthy Paws. "It turns out this little lump is indeed a true surgical emergency."

"Oh my God. What are you saying? Now Sox needs emergency surgery?"

Ms. Sauer drops to her knees, her permanent scowl resembling a downturned bass mouth, draping her arms around her boxer's neck as Sox sets to work, licking up her tears. My attempt at clinical levity has clearly backfired.

"No, no, no," I stammer. "Sox is going to be fine. The lump is what's called a cutaneous histiocytoma. It's totally benign. Most of them spontaneously regress." I can see I've lost her again. "Most of them disappear in a month or two on their own. See? It's an old veterinary joke."

Sniffling, wiping more drool off her eyes than tears, she says, "What is?"

"The need for emergency surgery. If Sox doesn't get surgery soon, it will be too late. You'll have missed the chance to make money because the lump will have disappeared."

I flash my brows, trying to convey "Get it?" but her thin lips compress into a pale and indignant grimace.

"That's not funny. You're telling me Healthy Paws wanted to make my Sox have risky anesthesia and put him through a pointless surgery on a lump that'll go away on its own?"

"Well, I'm sure that wasn't their intent when—"

"I knew it. I knew that bitch doctor was trying to rip me off." I guess Ms. Sauer is angry enough to actually use the b-word.

"Please, Ms. Sauer," I say, hamming up the ecclesiastical open palms spread wide before me. "Let's just be glad I could make the diagnosis." But then, unable to resist, I add in my most syrupy voice, "At least you know Sox will be well taken care of at Bedside Manor."

I'm pretty sure she sees that my fake smile is more about gloating than sincerity.

Ms. Sauer sniffs deeply, gets to her feet, and deliberates before picking up Sox's leash.

"I'm grateful," she says, somewhat tersely. "And yes, I'll be transferring Sox's care to you. But that lot over at Healthy Paws haven't heard the last from me."

Though this threat of negative publicity for our rivals might prove useful, it doesn't sit well with me.

"Ms. Sauer, can I be frank? I'm not sure going to the State Veterinary Board or the

**Eden Falls Gazette** is the best way to deal with this."

Sox shakes his head, saliva strands cart-wheeling end over end, flecking the front of my shirt. Ms. Sauer looks appalled.

"Oh, don't worry. I wasn't thinking of either of those."

I reach forward to shake her hand. "That's great. I'm relieved."

She holds my grip, and I watch as the devil dances in her eyes.

"I'll simply be chatting to Doris on the way out."

Her smug grin coincides with the paralysis affecting my lower jaw as it becomes my turn to impersonate a heavily jowled and drooling boxer.

**Everybody knows everyone in this town**. And no one more so than Doris. The tale of what I imagine will soon be Sox's near brush with death is about to go viral.

« **3** »

When I return to the waiting room, the man jumping out of his seat and charging my way is not the man I expected. This man is stocky and mustachioed, hand outstretched and ready for a shake, all business. I try to look past him to see what became of the sickly man and his devoted standard poo-dle. I wonder why they decided to leave.

"Cyrus. Pleasure to finally meet you. Guy Dorkin. I was in the neighborhood and thought what the heck, take a chance on introducing myself even though I don't have an appointment." Dorkin makes a show of turning left and then right as though he's sizing up the empty room. "Looks like I didn't need one."

And that's when he lets loose with a feral, distinctive laugh that I instantly recognize. It's that skin-crawling mix of wheezy donkey bray on the inhalation and hyena cackle on the exhalation. It's the one I heard at the bar last night. The man refusing to let go of my grip is none other than the office manager of Healthy Paws.

I make three quick observations about his greeting. He's trying to crush me, he's trying to pull me toward him, and he's twisting his wrist so his hand lies on top. What's that all about? Managing to break free, I sense an unpleasant stickiness lingering in my palm. Hopefully it's only a remnant of the stiff gel he's using to enforce the **Tintin** cowlick at the prow of his hairline.

"Pretty ballsy play you made the other day." Dorkin's got to be my age—late thirties, early forties—his black cashmere coat over a pin-striped suit and matching silk tie a little too dapper, a little too sharp for these parts. And the mustache has to be an experiment that went wrong. Perhaps it started out as a full beard, morphed into a goatee, and got downsized to its present state. Not quite seventies porn star specifications, it still draws the onlooker to Dorkin's meaty lips and the sizeable gap between his two front teeth.

"Not sure I'm with you, Mr. Dorkin."

"Guy. Guy. Lighten up, fella." There's a mischievous slap to my upper arm. "The free clinic you ran last week. I totally get it. Speculate to accumulate. Either folks flock to you in droves or they take advantage and you never see hide nor hair of them again." He throws up his hands, the laugh replaced by a sympathetic consolatory headshake. "Guess you got your answer."

"We're doing okay . . . Guy," I say, accentuating his name while jutting my chin toward the front desk. "Busy enough. In fact, one of your new clients is just leaving," I say, nodding toward the reception desk.

Ms. Sauer, caught in a conspiratorial huddle with Doris, glances our way, the sibilant hiss of their whispers falling silent. I watch with satisfaction as Dorkin's expression begins with indifference, passes through a moment of confusion, explodes with a flash of recognition (not sure if it's the dog or the owner), and finishes with a mask of supreme concern. It takes him a few seconds to shake it off.

"Look," he says, still striving to be Mr. Congeniality, "I dropped by 'cause I got a phone call from Critchley at Green State Bank. He says you're definitely no longer interested in selling."

Dorkin's grimace insists Mr. Critchley must have made a mistake.

"That's correct. Bedside Manor is no longer on the market."

Dorkin shifts his weight and acts surprised. "Really?"

"Yes, really."

His theatrical moment of hesitation is broken by another signature burst of laughter, followed by a playful punch to my upper arm.

"Good for you, Cy. Good for you."

Cy. No one has ever referred to me as Cy. In a matter of minutes Dorkin's gone from total stranger to baptizing me with a new nickname. And what's with all this physical contact? Is the frat boy yearning for the good old days at Tau Kappa Epsilon?

"No, that's great. But—full disclosure—your timing could have been better. Okay, your timing sucks. I mean, I wish you the best, but it's a tough market, you know?"

In my head I can hear Lewis telling me, **They want to wipe us out. They want to bring Bedside Manor to its knees**. I can't help myself.

"So why was Healthy Paws interested in buying this place then?"

Dorkin makes a gun out of his cocked thumb and pointy index finger, aims it my way, and clicks his tongue. "Good question. But to answer it, you should know who you're dealing with."

I almost say, "A total douche bag?" but keep quiet.

"Last quarter, my practice kicked serious ass."

The "my" is not lost on me.

"Number one Healthy Paws in New England when you figure in per capita head of population."

I'm not much of an actor, but my attempt at awe may have come across as disbelief.

"Cause for celebration, I imagine."

"You betcha," says Dorkin. "Me and the vets went out the other night. Had a blast."

I nod, flashing back to the scene at the bar, wishing I could hit the rewind button and start over with Amy. Given the amount of background noise fueled by drunken revelry, I wonder which veterinarian forgot to put his pager on vibrate and missed the emergency call for Tallulah, the stoned mastiff.

"Anyhoo, my point is I crunched the numbers, so you know they're solid, and yeah, so long as I used one of our existing doctors from Patton, not a new hire, this place could serve as a satellite."

"Satellite?"

"Yep, deal with the minor stuff here, but essentially feed the decent cases back to the mother ship, where we can do things right."

Dorkin leans in close enough for me to fully appreciate his coffee breath. "You see, Cyrus"—his voice has dropped to a deferential whisper—"I calculated this place to be unsustainable as a full-time facility. Why? Easy. Eden Falls doesn't have the population to draw on, and what you do have is never going to fork over the big bucks."

Dorkin flashes his brows as if he has provided proof positive, waits a beat, and then hits me with: "Hey, you and I should go out sometime, grab a beer."

If he punches me again, I might actually have to punch him back. Only I'll be aiming for his face.

"Yeah, you can be my wingman." Dorkin begins to sway at his hips, his hands open-palmed and stretched out before him as though he's beating out a rhythm on imaginary bongos. "You've got that brooding thing going on—good-looking and, best of all, that southern accent. Let me guess— Charleston?"

Clearly Dorkin's done his homework because Charleston is no guess. But good-looking? I've been told I have my father's kind blue eyes but I have nothing "going on" around the opposite sex. Just ask Amy.

And wingman? **I feel the need . . . the need for speed.** I swear I will never be Goose to his Maverick.

"Yes, Charleston. But you're telling me Patton, a town five times the size of Eden Falls, can support four full-time veterinarians, whereas Eden Falls can't support even one?"

Dorkin forces a sigh, as though he can't believe I still don't get it. "See, we're coming out of a recession, people have to cut back, cut corners, and, for the first time, pets are paying the price. Look, I was invited to spearhead a national advisory committee on the future of veterinary practice for Healthy Paws, so this heads-up is current, accurate, and free of charge. Two words: buckle up. If the likes of corporate practices are bracing for a bumpy ride, mom-and-pop places like this are going to get tossed aside and left for roadkill."

There's the chime of the front doorbell. Ms. Sauer and Sox are finally heading out, Doris shouting after them, "I'll give you a call when it's time for his vaccines." Funny how Doris has cranked up her volume control to eleven, broadcasting Sox's imminent return to Bedside Manor for his future care.

By now I've had more than I can stomach of Mr. Guy Dorkin, and if I were sensible I'd excuse myself, politely thank him for stopping by, and avoid the risk of further confrontation. The trouble is he said precisely the wrong words—mom and pop. I bore witness to the sweat and tears my late mother and father invested in this place. Their presence fills every paint-peeling, water-stained corner of every room, and, for right now, I still need them by my side.

"You know, Guy, part of me suspects

Healthy Paws is worried about the competition. Maybe you've got this the wrong way round. Maybe Bedside Manor is going to start drawing on some of that wealthy clientele in Patton."

I brace for a derisive laugh but it never comes. "Which bit of four—that's right, four—full-time veterinarians are you forgetting about, Cy?"

Though his expression remains wooden, the switch up from comical banter to sarcasm tells me I've struck a nerve.

"Four means we can provide care twenty-four/seven. Four"—he flutters the fingers of his right hand—"means you can get an appointment on a Sunday. And, FYI, Healthy Paws is a publicly traded company, I'm talking, 'Hello, Mr. NASDAQ.' We operate state-of-the-art facilities in thirty-six states. We buy in bulk, direct from all the major drug companies and pet food distributors, so the prices we offer to our customers cannot be beat. Do you know what drives profits in veterinary healthcare? Food and drugs. Everything else is gravy, and let me tell you, pet owners lap up our gravy."

If he's waiting for me to counter with

something unique to Bedside Manor, I'm not sure what I'm going to say. Our fax machine works? Just bought a new batch of hazardous chemicals for our archaic X-ray machine?

He concludes his monologue with, "You should drop by sometime. Love to show you around."

Though I'd rather take a cheese-grater to my eyeballs, I force a smile and say, "Sure. And I appreciate your . . . insight, but I think I'll stick it out, give this place a shot."

Dorkin purses his lips and shakes his head, pained by my great mistake.

"I gave your father a chance to sell up, but he blew it, determined to stay the course, plying his outdated techniques even as they were going extinct. Remind me, how did that work out for him?"

He spreads his arms widely, as if to a congregation.

"What kind of a legacy did he leave for you to salvage?"

I look away, grind molar on molar, meet his eyes, and say, "The kind that matters. The kind that comes without a price tag."

I can't tell whether it's what I've said or

his reading my sincerity, but I'm treated to the hyena-donkey hybrid laugh.

"I'm sorry, Cy. I respected your father, but times have changed. We live in a world of doggy day care, canine fashion accessories, Halloween costumes for pets, pet psychics, pet sitters, the list goes on and on. Veterinary medicine must evolve. The public demands it. If Fido's getting a pacemaker, then Fido's mom knows she can't just trade for a cup of tea and a slice of cake."

I wonder if Fido's pacemaker also comes with a soothing doggy massage.

"The days of James Herriot are over. He's dead and buried, and with him went his fossilized style of practice."

There's a hand squeezing my shoulder. I flinch, but he won't let go. "It's survival of the fittest, Cy, a dog-eat-dog world. Healthy Paws can offer you a path forward. Keep this place. Just operate with a different business model."

My eyes slide left and focus on his hand like it's a hairy tarantula.

"Don't say a word, just promise me you'll think about it. Here, take my card."

He reaches into his overcoat pocket and

pulls out a business card. I stuff it in the front of my chinos without even looking.

"Cell number's on the card. And check out my Twitter account. Fifty-eight followers can't be wrong."

He's backing up toward the front door, unwrapping a stick of Juicy Fruit and jamming it in his mouth. Why do I wish he'd found something more carcinogenic, like chewing tobacco? Extending the thumb and pinky finger of his right hand, Dorkin mimes a telephone while mouthing, "Call me," before disappearing through the chiming front door.

Watching as Dorkin's black Audi spins out of the lot, I smell the nicotine before I feel Doris's presence by my side.

"Piece of work, isn't he?" Doris looks as though she can will his car to crash with her eyes. "Vulture. Bided his time. Waited until your father was ready for the hospital before swooping in. He called it a mercy offer, an act of charity for a practice about to die. You believe that?"

Now she's looking at me, and for the first time it's a different type of scrutiny. Her defiant streak has been directed else-where, at a common enemy, and I am being invited to join the rebel alliance. It feels like an olive branch, even if it comes with a painful reminder of my failings as a son.

"He still wants me to sell. Funny, last week his offer came with all kinds of stipulations—in particular, decent monthly production figures. Now he can't wait to get his hands on the place."

Doris reaches into the pocket of her ski jacket and pulls out her Zippo lighter and pack of Marlboros. "That's 'cause you've got him rattled." And then, after a beat of deliberation, "Some folks must be saying nice things about you."

This last remark comes out as more of a statement than a compliment, as though by stressing the "some" she wants me to know she's an undecided juror. Doris and I have a long way to go to achieve a decent thaw. Still, I'll take it. I watch the craving ignite in her eyes as she plucks a cigarette and tamps it down on the lid.

"Well, Dorkin's going to be disappointed. I'd rather burn the place to the ground than become a disciple of the Church of Healthy Paws."

Doris pulls tightly on the invisible drawstring of her sticky orange lips, forming an uneasy pout. "I've been here before, with your father. You ready for payback?"

I drift off, working on a slow, gravelly Russell Crowe impersonation from the movie **Gladiator**. "And I will have my vengeance, in this life or the next."

"What you goin' on about?" says Doris, showing me her unlit cigarette and heading for the front door.

I clear my throat without explaining. "Hey, what happened to that guy with the standard poodle?"

She shrugs. "No idea. Dog felt better or maybe his owner got cold feet about seeing you?" The bell chimes and she catches herself. "Eleven o'clock. Dr. Lewis wants you to meet him at Garvey's. Remember the way?"

"Of course."

"The farmhouse, not the main entrance."

"Got it."

And that's when she relinquishes a scary, lemon yellow smile. "And Dr. Lewis suggests you bring your wellies."

Whether Doris believes no explanation is needed or merited, I cannot tell, but I'm seriously worried. The prospect of what awaits me actually makes her giggle like a naughty schoolgirl.

\* \* \*

Eden Falls is a "blink and you'll miss it" kind of place. No stop signs, no lights, no reason not to keep going. In fact, Main Street might be more accurately labeled Only Street. But Garvey's Nursery and Garden Center lies on the other side of a covered bridge on the far side of town, which is more than enough time to try calling Amy. Once again, it goes to voice mail. She must be screening my calls. I'm about to hang up, try back later, but even as I'm justifying my cowardice, I realize that's precisely what she would expect. Now might be the moment to be something I'm not—unpredictable.

"It's me." This time I overpower my insecure desire to clarify that "me" is Cyrus. "Thought I might drop by the diner at lunchtime. Not sure if you're working, but if you are, great. If not . . ." Keep going, easy-breezy. "Then . . . no problemo." **No problemo? What idiot says no problemo?** "Hey, I'd love to try to get together again sometime." Better, upbeat but still casual. And then a thought hits me. "Think of it like me coming home to Eden Falls. It's all about second chances." I pause for a minute before pressing End.

What's gotten into me? I should be scheming for ways to beat back an imminent attack from Mr. Guy Dorkin. Instead I'm obsessing over a woman I barely know. Worst of all, I spent a restless night convincing myself that my decision to give up my former life in Charleston, to return home and breathe new life into Bedside Manor, was in no way influenced by something as cliché as an attraction to a potential mate.

In a moment of clarity, I tried to break Amy's spell by deconstructing the elements of her allure. Unfortunately her self-lessness is hard to overlook. Here's a woman happy to put her education on hold (she was in a master's program over at UVM) and work a minimum wage job at our local diner in order to be there for her dying grandfather. There is, however, no denying her acerbic "take no prisoners" tongue, with words unleashed like bullets from an Uzi. Some say she speaks her mind. If I'm being honest, I think she speaks her heart. And yes, her facial features bear the perfect symmetry of an attractive woman, excluding her heterochromic (one's blue, one's brown) but no less hypnotic eyes, while she conveys an outward indifference to her looks. In another world this woman might not give me the time of day, yet here, in the northernmost reaches of rural Vermont, her beauty is not a tool to use or flaunt. If anything, she brandishes it like a test, daring you to look deeper.

Obviously, women are not my area of expertise. Taking this dare went against my better judgment. When I open up, I do so in carefully controlled increments; however, Amy makes . . . made me want to try. Okay, it's a ridiculous reaction to a woman I barely know from a diner and from being trapped with her in an X-ray darkroom, but I stopped redacting the bits of me I didn't want her to see—yes, even the intangible, emotional bits—because I could sense the possibilities. In short, I let down my guard.

I check the screen on my flip phone— plenty of battery and a decent signal. No excuses. Clearly this preoccupation with Amy is pointless. Best to go back to what works—clinical objectivity. Take in the bigger picture, weigh the options, spot the distractor, discard, simplify, and move on.

The vehicle in the cracked rearview mirror caught my attention long before the covered bridge. It's a gray minivan; and though the funhouse reflection makes it tricky, I'm pretty sure I can make out two figures inside—one white and one black. They've been on my tail since I left Bedside Manor, keeping a safe distance but now I'm certain I'm being followed. Two thugs looking to collect on one of my many debts, or a pair of contract killers hired by Dorkin? I indicate right at the sign for Garvey's. The minivan slows down then drives on, past the entrance. Maybe I'm confusing paranoia with astute observation.

In **Back to the Future**, Michael J. Fox used a DeLorean sports car as a time machine. My version is Dad's old Chevy Silverado truck, but it delivers me to a Garvey's far different from my childhood memories. For starters, the numerous post-and-beam buildings and glinting greenhouses are new, creating the sense that Garvey's is a little village rather than a local store. This was the place Mom and I would visit for apple picking, hayrides, Halloween pumpkins, and our Christmas tree. Now it looks more like a theme park—a Disney version of Vermont.

The once run-down miniature golf course has been artificially enhanced by water fountains and an Eiffel Tower. Remnants of the seasonal maze that used to stand in a field of fitful cow corn has gone, replaced by a wall of twiggy but manicured privet more suited to an English stately home. There's a building devoted to skiing and snowboarding equipment and one for fishing and hunting supplies. The rusty swing-set and slides have given way to a state-of-the-art playground, the need for a dab of Mom's spittle or a tetanus shot traded for hand sanitizers at the entranceway.

As I curb crawl past the petting zoo, a young mother carrying a toddler in her arms delivers the kind of death glare she might reserve for a suspected pedophile. She's obviously misread my look of surprise. Run-down stalls, a pigsty, and barbed wire have been superseded by imposing barns and white picket fencing. In the background I can still make out the remnants of the original farm—stanchions for livestock, silos, a milking parlor—but everything is conspicuously shiny, not a rusting piece of farm equipment or an abandoned tractor tire in sight.

When the asphalt of the neatly plowed

and salty parking lot ends, the wheels of the Silverado lock into the icy ruts of a trail leading directly to the farmhouse. Lewis's empty vehicle is parked out front, and I pull up alongside. As usual, I make sure there's plenty of room to turn around without the need to back up. That's because Dad's old truck might be the only part of his legacy that always looked forward—its reverse gear doesn't work.

It's one of those bleak, pencil lead— gray mornings; the threat of more snow hangs in the bitter January air like a raised dagger poised to descend. Direct sunlight has been banished, and that's why the man in the sunglasses, who comes crashing out of the house and charging my way as I pull on a pair of my father's green Wellington boots, instantly strikes me as strange.

"No. No," he screams, hands waving over his head as though I'm about to step on a land mine. "No solicitation. Not here."

Feet rooted to the spot, I raise a "I come in peace" wave that he chooses to ignore, almost barreling into me.

"Which part of private property don't you understand?"

The man has receding dark hair, center-parted and gathered in a ponytail, as though he's determined to keep every filament left on his head. The Kirk Douglas dimple chiseled into his chin is striking, but it's his mirror aviator sunglasses that have my attention. I haven't seen a pair like these in years. In my mind I flash to the prison guard in the Paul Newman movie **Cool Hand Luke**.

"I'm Dr. Mills, from Bedside Manor. I work with Dr. Lewis." I gesture to Lewis's truck as though this inanimate object will substantiate my claim. "Lewis asked me to meet him here to see a case."

For what seems like an eternity we stand there, inhaling each other's breathy clouds, the man apparently derailed by my explanation. He's about my height, six feet (like most men of five feet, eleven inches, I prefer to round up). I have no clue what's going on behind those mirrors, but without warning he winces and pounds a clenched fist into the center of his forehead.

"You got anything for a migraine in that bag of yours?"

He's noticed I'm carrying my late father's "doctorin'" bag.

"Might have some Advil."

I swing the bag up on my thigh and open it up.

"Don't bother," the man snaps. "Took eight hundred milligrams this morning. Didn't touch it. Got something stronger?"

"Afraid not," I say, beginning to notice an aroma hanging in the condensation between us. It's striking, the sweet smell of nail polish remover that is characteristic of a specific clinical disorder called "ketosis."

The man curses and stamps one foot into the snow like a warning from an angry goat. He's only wearing slippers.

"Test your glucose level this morning?" I ask.

The man eases his head back ever so slightly, but it's impossible to tell if he's impressed by my deduction. Blowing off ketones in the breath suggests poor glucose regulation, probably because he needs artificial insulin. Given the man's skinny build and the presence of visible scar tissue on the tips of his fingers, I'd go with juvenile diabetes, the scars the result of decades of monitoring his blood glucose with daily, tiny, painful pricks.

"Course I did," he snaps. "This"—he drills

a forefinger into his temple—"has nothing to do with it." Then he growls, scoops up a snowball, and pounds it into his temple, holding it in place, savoring the temporary relief as a trail of icy water runs down his wrist and forearm.

"If it's that bad, Mr. . . . Mr. . . ."

He makes no attempt to bail me out.

"I'd suggest a visit to the hospital."

Off in the distance two men are headed our way. One of them is Lewis.

"Ah, there he is, I won't bother you any . . ."

But Mr. Ponytail is no longer listening. His back to me, he lopes off to the sanctuary of his house. The hostility and the social miscues make me wonder if he has some mental health issues and fears getting caught talking to a stranger.

Lewis saunters over, dressed like a farmer from central casting—ruddy faced from the cold, wearing a flat cap and green Barbour jacket.

"Cyrus, this is Mike Garvey Junior."

"Nice to meet you," says a heavyset man in a Blue Jays baseball cap. He also has that Kirk Douglas dimple in his chin.

We shake hands.

"Was that your son I was speaking with?" I ask, gesturing to the house, catching sight of a shadowy figure at the screen to the front door.

Mike Garvey Jr. waves, but the shadow disappears.

"Yeah. My son. Michael Garvey the Third. We call him Trey. Afraid he's not been himself lately. Acting a little weird."

"Doris mentioned the incident in his truck," says Lewis. "When does he get his license back?"

"Never lost it," says Mike, and then to me, "He failed a sobriety test, but his blood alcohol level was zero. Chief Devito had to let him go."

Interesting.

"Maybe your son's odd behavior reflects a problem regulating his diabetes," I say. "How old was he when you got the diagnosis?"

Garvey considers me, his expression caught somewhere between worried and impressed. "Two. But he never said he was a diabetic, did he?"

Lewis sees where this is going and begins to grin. "Told you he was smart, Mike."

Mike looks unconvinced.

"Maybe," he says. "But you can talk to Trey. Get right next to him. Not so easy with Ermintrude."

**Ermintrude**.

Lewis's grin refuses to wane.

"I'm sure Cyrus would be happy to take a look," he says, and they both turn to me.

"Sure," I say, sounding anything but.

Mike leads the way around the back of the house and down a trail plowed through the deep snow toward the main farm buildings that lie beyond the public's reach.

"Lewis tells me it's been a while since you lived in Eden Falls."

"Twenty-five years," I say.

"Ah, back when my old man was running the place."

"He was a smart man, your father," says Lewis. "Saw what was going to happen to dairy farms in this part of the world and did something about it."

Garvey cringes at the compliment, and for a few beats the only sound is the satisfying squeak of compacted snow under our every footfall.

"Guess so," he says, "at least he started out that way. Dad pushed the all-natural angle, the antibiotic-free milk, cheese, and yogurt long before it was popular. And no one was trying to sustain rare breeds of cattle, sheep, or goats. Throw in organic fruit and vegetables, expand into plants and trees, and he reckoned he could keep doing what he loved, keep farming, keep working." Garvey forces a laugh and shakes his head.

"Garvey's is part of Eden Falls culture," says Lewis as we walk three abreast.

"Oh yeah," says Garvey. "If you like minigolf and a petting zoo. Dad got out because of falling milk prices. Cost him more in fuel and fertilizer than he could make in milk. Started selling off the herd, looking at other ways to work the land. Hey, now it's mine, I'm no better. See over there?"

He points to a clearing in the hillside.

"If we're still in business this time next year, I'll have a tow rope and floodlights, and with luck, kids will be tubing down there all night long. Not exactly my idea of farming."

"Maybe not," says Lewis, "but it's definitely mine."

Lewis catches my skeptical glance.

"It's true. I never liked farmwork. Hated the economics of whether a cure could be justified versus cutting your losses at a slaughterhouse. Garvey's is different. What's not to love when farm animals turn into pets?"

Pets? Now he's got me worried.

"This place has certainly undergone a major facelift since the last time I was here," I say.

"Had to," says Garvey. "Department of Public Health and Safety insisted on some of the upgrades. Insurance helped out when we took a hit from Hurricane Irene, but most of this is thanks to an equity loan from Green State Bank."

Ah, Green State Bank and the charming Mr. Critchley.

"I'm afraid the public likes its slice of farm life sweet smelling and pretty on the eyes. Here we are."

We've passed a row of stables (I'm relieved Ermintrude is apparently not one of the giant Clydesdale horses housed there), and Garvey leads the way into a large, airy barn. It's like walking into an animal husbandry class—steamy livestock busy chewing cud mixed with that authentic aroma of mud, manure, and damp straw bedding. The place is bright and warm, the

**V** of the ceiling a good twenty feet overhead. Our presence incites a chorus of bleats and moos reminiscent of kids singing the Old MacDonald farmyard nursery rhyme.

"She's way down at the end," says Garvey, but I'm distracted, checking out the animals segregated behind metal rails on either side of the central aisle.

There's a spotted black and white sheep bearing four horns. **It's a Jacob, a breed thought to have originated in the Middle East around three thousand years ago.** Nearby stands a small black cow with a band of white fur wrapped around her belly. **She's a belted Galloway. Her coat packs four thousand hairs into every square inch, making it highly resistant to severe cold.** Aside from these useless factoids and an ability to identify obscure breeds, I haven't thought about the diseases of farm animals since I was back in veterinary school.

"C'mon, Cyrus," says Lewis, the two of them ahead of me.

I trot to catch up. "Are those pigeons, Mike?" I ask, pointing to the crossbeams near the ceiling. Hundreds of raucous gray birds appear to be roosting (and actively defecating) at the far end of the barn where we are headed.

"'Fraid so," says Garvey.

"Flying rats," says Lewis. "Best not to look up, if you know what I mean." He doffs the peak of his cap. "You should have worn one of these."

"But there's so many of them. Are they a homing variety?"

"No idea," says Mike. "But they're good for business. Folks love having their picture taken with them. Sprinkle seed along your arms; see how many pigeons will land on you. Trey still holds the record—thirty-two. They seem to flock to him. Here she is. Dr. Mills, meet Ermintrude."

In an isolated stall, walled off from the other cows by bales of straw and hay, stands a fawn-colored cow with black hooves and a dark switch of hair at the end of her tail. I'm guessing a Jersey, but what concerns me is the way she's pressing her head into the wall. Based on the twitch and swivel of her leafy ears she obviously senses our presence, but it looks as if she's consumed by the worst hangover of her life.

The three of us cozy up to the fence, resting our elbows on the top rail.

"I remember you telling me you like comparative pathology," says Lewis to me.

"Me?"

"'Disease is disease,' you said, 'whether you're human or a duck-billed platypus.' Well, here's your chance with a Jersey cow. Ermintrude's twelve years old and as you can see, she's lost a lot of weight despite a good appetite. What disturbs me most of all is what's happening inside her head."

Lewis consults with Mike, something passes between them, and Mike claps his hands together and yells out loud.

Ermintrude startles as if she's snapped out of a trance, ears twitching, all four legs scrambling and uncoordinated as she skitters across the slick mud, going down on her front legs, bug eyes rolling back inside her head, black to white and black again. She's petrified and desperate to reach the sanctuary of the farthest corner.

"Not pretty, is it?" says Mike.

"How long has she been like this?"

Lewis does that thing with his upper incisor chewing on his lower lip.

"She's only been this bad for a few days. Right, Mike?"

"Right. But she's been acting weird for a while."

"Weird?" I raise my eyebrows and give the farmer my best "you're going to have to do better than that" glare.

"It started in the fall. Trey takes care of her, always has, and he noticed how she was . . . I don't know . . . pushy, rough, even a bit aggressive, especially around feeding time. We thought she's getting old, getting crotchety—hey, don't we all?"

"Speak for yourself," says Lewis.

"So we cut her some slack—until the incident in the petting zoo. Ermintrude's been a permanent fixture for years, not least because she's bombproof around screaming, pinching kids. But on this particular day she went postal on a five-year-old boy. Nearly kicked him into kingdom come. Trey saw it, but thankfully his mother did not. Otherwise, I'd be on the wrong end of a lawsuit for sure."

"I know this is not your area of expertise, Cyrus," says Lewis, "but I've seen how your brain works. You love the weird details about obscure diseases. Her calcium, magnesium, and glucose levels are fine. She's never had a fever, her diet is good, her lymph nodes are normal, and her pupil reflexes are normal. Her most striking clinical sign is her sensitivity to sound and light—"

"And the way she's become scary to be around."

"What d'you mean?" I ask.

"Put it this way," says Garvey. "You shouldn't go in there unless you've been trained as a matador."

"That's right," says Lewis. "I just wanted you to look at her, see for yourself, and maybe something will cross your mind that hasn't crossed mine. I've tried changing her diet, I've tried antibiotics, multivitamins, dietary supplements, you name it. And I've ruled out pretty much every common cause of neurological disease I can think of."

"She's going downhill and fast. Look at her," says Garvey. "If you can't help her, Dr. Mills, and soon, she's going to have to be destroyed."

If I look anxious, I hope that Lewis and Garvey will think it's just the burden of this responsibility. Truth be told, that's the least of my concerns. Lewis is right, I've always been obsessed with the minutiae of bizarre diseases, and though I came here out of a sense of obligation to my colleague, secretly I'm totally intrigued by this case, even if it is a cow.

"I'll do my best," I say, and even to my ear, this reply sounds totally insincere. Perhaps that's because I'm following my gut reaction, the knee-jerk response to what I just witnessed, Ermintrude's hypersensitivity to any kind of stimulation and the way it's identical to my recollection of a grainy video of similarly afflicted cows from Great Britain in the late eighties. Could the poor cow's affliction have anything in common with her caretaker, Trey?

**Afraid he's not been himself lately. Acting a little weird.**

What if Trey and Ermintrude have variations of the same disease? If so, and if this is what I think it is, the ramifications for me, Eden Falls, and a multibillion-dollar industry are incalculable. For one scary news cycle I might inadvertently steal more media coverage than the Kardashians. Air my suspicions to the FDA, prove them correct, and every single animal on this property will be destroyed before Garvey's, this third-generation Eden Falls fixture, gets razed to the ground.

"What's going on in that head of yours?" asks Lewis with a smile. "You on to something?"

I shake my head. It's scary enough even to think about my number one suspicion, let alone to air it. I'd best be wrong, because if not, Ermintrude, Trey, and Garvey's farm will be a national sensation for all the wrong reasons.

## « 5 »

Twelve thirty and the Miss Eden Falls diner is chock-full of a rowdy lunchtime rush intent on receiving sustenance. I reckon I'll be lucky to catch sight of Amy, let alone chat with her. I attempt to flatten the top of my crown where an unruly cowlick always lurks, berating myself for not looking my best, when a bear claw lunges in my direction and grabs me by the sleeve.

"Cyrus, quick, take a pew."

The order comes from Peter Greer, editor in chief of the **Eden Falls Gazette**, and a good friend and supporter of my late father and Bedside Manor.

I plop into the seat opposite him in a tight two-man booth. It doesn't help that Greer's a big guy, spilling over the red-checkered tablecloth between us to initiate an awkward hearty handshake.

"Marvelous to see you, old boy."

"Is it usually this crowded at lunchtime?"

"Always a little argy-bargy around the trough in these parts. Not to worry, you get used to it."

Did I mention Greer was English, complete with an accent posh enough to read the news for the BBC?

"How's business?" he asks. "Thriving after my stroke of genius?"

Greer's referring to last Saturday's free clinic. It was his idea of a way to introduce me to the community.

"If I ignore the fact that everyone thinks Bedside Manor offers complimentary pet care and we never ask for money, then business is booming."

Greer leans forward, sweeps his hand back and through his dapper mane of hair.

"Look on the bright side, you've got the opposition well and truly riled."

"The opposition? Healthy Paws?"

Greer chuckles. "Oh, it gets better, but did you order yet? You should, or it's going to take forever."

My waist-high view of the bar and other booths is blocked in all directions by a writhing sea of overinflated down jackets. Where's the main reason I came here for lunch?

"There she is."

Though seated, Greer's height gives him an advantage as he waves for attention like he's hailing a London cab.

"Here you go," says Amy, sliding a plate across the table. "Bacon burger and onion rings on the side."

"Marvelous," says Greer, "and I wonder if my dear friend, Dr. Mills, might place an order too."

Amy turns to me as though she never noticed I was there. No smile, no recognition. I stare into the magic of her distinctive eyes, rewarded with a blasé shrug.

"Um . . . what's good?" I ask, unbalanced by her distance and impatience.

She leans closer. "What's good?" she repeats.

I nod, but now I'm worried.

"Hmm, implicit in that question is the fact

that you not only trust, but you value my opinion. Wouldn't you agree, Mr. Greer?"

"Wholeheartedly," says Greer, squirting ketchup onto his plate, onion ring in hand.

"It seemed like a simple question," I stutter.

"But it's not. It's about personal taste, preference, and mutual understanding. Oh, I could tell you what I'm supposed to say, 'Yes, the fish sandwich is fantastic,' because the chef noticed the frozen cod has passed its sell-by date and wants to get rid of it, but I'm not that person. Now, if you want to know what I'll be having for lunch because I like how it tastes, I'll tell you the Greek salad."

I glance over at Greer, who's got the ring halfway to his mouth and looks afraid.

"Greek salad it is. And . . . thanks for the clarification." I say this with an absolutely straight face and watch as Amy tries to work out if I'm being sincere. It takes a while but there's a spark, the flicker of a weak connection between her lips and her eyes.

The crunch of the batter encasing the onion ring brings me back.

"My, my, that was rather strange. I take it the first date didn't go well?"

I rock back in my seat. "How did you know I went on a date with Amy?"

Greer chomps into his burger, chews, swallows, and says one word. "Doris."

It seems my failed attempt at a love life has become public knowledge thanks to my receptionist.

"It could have gone better," I say, peeling off my gloves and jacket.

"Well, I wouldn't be too concerned," he says.

"How can you say that? You weren't there."

Greer speaks from behind his fingertips to spare me the sight of half-chewed food.

"Because Amy's wearing lipstick. When she took my order she wasn't. I suspect she's powdered her nose just for you."

This disclosure makes me smile, pleased enough to snag one of his onion rings.

"The evening was a disaster," I say, drawing air into my mouth to cool off the steaming batter burning my tongue. "But it wasn't all my fault."

Greer's got a red dribble of ketchup on his chin that's hard to ignore.

"Go on," he says, happy to bite and chew, waiting for my story. His air is attentive, one of an experienced Don Juan, eager to share his wisdom on how to properly woo a lady.

"Things were going well until Amy got a phone call and insisted she had to take it."

"Obviously important."

"Obviously. And exciting and flirtatious and highly amusing."

Greer grabs a napkin and wipes his lips but misses the stray ketchup. "You were eavesdropping on a private conversation?"

"Of course not. The bar was noisy. She talked in a corridor outside the bathrooms, but I had a perfect view of her body language. Twirling her hair around her finger, playing with her necklace, getting all wide-eyed, even . . . giggling."

Greer recoils, a little too dramatically. "Not giggling."

"Hey, she's never giggled with me. I can only assume this pivotal phone call was from an old flame and she was thrilled to reconnect. Even though she was on a date with me."

"How do you know it was a man? How do you know it wasn't a long-lost cousin?"

"Because I asked. She said it was someone from her past. Someone very special.

Fine, but you leave me hanging for twelve minutes and then refuse to elaborate, that's just plain rude. What?"

Greer looks appalled.

"Hence Amy's lecture on the virtue of trust. Makes perfect sense."

"Hey, I was nervous. I wanted the date to go well, to be special. But the place was a zoo, and to top it all, she was obviously far more interested in someone on the other end of a phone than she was in me. Believe me, I'm not a control freak. I don't need to know every detail of her romantic past."

"And what do you know about her past, romantic or otherwise?"

"Next to nothing."

The ketchup finally dribbles onto a receptor that Greer senses, the napkin finding its target.

"Let me assure you she's well liked in this community, not least because she's taking care of her ailing grandfather, Harry. There's no one else. Her mother ran off with some guy to Montreal, and her father died of carbon monoxide poisoning."

Reading my horror, he adds, "Snowstorm accident. Few years back. Trapped in his car. Snow blocked off the exhaust pipe. Just went to sleep."

"That's awful."

Greer nods and swallows his last bite.

"You two have more in common than you know. Parents are deceased or estranged and . . ."

"And?"

"You're both . . . difficult to read."

I think about this. He's right, and I've got no comeback. However, I pick up on his use of the word **both**.

I lean in and lower my voice. "I've never known a woman like her. I've worked behind a microscope for the last fourteen years, and the only women I got to know were . . . well . . . straightforward, polite, scientific . . . okay, nerdy, if not demure. And southern women are just different. Tell you exactly what's on their minds. Not that that made my love life any easier."

Greer laughs.

"Let's hope Amy likes mint juleps, otherwise you've got your hands full with a bird of another feather."

"Glad you find this funny. My point is, if she'd rather be with someone else, then let's not waste each other's time."

Suddenly Amy swoops in with my salad. "Who's wasting your time?"

Her presence instantly shuts me down, my silence not helped by a guilty blush of embarrassment.

"Is it me or is it hot in here?" is all I can think to say.

Amy meets my eyes, and this time I sense she's traded frustration for mischief. "It's you." She's still holding the plate. "One Greek salad."

I reach out to take it, the tips of our fingers touching, the contact a second more than necessary before she lets go. I thank her in a boyish whisper.

"You all set, Peter?"

"Stuffed like the proverbial pig. My compliments to the chef."

Amy rolls her eyes. "Here's the check. When you're ready." She slides a slip of paper across the table and disappears.

Greer snatches it up and hunches forward, elbows on the table, his face inches from mine, a green leaf-laden fork hovering between us.

"Take it from a man who knows a thing or two about women, this woman"—he thumbs over his shoulder—"is still interested in you."

My lips work on a mouthful of vegetation as I mull this over.

"If I were you, I'd ask for a second date, somewhere quiet and relaxed. For God's sake, this time keep the conversation light. Seducing a woman is not a medical emergency. It's rare for one's services to be required stat or for the situation to necessitate a painstaking history of everything that led to this moment. Simply put, let her come to you. Believe me, women want to reveal themselves, but to get to the precious fruit inside, you must peel back the layers with skill and tact and patience. Remember, old boy, romance needs to be cultivated, nurtured, and never rushed."

I stab a piece of feta and shake my head. All this from a man whose red silk boxer shorts were consumed by his mistress's Labrador while her husband was out of town.

"What were you going to tell me about Healthy Paws?" I ask.

"Oh, that's right." Greer reaches for his wallet and deposits a ten-dollar bill on the table. "Got a phone call from a Mr. Guy Dorkin this morning, office manager over at—"

"I know who he is."

"Huh. Well, Dorkin wants to follow your lead, wants to offer a free clinic and tour of his fancy digs over in Patton. Thing is, he wants to advertise in the **Gazette**. He's trying to win over the pet owners of Eden Falls."

I put my fork down. "What a total—"

"My thought exactly."

"But you know Bedside Manor is hanging by a thread. We can't afford to lose what clients we have left."

"I know. But what am I to do? Dorkin wants a full-page ad to run this Friday."

"Tell him he's missed deadline. Tell him there's no available space."

"Too late. He dropped by in person. One of my lackeys already took his money."

The curse slips between my clenched teeth.

"Sorry about that."

"Not to worry," says Greer, reaching across the table to pat me on the forearm. "I'm already working on a cunning plan. The Dork is going to rue the day he advertised in the **Gazette**."

And with that, Greer eases himself out of the booth and, seeing Amy headed my way, winks and wishes me luck.

"All set?" she asks, even as she grabs my plate.

"Yes, thank you."

"Just the check?"

"Please," I reply. As she turns away I blurt out, "How are Clint and Harry doing?"

Despite the name, Clint is the **female**, funny-looking Lab mix her grandfather Harry calls his best friend. Last week Clint had a bad run-in with a wayward pork chop.

"They're great," she says, considering me, and it's like I'm watching a security gate slide back, getting my first unimpeded look at the person on the other side. "Kind of you to ask."

"Not at all," I say. "Give them my best."

She waits a beat. "Fixing Clint, you were cool under pressure," she says. "Now I've seen what you're capable of."

I do this nervous porcine snort thing that is definitely not cool. "I'm not sure that's true."

"No? Well, you've proven you can handle at least one tricky bitch."

She smiles. I hope she's referring to Clint.

Once again she makes to leave.

"Wait. Did you get a chance to listen to your voice mail?"

Amy comes back to the table looking confused.

"Um . . . see . . . I left you a message. Look . . . I know the other day, well, it didn't go as planned."

Nonchalantly she fingers the top empty buttonhole of her shirt. "Oh, so you thought you'd get to sleep with me on the first date?"

"No," I shout, causing a few heads to turn before regaining my composure. "Never."

"Never as in it never crossed your mind because I'm not your type?"

"No, I mean, yes, it's crossed my . . . I mean, no, I'm not that kind of man."

The smile wriggling into the corners of her mouth takes its time, enough for me to achieve maximal blood flow to my cheeks.

"And what kind of man is that exactly?"

Her standing over me, forcing me to angle my head upward, only exaggerates my discomfort. To my surprise she reads it, deciding to squat down so we're face-to-face.

"Hey, I'm sorry if I came across as . . ."

"Rude," I offer.

Amy puckers her lips. "I'll give you abrupt, maybe even snippy. But believe me, my behavior was for your own good."

I manage a slow nod, forcing the next question out of my mouth to change from "What's that supposed to mean?" to "Can we have a do-over?"

In her dispassionate deliberation, the room falls silent, joining me in a moment of breathless anticipation. Though there may be some truth to the notion that attractive women can go overlooked because they appear unapproachable, even unattainable, I wager Amy's single status is based on a frank, brutal honesty that is as unsettling as it is beguiling.

"Sure, why not?"

Is it me or does the background noise return to its former volume?

"Just as long as the green-eyed monster doesn't rear its ugly head."

"Green-eyed monster?" I ask.

"'O, beware, my lord . . . the green-eyed

monster which doth mock the meat it feeds on.'"

Did I mention Amy was an English major?

"Shakespeare," she says. "**Othello**. Referring to jealousy."

"I wasn't . . ." I catch myself in the nick of time and push down the urge to act defensive. It was being the voyeur, having to witness her irresistible smile and laugh, the ease with which this mysterious man on the other end of a phone captivated her in a way I doubt I ever could.

"Of course," I say. "Fresh start. Clean slate. Don't suppose you're free this evening?"

She winces, inhales between clenched teeth. "Afraid not, got plans."

And I can tell she's watching me, like this is a test, her unavailability bait, to see if the monster lurking inside me will bite.

"No problem," I manage, though I'm not sure she's convinced. "Another time."

"That would be nice," she says, softening. "I'll have my people call your people. And soon, okay?"

*    *    *

I knew it. I knew I wasn't being paranoid. Parked on the other side of the street from the diner is a dishwater gray minivan. It has to be the one that tailed me to Garvey's. There's a figure reclining in the driver's seat, lying low, gangsta-style, behind the steering wheel, but I can't see his partner. Peeved, I succumb to a rare moment of spontaneity, schlepping across the mushy brown snow to confront them, squinting through the condensation on the inside of the window, only to be greeted by white teeth and an explosion of booming barks.

"Easy, Stash," commands a voice, winding down his window, bringing one hand up to his windpipe in the manner of a fake karate chop. The barking instantly stops, and that's when I recognize the gaunt, sickly guy I saw earlier this morning in the waiting room. Riding shotgun, sitting square and to attention, is his black standard poodle.

"Hey, Doc," says the man, looking pleased to see me. "I've been hoping to catch you. Wondering if I can have a word. In private."

"What's this about?" I ask.

The man hesitates, checks in with his partner, Stash (strange name), before coming back to me, giving new meaning to the phrase **deadpan expression**.

"I have a favor to ask. A big favor. Something only you could appreciate."

If the request is meant to sound ominous, it does.

"You'd better explain," I say.

A car barrels past, spraying a frosty slurry down the back of my pants as a couple of satisfied customers exit the diner and head our way.

"Sure. Somewhere quiet?"

I'd offer to come around and sit in the passenger seat, but the dog doesn't look like he's prepared to move.

"I'm headed back to the practice. I can meet you there."

Before the man can reply, my cell phone rings.

"Where are you?"

No introduction. No pleasantries. Straight to it.

"Good afternoon, Doris. I just finished up lunch at the diner."

I drift around to the front of the van to avoid another oncoming car.

"Any chance you could . . ."

The request gets lost in a burst of static.

"Hang on." I walk up the street as though I can somehow divine better reception. "Can you hear me now?"

More disjointed, garbled consonants. I jog over to the diner side of the street.

"Any better?"

"I said can you pick me up a packet of Marlboros from the gas station across the way? And then you're needed on a house call."

"Doris, I'm not comfortable enabling your drug habit."

"Suit yourself, but I'll have to leave the practice unattended to get them."

She always knows just what to say. "Okay, fine, what's the address?"

She rattles off a street name I don't recognize.

"It's off Route 62, closer to Patton than Eden Falls."

"Patton?"

"Maybe you're starting to get a reputation."

I'm speechless. Did Doris just give me a compliment?

"Or maybe they just don't know any better."

She hangs up before I can reply.

I look back across the street for the gray minivan.

It's gone.

The home of one Marmalade Succabone (yes, I asked Doris to repeat the pet's name) is a conspicuously lonely colonial surrounded by empty lots, abandoned half-finished wood construction, and what appears to be a green plastic Porta Potty lying on its side. Though the turn into their street boasts the professional masonry of a new stone wall, and rows of arborvitae welcome the visitor to desirable Deerfield Meadows, clearly the developer went belly-up after completing one property, leaving no sign of getting the rest of the project finished any time soon.

In the driveway sits a brand-new pink Jeep, a life-sized version of something Barbie might drive. I walk past thinking someone's awfully confident of herself.

"Dr. Mills?"

A girl stands at the front door, sixteen, maybe seventeen years old, wearing a flimsy leopard-patterned shirt over skin-tight black pants the likes of which I haven't seen since Olivia Newton-John in the final scenes of **Grease**. The trouble is, that's where the similarity to Ms. Newton-John ends. I don't know how to put this, and please, I'm simply being objective, not judgmental, but she's about five-two and I'm guessing two hundred pounds.

"That's me."

"Thought so," she says. "Come in," offering her hand to shake, an act that strikes me as a little odd for her generation and, at the same time, completely wonderful. She has a pretty face and there's nothing but warmth in her smile.

"I'm Charlie, Charlie Brown."

I must look confused.

"Short for Charlize," she adds, for explanation.

"Ah."

We stand in a foyer, with a formal dining room to my left and what looks like a family room to my right. The place is neat but cavernous and way too empty, as though it needs a lot more furniture.

"Your parents not home?" I ask.

"No," says Charlie, "it's just me and my mom, and she's at work."

I make a show of checking the time on my wristwatch.

"School's out early today?"

She purses her lips as though contemplating which excuse to use. "Gym. Last class. I skipped."

"In the pink Jeep."

"You like?"

"It's very . . . eye-catching," I say.

"Thanks," she gushes as though I've paid the finest of compliments. "Hey, come on through, and I'll show you Marmalade. Can I get you a drink? Coffee, tea, something stronger?"

Something stronger? I catch the way she's watching for my response. The kid's trying to get a rise out of me.

"I'm fine," I say, following her into an open kitchen, noticing a couple of framed photographs on the walls. They're of a woman, a stunningly attractive woman. And please, before you start to think I wear rose-colored glasses around the opposite sex or that northern Vermont is an oasis of beautiful people, let me differentiate between Amy and this particular female. Amy's beauty is a package deal. This is airbrushed into a professional glamour shot.

"That's my mom. Trying to look hot after the divorce."

"Really? Why? Not that she doesn't look hot . . . sorry, I shouldn't have said—"

"It's cool. Her therapist says it's a normal part of her recovery. They're both better off. It just sucks that Mom's either working or embarrassing herself meeting total losers online and Dad went off to live in Wisconsin. Married a bimbo and started a new family. Twins. They're actually really cute. There she is."

What looks like a furry orange medicine ball lumbers past only to be swept up into Charlie's arms (with some difficulty, I might add).

"Dr. Mills, meet Marmalade Succabone."

I reach out to pet an overinflated blimp of a feline.

"Wow, she's . . ."

"What?"

I struggle to find the words to capture Marmalade's dimensions.

"Voluptuous."

Charlie beams. "I like that," she says.

"Voluptuous." She runs a hand over the creature's girth and the cat approves with a Geiger counter purr.

"What seems to be the problem?" **Aside from her morbid obesity and the real possibility of challenging the Guinness World Record for fattest living feline, which happens to be 48.6 pounds.**

"You're kidding," says Charlie Brown, having to readjust the position of the mammoth in her tiring arms. "Look at her. She's totally overweight. And no one knows why."

I could have breezed by this last comment, but my mind jumps all over it.

"You've already sought veterinary advice?"

For the first time I catch Charlie's confidence begin to slip, just like her grip on the uber-cherubic cat spilling onto the floor with a seismic thud.

"Yeah, well, we went to the local vet, but they're, like, useless."

"You mean Healthy Paws?" I say, and I realize that I'm at risk of breaking into a smile.

"Yeah, they haven't been able to help at all. You know they have hidden cameras in every exam room."

I'm surprised by this unexpected tidbit. We don't even have an alarm on the door at Bedside Manor, and they have cameras in every room?

"I'm not kidding, my friend Gabe came with me one time. You've met him."

Gabe. Mr. Pot Brownie.

"Yeah, he told me he met this vet last night who didn't snitch on him to his mom. And that you were cool and maybe could fix Marmalade?"

So Gabe's the reason I got this house call. It makes sense. High school "freaks and geeks," the ostracized, pretty, but overweight girl is best friends with the nerdy computer whiz with an affinity for marijuana.

"Gabe's into spy stuff. He spotted the camera in the ceiling."

Sounds like Napoleon Dynamite has been watching one conspiracy movie too many.

"Not sure what to tell you, but let's have a look at Miss Marmalade."

I don't have far to go to find the cat that ate Vermont.

"Is this a pantry?"

"Yeah. That's where we keep her food."

Marmalade sits in front of the door, grooming a paw, though I sense she would rather be chowing down on a juicy T-bone or a baby wildebeest.

I kneel on the hardwood floor beside her, sweep my tie over my shoulder (Marmalade seems to think it's a toy), and pull out my stethoscope to listen to her chest. Everything seems in order. Though I might best describe palpating her abdomen as like kneading dough, again, no abnormalities jump out at me.

"Anything?"

"Not really. Can I assume she's had her blood tested?"

Charlie reaches across a counter and picks up a file. She shakes it in my direction.

"Yeah, blood, pee, you name it, she's had it tested. I like this cat, but Mom? Mom adores this cat. She worships her.

This cat can do no wrong."

I take a look, see the familiar Healthy Paws logo on everything, and once again note the doctor on the case, the "useless" doctor on the case, to be none other than Dr. Honey. Still, the data is not pointing to an obvious cause for the cat's weight issue.

"What's she fed?"

"Regular cat food. It's even diet. Take a look for yourself if you don't believe me."

"Of course I believe you," I say, noting her defensive tone.

We face one another, the orange colossus in my peripheral vision happy to bide her time at the pantry door.

"Why haven't you asked the obvious question?"

"Which one?" I ask, totally confused.

"Her name. Marmalade Succabone. Don't you think it's strange?"

"A little. But I've learned not to second-guess the names people give to their pets."

"Really? Not curious?"

It's pretty obvious she wants me to indulge her.

"Sure. Why Marmalade Succabone?"

She lights up. "It's her porn star name."

"I beg your pardon?"

"Her porn star name. You know, you take the name of your first pet, then you add the name of the first address you lived at and you get your porn star name. She's my first pet, and when I was born we lived on Succabone Avenue. Let's do you."

"Uh . . . no, no, I really don't think that's—"

"What's the name of your first pet?"

The shake of my head is met with narrowed eyes.

"Tommy," I relent, with a sigh.

"Very good. And the first place you lived?"

I think back, my memory pressing the Play button on a conversation with my late mother, Ruth, back when I was ten, her pointing out the car as we passed a street, saying, "That's the apartment where we lived until you were nine months old." The street sign flashes before my eyes, and my mind makes the connections, the blood rushing into my cheeks as I see the excitement, the thrill, ignite in Charlie Brown's eyes.

"I should be going," I say, straightening out my tie, putting my stethoscope back in the bag.

"Oh, come on. Not before you tell me."

I inhale, long and deep. "We first lived at Apartment Four, Lovelace Terrace."

Her nose wrinkles as she pumps a fist. "Works every time."

I shake my head and begin walking back toward the front door.

"Any chance I can hold on to this file? Take a longer look, do a little research?"

"Yeah. Sure."

We make it to the front door.

"You got a girlfriend, Dr. Mills?"

"That's a very, uh, forward question to be asking someone you've only just met."

"Well, do you or don't you?"

I think about Amy. I think about how she would respond to someone catching her by the arm and asking, "Hey, aren't you Cyrus Mills's girlfriend?"

"If you must know, and clearly you absolutely must, the answer is . . . not really . . . not definitively."

Charlie Brown seems inordinately pleased. "I'll take that as a no."

It's time to steer this conversation back to business. "I'm afraid there is a fee for this visit. Should I call your mother?"

"No," she says, way too fast and way too loud, reaching into the front of her pants. There's a whole lot of squirming and writhing to extract what I think will be wadded-up bills. It's not. It's a voucher from Garvey's for ice cream.

"Um, I can just bill you. It's not a problem."

She shakes her head and says, "Here, give me your cell phone."

Suspicious, I hand over the phone.

She takes it like I handed her a religious artifact.

"Wow, Gordon Gekko called, says he wants his phone back."

Though I should be insulted about the criticism of my outdated model, I'm impressed by the reference to the movie **Wall Street**.

"You an Oliver Stone fan?" I ask.

She frowns, rocks her hand side to side. "**Platoon** was okay, but as Vietnam movies go, I'm all about **Apocalypse Now**. Martin was better than Charlie any day."

Wow, a fellow movie buff. I'm impressed. But not surprised. Probably too many nights spent at home alone.

Her thumbs begin clicking on the phone's keypad like she's typing code.

"It's okay," she says. "I'm a professional."

I'm left in no doubt.

"Here's what I'm going to do. **I'll** call my mom and have her drop off the money. I've put my phone number in your contact list so that if there are any problems, you go through me, **capisce**?"

If she's trying to distract me from her sketchy behavior with a famous phrase from Coppola's **The Godfather**, it's not working.

"And, um, this just in . . . you need to get some friends. In the meantime, treat yourself to a sundae."

Charlize hands over the ice cream voucher, along with my phone. There are nine perfect holes, three rows of three, punched into the card, and the announcement—tenth sundae is on the house.

I thank her and step out into the cold.

"No," she says, "thank you, Tommy Lovelace."

« **6** »

It's the only other vehicle in the practice lot—the gray minivan. It's got windowless double doors at the back and what was probably a business ad or a logo brushed out by hand with mismatched house paint.

Looks like someone still needs that **big** favor.

I jump down from the Silverado as the driver's side door swings open.

"You free to see me now?" asks the gaunt man behind the wheel.

Even though the dog next to him doesn't move a muscle, I can almost sense the creature's anticipation.

"Sure. Come on in."

The man swings his legs out to the side and shuffles to the edge of his seat, preparing to rise. His jeans ride up above his socks, exposing bony ankles and blue bruises on alabaster white skin.

"Need a hand?"

"No," insists the man, "we've got this. Stash, stick."

The command is quiet and relaxed, a throwaway line, but Stash leaps between the front seats and into the back of the van before emerging with a wooden walking stick balanced between his jaws. Somehow the dog negotiates the ninety-degree turn, the seats, and the steering wheel like a skilled waiter carrying a platter through a crowded restaurant. What the dog lacks in appearance (he sports a wild dreadlock coat) he makes up for with remarkable dexterity, depositing the curved handle in his master's open palm.

No reward, simply on to the next instruction. "Stash, stand." On a dime, the poodle spins around and comes to rest in a standing position adjacent to the open door. I note the way Stash drops his head and neck ever so slightly, bracing, locking his

elbows, before taking the brunt of the
man's trembling weight as he eases into a
full upright position, the walking stick more
for balance than support.

Seconds pass as the man sucks down
mouthfuls of icy air before saying, "Stash,
come." I hold the front door open and the
two of them amble into the waiting room,
no leash necessary, the dog's nose never
more than a few inches from the man's left
thigh.

"Why don't you give Doris here your details. She'll make up a file and then we can
head over to the exam room. Just got to
dump my stuff."

I raise my doctor's bag and keep moving toward the door marked PRIVATE that
leads to the central work area.

"Won't need a file," says the man. "Only
want a quick word. In private."

It's not easy to guess the man's age, but
I'm betting he's a whole lot younger than
he looks. A black woolen cap accentuates
his baby-bird features and jug-handle ears,
and I can't tell the color of his eyes because
they live in the eclipse of his sockets. His
leather bomber jacket looks empty and
stiff, as if it's full of helium, the white fur col-

lar drawing the eye to a garish Adam's apple, slung under the angle of his wishbone jaw, the cartilage sharp and agitated.

The pathologist in me imagines all sorts of grim diseases. He reminds me of one of those tragic final photos of Rock Hudson or Patrick Swayze. **A quick word**. How big can this favor possibly be?

Doris stares at me. Stash stares at his master. Doris is hard to read—leery or irritated or both. I'm pretty sure she thinks he's not going to pay for my time.

"Okay," I say. "This way."

I ignore Doris as she shakes her head and clucks her tongue. If the man catches her disapproval, he doesn't let on.

I gesture for the man to take a seat on the wooden bench, but presumably for practical reasons, he waves the offer away.

"What can I do for you, Mr. . . ."

"Better you don't know my name, Dr. Mills. Better you don't know nothing about me, period."

Uh-oh. Maybe Doris was right.

"Okay. Why don't you tell me what's on your mind?"

The man leans into the exam table for support. He flexes the fingers of his left hand, a subtle beckoning gesture, and Stash instantly sits and backs into a position so his flanks are touching the leg of his master's jeans.

"See, I spoke to people round town. They told me about you, said you were a good man, said you helped out a pregnant girl, found a missing dog, ran a free clinic."

Boy, everyone loves free.

"Figured you for the kind of guy who'd be receptive to my proposal. Figured you for a doctor with a heart. A doctor with a conscience."

Where is this headed? I flash back to when I was maybe six or seven, my mother taking the stranger-danger lecture to the next level.

**Beware of compliments from people you don't know. They want something you won't want to give.**

I glance at Stash. This cannot be good.

"It's an unusual request, but you and I have a whole lot more in common than you know."

Now we're cut from the same cloth?

"I grew up round here as well. Like you, I eventually came home, only you got this practice and I got this dog."

I got Bedside Manor and he got Stash? What's that supposed to mean?

"And I wouldn't ask unless I was totally desperate and had nowhere else to turn."

"Let me just stop you right there, whoever you are, because if you're going to ask me to put your dog to sleep and this dog doesn't have a painful or terminal illness, then you're wasting your time."

The man recoils. "Not him. Not Stash. I want you to help put **me** to sleep, in so many words."

Should I be looking for the hidden camera? Is this a joke? Then the man arches into the table and the overhead light chases away the shadows, just for a second, and I see what lies beneath—the black hopelessness of eyes that are already dead.

"You're a man who can end suffering." His tone is in control, not accusatory. "Well, I think I've suffered enough. Modern medicine has given me a life in which I can lose everything and spend my days fighting insurance companies. Only thing of value left is this poor dog, and what kind of a life does he have?"

Maybe I could extol the dog's talents, drop a few platitudes about the way companion

animals help us look forward, give us purpose, but in this moment it feels wrong—
trite and woefully inadequate.

"You want me to help you kill yourself?"
I ask, unable to keep the shock out of my
voice.

"I'm not a well man, Dr. Mills. And I'm
never going to get better. We're talking
days, not weeks. What remains for me is
miserable and inevitable and, most of all,
undignified. I don't need pain relief. I need
the pain to stop forever. I know you know
what I'm saying. It's what you do. Delivering a dose of mercy because nature can
take its course and shove it."

I'm not sure where to begin. Last week I
was a doctor disturbed by the way pet
owners get so personal, trying to suck me
into their overwrought lives. Now I'm being
asked if I'll be Dr. Kevorkian.

"Oh no," he says, clearly reading my
shocked expression, "I didn't mean for you
to do it." He laughs, as though I should be
relieved by this clarification. "I just need
the euthanasia solution, the barbiturate.
Point me in the direction of the drug box,
leave the key out or tell me where I can
find it, and I'll do the rest. It'll be a break-

in. You've got insurance, right? Police won't care. They'll blame kids looking for Special K."

Ketamine. Special K. He's serious, in the worst possible way; a tragic, disturbed, unreachable serious. This total stranger wants me to help him commit suicide, and his tone is so casual, so relaxed, he's like a neighbor who drops by to ask if he can borrow your stepladder or whether you can help him move some heavy furniture. It's surreal. But then Stash glances my way for a split second, and the reality of this predicament becomes plain and simple.

"I can't help you. I'm sorry."

The man cants his head to one side and a trace of acquiescence crawls between his gray, cracked lips, careful not to let me see his teeth and gums. It's as if he knew this was a long shot but worth a try.

"Hell," he says. "If the plane's going to crash, might as well lay down and go to sleep."

This is a man resigned to his fate. The time for anger and fighting has past.

"Thanks for hearing me out," he says, heading for the door, Stash right by his side.

"But what about your poodle?" I ask.

The man hesitates and turns my way, visibly disappointed.

"He's a doodle, not a poodle. Australian. Fourth generation."

Uh-oh. In the sheltered world of veterinary pathology I've noticed the popular trend of mixing poodles with all manner of different breeds, earning the moniker "designer dogs." I've never met one in the flesh. Or should I say the fur. That's why it's so ratty—he doesn't shed and, by the looks of things, doesn't get groomed.

"Stash has Labrador loyalty with standard poodle brains."

"Got it," I say, noting the pride in his voice. "What's going to happen to him?"

The man shrugs inside his jacket, but the shoulders barely move. He turns away and doesn't look back.

"That's up to you," he says as the front door chimes and the two of them slip away.

**What a strange comment**, I think. **Why or how would his dog have anything to do with me?**

Doris sidles over as I watch Stash help the man get back into his van.

"Before you start," I say, "that is an incredible dog. Faithful, attentive, and really smart."

"Smart enough to be billed for your time?" Doris lets the question simmer for a few seconds before adding, "By the way, there's a doctor been holding on line two. Wants to talk to you about a case. Says it's important."

"Doris, why didn't you say so?"

I practically sprint for the phone in the work area because, for the second time in one day, my expertise is being sought as a second opinion. Perhaps I have misjudged general practice, thinking it would never tax my brain, days blurring with the endless monotony of vaccines and health checks. Yes, I'm rusty with the hands-on stuff and the challenge of extracting a meaningful history from well-intentioned but long-winded owners, yet fellow professionals still want a slice of what counts—insight, knowledge, and the ability to uncover the truth.

I press the red line two button on the phone.

"Hello."

"Is this Dr. Mills?"

A reserved female voice.

"It is."

"Well, well, well, you've got a nerve. This is Dr. Honey over at Healthy Paws, and I don't know where you came from or what kind of voodoo medicine you like to practice, but around these parts we don't go poaching cases from one another."

My silence is borne of genuine shock, but she keeps going. "Oh please, I'm referring to Sox Sauer, the boxer, small lump on the shoulder. Are you really so desperate? Would it help if I handed out your business card at our local dog park? You're like the veterinary version of an ambulance-chasing lawyer. Do not, repeat, do not let this happen again. If you do, I will be forced to seek legal counsel."

The line goes dead before I can say another word.

No bribe, no negotiations, no preemptive white flag. Right now I'm angry enough to risk life and limb, charging straight into enemy territory, a human microburst, rifling through Doris's reception desk in search of the Sox Sauer file.

There's a savage rap on the glass and then a pointy finger insists I cease and desist followed by an aggressive shooing motion that makes me retreat to the other side of the waiting room. Doris is on the other side of the window looking in with a murderous glare, my crime so serious, I watch as a half-smoked cigarette (you heard me right) swan dives off the ends of her fingertips and lands in the snow.

The front door chimes.

"What on earth are you doing, Dr. Mills? There's a precise system to my record keeping."

"Sox Sauer. I need his file. Now."

Doris comes around the desk and, making a point of keeping her eyes on me, shuffles a sheet of paper here, a bill there, and suddenly there it is in her quick yellow talons.

"You mean this, Dr. Mills?" Her words are clipped, an angry hornet determined to sting.

I take it, my nod all the thanks she will get. It's not the case notes I want. It's the phone number for Ms. Sauer.

"If Healthy Paws thinks I'm out to steal a client, I'd best find out what this client has been saying to them."

"Marjorie Sauer might act confrontational," says Doris, "but she prefers to whisper. Not like me. I prefer to see the fear in their eyes."

Why am I not surprised?

Back in the work area I dial the number from the page marked "Client Information."

"Hello, Ms. Sauer, this is Dr. Mills from Bedside Manor. Tell me, have you been in contact with Dr. Honey following our consultation this morning?"

"No."

"Oh."

"But that office manager called me up. Dork, Dorkus, or something."

"Mr. Dorkin."

"Yeah, him. Asked what I was doing at Bedside Manor this morning, and I told him, and he started out acting sympathetic, apologizing, wanting to know how Healthy Paws could do right by me and Sox, and I told him he could start by not trying to rip off conscientious and vulnerable pet owners by recommending unnecessary surgeries. And that's when he went off on me, telling me we're not welcome at Healthy Paws—fired is what he said, 'You're fired.' Like he was Donald Trump."

There's a sniffle, a series of jagged little breaths, as Marjorie Sauer begins to lose her composure.

"Then, get this, he says he'd be happy to recommend alternative veterinary practices. I said, 'Don't bother, we'll be going to Bedside Manor from now on,' and that's when he did this weird laughing thing and said, 'That place will be in foreclosure by this time next week. You just burned your bridges, lady.' And then he hung up."

I was right. Dorkin did recognize Sox as a Healthy Paws client. And the guy's got an ugly temper. But here's the upside: he'd only be this serious about our rivalry for one reason—he's worried.

My cell phone begins vibrating in my pocket.

"Have no fear, Ms. Sauer. Dorkin's full of hot air. We're not going anywhere."

I hang up on one call and pick up the next, not recognizing the number on the screen.

"Hey, Doc, you free to talk?"

"Um, who is this?"

"It's Charlie Brown, remember? Marmalade Succabone, feline porn star."

"Right, Charlize."

"I, like, spoke to my mom, and she's going to be passing through Eden Falls on her way home. She's going to give you a check for the house call. Any chance you could meet her at the diner on Main Street?"

"I suppose so."

"Great. Seven?"

"Okay. But wouldn't it be easier—"

"I'm just repeating what she said. You still wearing that ugly tie?"

"I beg your pardon. I happen to like this tie."

I study the narrow strip of one hundred percent woven microfiber polyester dangling from my neck. It's white with bold red stripes.

"Please! It looks like a candy cane. But don't take it off. That's how she's going to recognize you. That and my description of how you're totally hot!"

I catch the laugh just before the line goes dead.

Five of Seven and I have my choice of several empty booths, picking one close to the front door with a view of everyone who walks in. I wonder if the diner's always quieter on nights when Amy's "got plans." Keeping my winter coat on but unzipped to adequately expose my "ugly" tie, I've barely settled in when a waitress I don't recognize appears by my side.

"It's Doc Mills, isn't it?"

She's young with spiky tangerine hair, some sort of sparkly piercing embedded in the skin adjacent to her right nostril, and a plastic tag that tells me her name is Mary.

"It is."

"Coming to see you tomorrow. My dog, Gilligan. Amy said if anyone can sort him out, it's Doc Mills."

I smile, buoyed by the idea of Amy talking about me behind my back, giving me compliments.

"I'll certainly try my best." I glance at my watch, nearly seven. "So Amy's off tonight?"

"Yep, she asked if I could fill in for her, and I can always use the extra money."

Ordinarily, I wouldn't push, but the twinge inside won't go away. "Oh, is she doing something special?"

Her nose twitches, making her piercing catch the light, and I fear she's on to me.

"Don't know, but she was picking up a dress from the dry cleaner and getting her hair done, so it sounds like. But listen to me going on, what can I get you?"

"Actually, I'm meeting someone. Should be here any minute." With Amy not here I have no intention of sticking around. As soon as Mrs. Brown hands over my check I'll be on my way. "I'll hang on if you don't mind."

"Coffee while you wait?"

"Why not."

"Cream, no sugar, right?"

How did she know? Just how much did Amy share about me?

"Great."

I ease back in my seat, wishing I'd brought something to read. I hate twiddling my thumbs when I could have been researching catastrophic diseases of cattle or Jenny Craig for cats instead of imagining Amy out somewhere nice, somewhere that necessitates a dress. Women get their hair done for one of two reasons—either to outdo the female competition or to attract a mate. What are the odds that this momentous date has nothing to do with the mysterious caller who could make her giggle?

"There you go," says Mary, placing the steaming mug before me. "Let me know if you change your mind."

I thank her and look up as a bearded man in a lumberjack shirt breezes by on his way to the counter. Five more minutes, that's all I'll give her and then this annoying Mrs. Brown can damn well drive over to Bedside Manor and drop off the check at my convenience, not hers.

Fifteen minutes later and I'm looking over my shoulder for Mary, wanting to pay for my coffee, when I notice a domino effect of male heads turning toward the front door. I join in and discover a woman hovering at the entrance—golden hair swept back and expertly pinned in place, meticulously applied makeup (the sort that's supposed to look like you're not wearing any), short white double-breasted trench coat, jeans, and knee-length leather boots. If this new arrival is Mrs. Brown, she either works for **Vogue** magazine or she's totally overdressed to drop off some money.

Why is she headed my way?

"Mr. Lovelace? Thomas Lovelace?"

"I'm . . . I beg your pardon?"

"The tie. Too funny. And so much more original than a pink carnation."

Pink carnation?

"I'm Dr. Winn Honey," she says, extending her hand for me to shake.

Winn Honey. Dr. Honey. Dr. Honey, the vet from Healthy Paws who hates my guts. Why on earth is this woman greeting me like we're on a blind date?

Dazed, fish-mouthed, and speechless, I

watch as my hand drifts up and completes the greeting.

"Mind if I take a seat?"

She's already unbuttoning her coat, hanging it on the brass hanger at the end of the booth, and sliding across the seat opposite, the tips of the fingers of her right hand performing a minor adjustment to her coif.

"So sorry I'm late. Work." I get the whites of her eyes again, a sharp intake of breath. "But let's not go there just yet. Should I begin or would you prefer to start?"

The only reason I'm not drooling like a total moron is the adrenaline coursing through my body and sapping my saliva. The logic is irrefutable. Given she used the name Tommy Lovelace, the mother of Charlie Brown and Doc Honey must be one and the same person.

It's the question I'm about to ask when my phone begins buzzing in my pants and I recognize the number of the caller. Amazing. At this precise moment, I can think of no one else in the world I would want to speak to more.

"Would you excuse me for one minute? I have to take this call."

"Sure. Want a refill?" asks my adversary, pointing to my empty mug.

"Why not," I reply, hurrying through the front door and out into the night.

I flip open the phone.

"She there yet?"

"Yes, Charlize, she's here all right. You want me to tell her how you set her up on a blind date with a veterinarian and not a porn star?"

There's a silence, followed by a sigh, followed by, "It was Gabe's idea. Okay, Gabe's and my idea. He figured I could use Marmalade as a way for me to check you out. We wanted to hook you guys up 'cause we both really like you, and Gabe wants to pay you back for being cool about the pot. And I'm sick of the way Mom's meeting weird men online and bringing them home on a first date like a sex-starved nymphet. It's embarrassing."

"You what? No, no, that's ridiculous and totally inappropriate. I'm sorry, Charlize, you leave me no choice but to—"

"It's too late. Gabe already set this up through a dating website: Loveatfirstsite .com. But don't worry, he didn't use your name or anything to create a profile."

Any sarcastic "that's a relief" rebuttal escapes me as the surprises keep coming.

"Mom thinks you're Mr. Tommy Lovelace. The site sent her an email saying the two of you were compatible and you were eager to see if there were any sparks, any love at first sight."

Her amorous intonation is not helping her cause as I pace back and forth in front of the entrance to the diner, the fog in my head as thick as the fog from my breath. "Let me get this straight—you guys secretly created a dating profile for me and lured me here to meet your mom and she has no idea?"

"Just listen," says Charlize. "You can walk away at any time. That's why we gave you a fake ID and put you together on neutral territory. Mom has no idea who you really are."

"Clearly," I say, flashing back to her angry phone call about Sox Sauer. "So your worries about Marmalade's weight, that was just to set this up?"

"No . . . not really," says Charlize, but I detect a shift in her tone, brazen and defiant turning more uncertain, even introspective. "My mom actually did all those tests and she still can't figure out why Marmalade's so fat. Maybe you're smart enough to find out where she went wrong."

I can't tell if that's a challenge or a request. Either way, if the second case I poach from Healthy Paws happens to be Dr. Honey's own cat, I'll need an ambulance and then a lawyer.

"Coming clean as a veterinarian from the nearby rival practice might prove a little tricky, don't you think?"

"Maybe. But based on the type of man she usually ends up with, if you two hit it off, she'll find a way to forgive you. Can you say low self-esteem?"

For all her scheming and the burden of the shameful and outrageous position she's put me in, I can't help but admire her chutzpah.

"Walk away and she'll be none the wiser. Wouldn't blame you, especially if she starts blabbing about work and more work."

And, unintentionally (at least I hope so), this is where Charlie Brown sets the hook.

"Go back a minute," I say, stopping in front of a bulletin board to the left of the diner's entrance. "What details did Gabe make up about this Mr. Tommy Lovelace?"

On a bulletin board outside the diner, next to a handwritten notice of someone searching for a runaway teenager, there's a poster that pulls me away from Charlie's reply.

Healthy Paws and the Eden Falls Knights
of Columbus
present
**Pet First Aid**
A lecture by local Healthy Paws veterinarian,
Dr. Winn Honey, VMD.
Refreshments will be served
Freebies for your four-legged friends
Dogs Allowed*

"He kept it vague. Except what you do for a living."

Dogs allowed. But there's an asterisk. My eyes dart to the bottom. Where's the asterisk, where's the exception?

"Doc, you still there?"

I can't find it. "Sorry, missed that last bit."

"Gabe put down your job as movie reviewer for an online magazine. He didn't know what else to write. If it helps, he did say you love animals."

Dr. Honey is going to lecture here, in Eden Falls? First they hit up the **Gazette** to advertise for a free clinic and now they want to do outreach to pet owners on my turf.

"Okay. I'm going to see what happens . . . but forget about a fairy-tale ending. Your mother may be an attractive woman, but I'm not interested. Right now, I'd love to walk away, but it would be rude and hurtful and unfair to someone who's been conned by her daughter into thinking a computer program just discovered her soul mate. And don't think I won't spill the beans if this gets messy."

The line falls silent, and for the first time since stepping outside in only a shirt and tie I feel the cold setting in.

"Sorry," she says, and I don't need to hear her weeping to know she means it.

"Charlie."

"What?"

"I'm not going to get paid for that visit today, am I?"

"No," she says, "not unless the sundae counts."

Back inside the diner, Dr. Honey has her back to me, sipping a coffee. The fact that she hasn't stormed off or come look-ing for me can only mean one thing—Mary the waitress hasn't blown my cover as Cyrus Mills. How long can that last?

"Very sorry about that," I say, squeezing back into the booth. "Rude of me, and I apologize."

"Not at all," says Honey, eyeing me with unnerving scrutiny over the rim of her mug before placing it off to one side. "Do I detect an accent, Tom? Sorry, do you prefer Tom or Tommy or Thomas?"

"Tom's fine," I stutter, "and yes . . . um . . . I lived in . . . Mississippi, for a while, slip in a little twang and drawl every now and then."

Dr. Honey sits up a little straighter, plays with the handle of the mug. "It's nice. I like it."

I'm guessing she's a little older than me, midforties, and I'm rewarded for staring with a big smile of overly whitened teeth. I'm speechless. This is why I've never been on a blind date. The only two questions that have popped into my head are "Do you work out?" and "How tall are you?" Both make me sound like a creep who wonders if she'll fight back or fit inside the tomb under my basement. I'm so not suited for this.

I'm glad I couldn't get a word in edgewise when she was reaming me out on the phone over Sox Sauer. Clearly she hasn't recognized my voice.

"Need anything else?" asks Mary, breezing by, glass coffee carafe in hand.

"I think we're fine," says Dr. Honey, placing her hand over the top of her mug. I pretend to sip, shake my head, and though Mary keeps going, she's not fooling me. I know I'm being watched. Amy's co-worker is obviously curious about the meeting between Dr. Mills and a beautiful stranger of the opposite sex. Suddenly that unpleasant writhing sensation in my guts at the thought of Amy out with another man lessens at the prospect of what Mary imagines she sees and might report back to Amy.

"You were about to go first," I say as though I'm familiar with the standard blind-dating protocol.

"Ladies first," says Dr. Honey, folding her hands in front of her on the table. "I like that." I fear she has her thirty-second elevator pitch down cold. "My name's Winifred, old-fashioned I know, but friends call me Winn. I'm a veterinarian, so naturally I love animals. I'm a hopeless romantic, but from time to time I like to let my hair down, if you know what I mean. I love good food, good wine, good books, and good movies."

"Good . . . good," I say, slow nodding and feeling anything but. She pretty much covered every base. If I said I was an abstinent illiterate vegan hermit I'm pretty sure I'd still be in with a chance. "You work here in Eden Falls?"

See how I did that? Fake left, go right.

"No, I work over at a Healthy Paws in Patton."

"You like being a vet?" After a lifetime of being on the other end of this question, I know how this inane line of inquiry goes. "What I mean is . . . it must be so rewarding, but also so very sad, putting animals to sleep all the time."

Winn Honey looks down at the table and back at me.

"I promised myself I wouldn't bore you with tales of woe from work."

"Don't be silly," I say. I can't believe I'm staring into the sparkling green eyes of the enemy. This is so wrong. At the very least I should get up and walk away. "I'm fascinated with what goes on at a modern animal hospital." I know, I know, but at least I'm telling the truth. "I always wanted to be a veterinarian when I grew up." See, so long as I don't actually lie, this façade doesn't feel too bad.

"Oh, I don't know," she says on a sigh. "My boss is a total dick, pardon my French."

"Your boss?"

"Sorry, office manager. Today he made me call the animal hospital down the road," she points over her shoulder, "stood right in front of me while I shouted at their vet for stealing one of our cases. He has some sort of vendetta against them."

"Wait, this guy stole your case?" As soon as the words leave my mouth I want them back. How would I know the vet is a he?

"It's complicated, but my boss thinks that if I lose a case I must be doing something wrong. It was enough to get a second written warning in as many days."

She missed it, so I pounce. "Second?"

"Tuesday night I was on call, but I forgot to turn my phone to vibrate. Ended up missing an emergency."

Ah, Tallulah, the pot brownie–chewing mastiff.

"One more strike against me and I'm out, fired, time to look for a new job, and, thanks to a noncompete clause, I'd have to move out of the area."

"Noncompete clause?"

"Forget it," she says, wafting a hand in front of her face. "All it means is I can't afford to screw up on Saturday. I've got this stupid lecture to give here in Eden Falls at the Knights of Columbus. It's meant to drum up business, an excuse to show off our place. You should come, if you're interested."

"I am," I say, and then, ignoring the fact that I'd be instantly unmasked as Cyrus Mills, I add, "I will."

She seems inordinately pleased, as though by making this promise we already have a future together.

"Your turn," she says, and then, reading the fear contorting my face as nervousness, she reaches across the table to touch my hand. "First blind date?"

I nod, and then it strikes me that it may be possible for me to go forward, to maintain this lie, so long as I stick to the truth.

"Take your time," she says soothingly. "No rush. Whatever comes into your head."

"Well . . . I'm from Eden Falls. Obviously I like watching movies." My awkward, nervous laugh is genuine.

"Obviously," she says, showing me her teeth again. It's like she's coercing a naughty boy to come clean about his crime.

"Um . . . well, I would say I have a certain . . . affinity . . . to animals."

"Affinity? Interesting."

**Only ten percent of men and women get a second date if they say they don't like pets.**

"Yes, that I'm intrigued by what's going on inside them."

"Really. Like a pet psychic?"

Oh dear. "A little bit," I say, trying to think of ways to return to the secrets of Healthy Paws.

"Tell me," she says, trying to bail me out. "What's your greatest strength?"

I make a show of bringing my thumb and fingers to my chin. Obviously trust goes out the window and so does honesty. Logical and intelligent seem a little self-aggrandizing.

"Good listener," I reply. Which is code for "I'd love to listen to you gripe some more about your place of work."

"Greatest weakness?"

It's painful to watch the sincerity, the hope in her eyes.

"That's easy. Stubborn. Judgmental. Occasionally impulsive."

"Impulsive?"

Dr. Honey seems to like the sound of that one a little too much.

"I tend to jump to conclusions," I add. "Not always the right ones."

Her head lilts ever so slightly to one side. "Has that gotten you in trouble in past relationships? With your ex-wife . . . ?"

Oh, okay, she's fishing here.

"Actually I've never been married. You?"

She hesitates. Maybe it's the recollection of what went wrong or the worry of what she must confess. "Guilty."

Strange word, like she's committed a crime.

"Married for nineteen years."

"Irreconcilable differences?" I ask.

"Irreconcilable hatred," she snaps back, and I can tell she means it.

"Children?"

For the first time she appears a little flustered.

"Just one—a teenage girl. But she lives with her father. Wanted to stay in the same school system. I see her every so often.

Essentially, it's just me, not forgetting the love of my life, Marmalade."

Well, well, I'm not the only one telling fibs. Has Winn Honey discovered that having a child seriously limits your dating options? And why was Charlie not referred to by name? Is the daughter caught up in some sort of misplaced anger at her ex? I know what it's like to play the blame game, changing my last name to my mother's maiden name and refusing to acknowledge my father's existence for fifteen years. It took his death and his dying veterinary practice before I realized, too late, what a fool I'd been. I wonder how far this jilted woman will go to compete with the much-maligned Mr. Brown in Wisconsin.

"Marmalade. I'm guessing an orange cat."

"Very good. Maybe you are psychic after all." This next smile is coy, not unpleasant, and, I imagine, has proven to be highly effective in the past. "Look, after my day I could really use something stronger than a coffee. You fancy a real drink? We could take this conversation to a bar or, if you prefer, I've got a nice Chardonnay chilling at home."

The recollection of Charlie Brown gagging over her mother's penchant for one-night stands comes to mind as one of my Bedside Manor clients stomps through the diner's front door. Ethel Silverman is a crotchety old biddy who makes Doris look positively discreet and compassionate. Her raptor eyes spy me. She bristles but heads straight for the counter. How long before I'm treated to a surly update regarding her husky Kai's ongoing skin issues?

"Yeah . . . um . . . that sounds perfectly . . . fine, but . . ." **Think, Cyrus, think.** "But . . . I'll be honest . . . I wasn't sure this . . . en-counter, was going to . . ."

"Let me guess, you prefer brunettes?" she says with a smile that barely masks her vulnerability. I see it, around her eyes, written in the fine wrinkles and lines of her carefully applied foundation, the insecurity, the permanent scar of being abandoned by your husband for another woman.

"No, of course not."

It's true, in a general, unprejudiced way, but she appears to catch the fact that my remark is more objective, less emotional.

"So what's the problem?"

"There is none. I thought this was a way to see if there was anything between us."

"And is there?"

"More than you can imagine," I say, reaching into my pocket and laying a twenty-dollar bill on the table. I want to get away before Ethel and Mary rat me out, even though I need change and don't want to give Dr. Honey the impression I'm trying to impress her with a big tip.

"Are you sure you're not married?"

"Absolutely not."

"Hmm." Once again she dazzles me with her smile. "You are very different, Thomas Lovelace. Strange name, but you have my attention."

"And you mine," I say, getting up. "So . . . um . . . email me, and I hope to take you up on your offer real soon."

At least at her house there's no risk of being unmasked as Cyrus Mills.

"I'm not kidding," I say, standing to shake her hand. And then, as a melding of truth and flirtation comes to mind, I can't help but add, "There's so much more about you I want to discover."

# Thursday

« **8** »

I didn't expect to see Mary from the diner quite so soon, but thanks to her tangerine hair, she's the first (and only) person I recognize in a rowdy waiting room. It's Lewis's morning to see appointments, and sometimes it feels like we are polar opposites when it comes to our appeal as veterinarians. Lewis consistently packs them in with his magnetic attraction whereas I keep them away with my magnetic repulsion. Still, five minutes ago, I was the recipient of an unusual greeting from the bottom of the stairway to my apartment.

"Hey, you awake up there? You've got one waiting."

Ah, Doris, my cup of morning cheer, what would I do without you?

I grab the file on her desk (it lies alone, crisp and thin, adjacent to an imposing tower of case files for Lewis) and march over to Mary, trying to get a read on her impassive features. What if, after I left, Doc Honey asked her about the mysterious Tommy Lovelace? Is my cover blown? If so, how much did Mary share with Amy?

"He's outside in the car," says Mary, as soon as I say hello, "gets easily stressed." She sticks her head out the front door and yells, "Drew! Drew, come on."

A redheaded man steps out of a pickup carrying a border collie in his arms like an awkward piece of furniture, and I usher the three of them back into the work area, making my apologies, claiming our other exam room is undergoing renovation (or at least it will if the practice can stay in business until the end of the month).

"This is my husband, Drew. He's apprenticing as a mechanic at the gas station down the road," she says, making the introduction sound like an apology for the calloused, oil-stained hand that reaches out for the greeting. It's heavy on crush, light on shake, the dog perfectly still in his arms. By still I mean rigid, as though the creature's been stuffed or needs to be defrosted. When Mary said stressed I think she meant scared stiff.

"And this is Gilligan," says Mary as Drew finally places the timid creature on the floor. The collie comes to life, running on the spot, a cartoon dog scratching for traction on the linoleum, scampering behind Mary like a shy child hiding behind his mother's skirt, or, in this case, black jeans.

"Come on out, Gil, come on."

Best I can tell, Gilligan is a handsome tricolor of black, tan, and white, with pricked attentive ears. His bushy tail is so tightly curled underneath him it practically screams "don't even think about taking my temperature." He won't allow me to make eye contact, burying his head into the back of Mary's knees. Perhaps Gil thinks if he can't see me, I can't see him.

"Very smart breed," I say.

"I know," says Mary, clearly taking this as a compliment.

"Fastest time to open a car window by a dog."

She looks confused.

"A border collie called Striker," I say. "Just over eleven seconds."

Mary consults with her husband, her expression suggesting they should leave while they have the chance.

I press on. "What's going on?" I ask, picking up pen and paper to take some notes when, as if on cue, Gilligan decides to give his version of the story. In the style of a cuckoo clock striking the hour, a snout pops around Mary's leg to deliver a snappy, ear-piercing bark.

I reel, a little theatrically, but get no response from either Mary or Drew.

"I'll start at the beginning," says Mary, as Gil lets rip with another bark. "Drew and I have been married about six months." Bark. "Few weeks after the wedding, we moved into my late grandmother's house." Bark. "Before that, Gil was fine, right?"

There's a pause, and Drew nods as Gil, the canine metronome, times another yappy keening to perfection. Seriously, he has to be cracking 120 decibels, easily. His bark's a health hazard, but worst of all, and what leaves me speechless (and presumably hearing impaired), his owners don't seem to notice. They don't even blink.

"Ever since we've moved he's been acting weird." Bark. "Both of us work, and it's like he has separation anxiety." Bark.

I narrow my eyes, wince, and press my index finger deep into my ear canal, to no avail.

"He stays in the exact same spot where I left him." Bark. "Standing at the dining room window, waiting for us to come home." Bark. And then, finally, my features having contorted past "unpleasant wince" and ending at "unbearable torture," she says, "Is there a problem?"

The welcome silence hangs in the air between us. Seconds pass without a bark, and I get to savor the after hiss ringing in my ears.

"Sorry, just, um, having a hard time concentrating," I say. Mary looks at Drew; they share a shrug and a frown and both come back to me looking confused. "Gil's barking." I feel like I'm explaining the punch line of a joke. "It's quite . . ." **Careful, Cyrus, don't offend.** "Extraordinary. Don't want to miss anything important you might say."

"Right," says Mary, stretching out the syllable as though totally on board, making eye contact with Gil while placing an index finger to her shushing lips.

"Really? That's going to silence your bad-mannered dog?" I want to say, but I bite my tongue and brace for the pending rupture of an eardrum.

"He's not eating much, and he's losing weight, don't you think?"

Drew nods but remains silent, and, to my amazement and relief, so does Gilligan.

"Then this time yesterday morning, he had like, I don't know, like a seizure. Scared the crap out of me. That's when I talked to Amy, and she said you're the man to see."

Was this the last time Mary spoke to Amy or was there a gossipy update regarding my "date" with a beautiful woman?

"When you say seizure, what do you mean?"

Mary deliberates, the recollection visibly upsetting. "He was lying on the kitchen floor, legs out straight and stiff, out of it, and he'd wet himself. I kept calling his name, and it was like no one was home. That look in his eyes, I'll never forget it, it was like . . ." A tear gets away from her right eye. "It was like he was dead."

I glance over to Drew, wondering why he's not putting a consoling arm around his young wife's shoulder. I read sympathy but reckon there's a blue-collar emotional toughness holding him back.

"So you never actually saw Gil shaking or trembling or flailing?"

"No."

"And how long did it take him to get up and back to himself?"

"Maybe half an hour. He was staggering at first, out of it, like he was really frightened."

All this time Gilligan has been watching me while his body remains neatly concealed behind Mary's legs.

"Okay, let's have a look at him."

I step forward and to one side, coming around Mary as Gil makes an equal and opposite maneuver so he can remain invisible. I catch myself, change direction, and we repeat our dance, Mary our maypole in the middle.

"Drew, perhaps you could lend me a hand." An oily, calloused hand.

Seconds later Gilligan has been corralled

as Drew kneels on the floor beside me. Based on the man's pallor and freckles, I'm betting on an Irish heritage, cheeks guaranteed to light up red with too much sun or too many pints. His dog is compliant but clearly terrified. I don't need a stethoscope to determine his heart rate; I can see it thumping against his rib cage like it wants out. And forget about palpating the contents of his abdomen. Gil's tummy is rock solid, constantly bracing for a sucker punch to the gut. I do, however, make two meaningful discoveries. The nerves from Gil's brain that control blinking, seeing, swallowing, licking, smelling, and, sadly, barking all appear to be in full working order. But I have a problem with the color of his gums.

"Perhaps you can help me lift his tail so I can take his temperature," I say, remembering one of Lewis's favorite tricks. **If you don't know what to say or do, take a rectal temperature, it will give you a few extra minutes to think.**

For a while Drew and Gilligan engage in their own version of Greco-Roman wrestling until the mechanic pins him and the collie submits to my thermometer.

Here's my problem. As a veterinary pathologist, I've always had a direct, physical path to the diagnosis. I was like the detective who always got his man, the culprit tried, convicted, and behind bars and I never had to worry about the motive. Now, in my second week of pretending to be a real veterinarian, unsolved cases are beginning to stack up. Ermintrude the crazy cow, Marmalade the fat cat, and now Gilligan, the neurotic collie. Yes, I've got clues, but I don't have nearly enough evidence to convict. I'm all speculation, hot air, and theories, surrounded by anxious relatives desperate for results. Where are all the easy cases? Where are the fleas or the worms when you need them?

"One oh three point two. To be honest, he's so nervous I'm surprised the glass didn't melt."

"What do you think?" says Mary, petting Gil as if she's offering an apology for the violation.

I take a deep breath. "His gums are too pale. He's anemic."

"What? Why?"

"Three possible reasons. Losing blood, not making enough blood, destroying blood."

"So which one is it?"

I consider what I've got to go on. No appetite, weight loss, seizure, and anemia. Each problem has dozens of possible causes—put them together and the permutations are endless.

"Not sure," I say, but as she deflates, I rush to add, "but I intend to find out."

Rather than relieved, Mary seems cagey. "Sounds expensive," she says. "What's your best guess?"

That's when I wonder if my referral from Amy was grounded in a respect for my clinical prowess or recognition that, in certain circumstances, I can be a soft touch. Happy to get extra hours at the diner, husband's an apprentice, lucky enough to be given a house to live in—more than enough clues to know money's tight.

"Tell you what, let me get a blood sample and I'll look at it myself. Hopefully I'll find the answer and save you the cost of sending it off to a lab."

They check in with one another, there are nods of approval, and the deal is sealed by a complimentary yip from Gilligan.

Despite the collie's fear and unyielding full-body rigidity, I get the necessary blood and see them out, Drew, as talkative as ever, offers a grim nod and a grungy handshake; Mary smiles, thanking me and insisting, "Amy was right," as Gilligan yanks her through the front door.

Right about what? Right to suggest I see her dog? Right about me being a bit of a nerd? She's gone before I can ask. At least that's my excuse.

With the purple tube of the blood sample safely inside my breast pocket, I head back into the work area, only to find Lewis perched in front of our microscope. He looks up as I approach.

"What, you think you're the only one who knows how to use it?"

"No, of course—"

"Look it."

Lewis gestures to the eyepieces. I take a peek and remark, "Otodectes cynotis."

Lewis shakes his head in frustration. "Keep it simple, Cyrus. Plain speak. 'Ear mites' makes a lot more sense to most people."

I straighten up, close my eyes, and wipe both hands down my face. "Right now I'd love to make a straightforward diagnosis like ear mites. Seems like every case is a mystery wrapped inside an enigma. I'm used to working for private diagnostic and pharmaceutical companies with deep pockets. Our clients demand quick answers or cheap solutions, preferably both, with nothing more than a laying on of hands."

Lewis gets to his feet. He's not much taller than a racehorse jockey, so I know he's used to angling his head way back to make eye contact.

"Trust me, folks will find a way to pay. What you need to worry about is how to spend their money. You might prefer to run every test in the book, but the best clinicians learn how to play the odds, cut the fat, and get to the answer by the shortest possible route."

"That's what worries me," I say.

As always, Lewis stands way too close for my comfort. I brace for some sort of physical contact. Oh, for a return to the eighties fashion of oversized shoulder pads to buffer these touchy-feely moments.

"You ever play Clue as a kid?" asks Lewis.

I flash to the classic children's board game, laid out with the cards and playing pieces on our dining room table, Mom sitting opposite. Did my father ever join us?

"Of course."

"Good. And I'm betting not once did you give up and open the black envelope because you couldn't wait to know whodunit?"

My silence gives him my answer, and there it is, the hand squeeze to the shoulder.

"Cyrus, you're blessed with an amazing clinical memory, remarkable, if bizarre, observational skills, and okay, your logic can be a little eccentric at times, but start playing this new game and, while you're at it, enjoy yourself."

I try to twist my lips into something approaching a smile.

"Hey, I meant to tell you, I had a visit from Mr. Guy Dorkin of Healthy Paws yesterday."

"Yes, Doris told me."

Silly me, of course she did.

"She also mentioned you had a phone call from an irate Dr. Honey. You know this woman is speaking in Eden Falls this coming Saturday?"

Hmm, now that's interesting. No doubt Ethel Silverman will have informed Doris that I was spotted in the diner last night with another woman. However, the fact that I am not being directly linked to Dr. Honey suggests Ethel did not know who she was.

"I do, and I did. I met Doc Honey for coffee last night. Turns out she was put up to the phone call by Dorkin, for losing a case to Bedside Manor. But I don't think she's a bad person."

"Ah, that's who you were with."

Of course he heard. This town is way too small.

"Yes, and if you don't mind, I'd like to keep that between us."

Lewis narrows his sage gray eyes.

"Would that have anything to do with a certain waitress at the diner?"

"It would have to do with a desire for a measure of basic privacy. If you must know, I was tricked into a rendezvous. Long story. But I thought meeting Dr. Honey might provide valuable insight into what makes Healthy Paws tick and how we can overcome their assault."

"Wait up, why would Doc Honey reveal their secrets to the enemy?"

"Valid question," I reply, "but it'll have to keep. Did you know they have hidden cameras in their exam rooms?"

"Yes. They claim it ensures optimal customer service. What it ensures is that every vet follows the script, maximizes every billable opportunity. Big Brother is watching your every move so if you try to give a client a break, cut a diagnostic corner, you're busted on candid camera."

"That's unbelievable. And what's with this noncompete clause?"

Lewis rocks his head side to side. "Sadly all too common these days, but less so in a rural community like ours. Did she mention the range and the time?"

"No," I reply, not sure what he's referring to.

"Usually two years and thirty miles. Regardless of whether she gets fired or leaves voluntarily, the clause intends to prevent her working as a vet for two years within a thirty-mile radius of Healthy Paws in Patton."

"Wait. What if you've got kids in a school system? What if your spouse has a job nearby? What about the mortgage on your house?"

"Unless you've put an awful lot of money aside, time to sell what you can and ship out."

"Wow, that sounds harsh."

"That sound is the juggernaut of corporate veterinary medicine, more than happy to mow you down. What else did your Deep Throat share?"

I flash to **All the President's Men. Follow the money**.

"That's a work in progress."

Lewis furrows his bushy brows. "My advice is to be careful. Dr. Honey may be finding out more from you than you from her. Remember, she works for Dorkin, and Dorkin plays dirty. If Bedside Manor's going to survive, we might have to get down in the dirt as well."

"What are you saying?"

"That kid, the computer whiz from the other night? Perhaps he could hack into a certain computer system that tells people how to act like a veterinarian."

"That's got to be illegal."

"Cyrus, I'm seventy-three years old, and as far as I'm concerned something is only illegal if you get caught."

I straighten up and blow out a disapproving breath.

"Hey, I'm floating ideas here," says Lewis. "Ignore me. You getting anywhere with Ermintrude the cow?"

There's a moment when I think about sharing my suspicions about the diagnosis from hell. But although it's based on some troubling evidence, it's still circumstantial. Until I build a better case, I'd just be fear mongering.

"Still working on it," I say. "You got other cases to see?"

"Unfortunately," Lewis replies. "Don't suppose you could pick up one or two of mine? The wife's seeing a doctor at noon, and I'd like to be there."

"Sure," I say, "happy to. How is Mrs. Lewis?"

Lewis smiles the smile of a man whose love for his wife hasn't wavered in over fifty years.

"She's good. Told her all about you. Perhaps you could visit sometime. Bring Amy."

And with that he disappears back into the exam room, the throwaway line a carefully lobbed grenade, his passive-aggressive way of saying, "Sort out whatever's going on between you and Amy and make it right." Even if I know how, I wonder if I'll get the chance. It's quite possible my date with Doc Honey has turned her into Miss

Scarlet, intent on killing me with the lead pipe.

"Here, Dr. Mills. Dr. Lewis told me you wanted to help him out, so I picked this case especially for you."

Doris smiles as she hands over the file, a smile borne of genuine pleasure. It's unnerving. I must be walking into a trap.

"Henry," I call, keeping a wary eye on Doris.

"Over here," says a man with a full head of white hair so curly it reminds me of Shirley Temple in **Heidi**. The man's beard is just as white, but the length more Hemingway than Santa. Still, he's packing enough pounds to make some extra money during the holiday season.

"You must be the new one. Heard about you. I'm George Simms; Henry's in the carrier."

George pumps my hand, and once again I make my apologies for using the work area instead of our "other" exam room that still bears a striking resemblance to a storage closet.

"Haven't seen you at the Inn yet."

"The Inn?"

"The Inn at Falls View. I own the place," says George. "Stop by, have a welcome drink on the house. And Chef's great. Though I leave him to it. I'm more comfortable with the bar and the front desk. Make sure our guests are happy. Should I let him out?"

"Sure."

George places the carrier on the floor, undoes the latch, and a miniature black panther yawns, stretches, and leaps onto a counter next to him.

"See the problem?" asks George.

"Can I assume it's the pink lesion on the tip of his nose?"

"Lesion." George grins. "If by lesion you mean the hideous deformity masking Henry's handsome features, then yes."

Henry has his back to me, tail up, busy investigating this new landscape. Finally, a problem I can solve, a physical abnormality I can see, touch, define, and treat.

"How long has he had it?" I ask.

"Months."

"Really?"

"Saw your father about it several times, Doc Lewis as well. Still growing. Getting bigger and uglier every day."

"Let's back up a little. Henry's what, an indoor cat?"

"Indoor and outdoor. Twelve years old and still a great mouser. Not a rodent on our premises, though he does have an annoying habit of bringing back his kills and leaving them on the doormat."

I watch as Henry leaps over a sink and discovers the microscope with much cautious sniffing and the occasional lick.

"And what's he been treated with?"

"We've tried creams, pills, and injections. Antibiotics, antifungals, steroids. Nothing's touched it."

We're having this conversation, but we're not looking at one another. We're both tracking the black cat with our eyes like he's an inquisitive toddler, disaster imminent.

"Has it been biopsied? If it's a tumor, I wouldn't expect any of those treatments to make much of a difference."

George chuckles. Definitely a Santa, he's got the "ho ho ho" down pat. "I'll be honest, Doc. Henry has certain . . . issues, when it comes to veterinarians."

And suddenly all I can see is Doris's nicotine-stained smile.

"Henry's smart, and he can tell the difference between being petted and being examined."

Henry begins swatting at a box of lens tissues, and I notice his paws.

"I see he's polydactyl. His paws. Extra toes." It's a genetic mutation. **Normal cats have eighteen toes. Polydactyl cats can have as many as twenty-seven.**

"That's right," says George. "I believe Hemingway was a big fan."

"Yes, sir."

Maybe George does prefer to impersonate a certain author from Key West.

"Well, I appreciate the warning," I say, picking up a clean towel, "but I'm pretty sure I can handle a kitty cat, even one with extra toes. If I wrap him up, swaddle him nice and snug, I'll be able to take a closer look."

"You're the professional," says George, stepping back as I unfurl my makeshift cape, ready to bring it on. "Only don't look directly in his eyes."

I do a double take. "Why not?"

"Just don't, is all."

Could be tricky, I think, given the location of Henry's problem on the tip of his nose.

Henry remains perched next to the microscope, grooming his neck in long, languorous licks, the barbs of his pink tongue catching in his fur. He seems totally unfazed until I close the distance between us to less than ten feet. That's when the grooming stops. I look back at George.

"What are you doing?"

He's zooming in with his cell phone, filming my examination. "Never know, might make you famous on YouTube. Go on, get in the frame."

Rather than lunging at Henry head-on, I come in at a tangent from his right side.

**Male cats are more often left pawed, just like more men are left-handed.**

Five feet away and the cat's ears begin to flatten.

**Thirty-two muscles control the feline outer ear, whereas only six control the human's.**

Using an oblique glance, I can see the lesion—fleshy pink, moist, and bulbous. It's as though the cat's wearing a red clown nose to impersonate Rudolph.

"Should exfoliate nicely," I whisper, inching forward.

"Exfoliate?"

Will I ever learn to stick with layspeak?

"If I can touch a microscope slide to his nose, I guarantee some of the cells from the lump will stick to the glass and I'll be able to make a diagnosis."

"Can't wait," says George, for all the wrong reasons.

This is it. This is the point at which I must commit to the capture and restraint of the mutant beast. In my left hand I brandish the towel like a net. My right hand is ready to lunge, to scruff the back of Henry's neck, evoke memories of kittenhood, the sense of submission, of being carried around by his mother.

What follows is brief and noisy, but I'm the one screaming, not Henry. Though I've always thought I possessed quick, if not catlike, reflexes, it takes a feline to prove my reactions are pathetically slow. Henry nails me with a swat I sense rather than see, the pain of claws piercing flesh delayed until I stagger backward, a towel pressed into the bloody scratches on my forearm.

"You were lucky," says George, switching off his phone, his tone disappointed. "Didn't get you with his teeth."

I huff. "More than one way to skin a cat," I say, washing my wounds in antiseptic solution. "Time for a little chemical restraint."

George comes at me, suddenly animated, waving his palms in my face. "Sorry, Doc. No can do. Henry's got a heart condition. Doc Cobb tried to knock him out one time and nearly lost him. Scared me to death."

"There's always a risk with anesthesia, Mr. Simms, but based on this display I'm not sure we have a choice."

George sighs, studies the floor, and smooths down his beard. "To be honest, I brought him in today to give you, or should I say Bedside Manor, one last chance. In case you knew what it was just by looking at it."

"I don't understand."

"See, I was thinking of going over to that big practice in Patton. I told them about Henry and how he might need sedation or anesthesia, and they promised me he'd be fine. Said they've got these fancy monitoring devices, use them to anesthetize cats older than Henry all the time. You don't have anything like that here, right?"

"No, but . . . they promised, eh?"

George fidgets, refuses to meet my eye. "Look, I've always been loyal to Bedside Manor, but I've got to do what's best for Henry. Could you give me a referral?"

I finish drying off my arms, but the scratches continue to weep tiny tears of blood. Will Healthy Paws stop at nothing to increase their caseload? As far as I'm concerned the doctor who says he never makes mistakes is either lying or an impostor. And the doctor who promises something more than to do his or her best is asking for trouble.

"Here's what I'll give you, George— my promise that I'll diagnose Henry's problem without resorting to sedation or anesthesia."

"How are you going to do that?"

"No idea," I say, more angry than defiant. "But my promise is just as valid as theirs."

George waits a beat, tips his head back. "Tell you what, I'll give you to the end of the week. No diagnosis and I'm taking Henry to Healthy Paws, referral or not."

And with that, St. Nicholas scoops Henry into his arms, deposits the cat in front of the open door of his carrier, and, after a moment of consideration, Henry chooses to stroll inside and lie down.

"Deal," I say, shaking his hand and leading him back into the waiting room, just as there's a strange trilling sensation in my pants. It's my cell phone; not a call, but a text.

> Hey, want to get together this afternoon?
> Take me on a date?

Panic might have set in if the text had been sent from Doc Honey. Instead I succumb to shock—it's from Amy.

« **9** »

"Thought you might appreciate somewhere a little quieter," says Amy as I hold
open the door to the so-called Scoop-
Shack. "January in Vermont; won't get
much quieter than an ice cream shop."

We step inside one of those new buildings on the Garvey estate—half a dozen
plastic tables and chairs sit empty, hedged
in by glass-fronted refrigerators displaying
assorted quarts and pints of sorbet, ge-
lato, frozen yogurt, and ice cream. There's
the sweet tang of vanilla in the air and the
cheery flamingo pink and azure blue paint
job does its best to help me forget the

season. Finally we're alone, without distractions, and all is right with the world.

Amy takes off her scarf and unzips her jacket. "If we're frozen on the outside, might as well try on the inside, yeah? Oh, and if anyone asks, I was never here."

Is she embarrassed to be with me?

"What, you think this just happens? My trainer would kill me."

Amy drags the back of the tips of her fingers down the contours of her hips and thighs, showing off her figure, the defiance in her heterochromic eyes tempered by the flash of a smile.

"Flavors on the left, fixings on the right," she says, pointing to a chalkboard behind the main counter. "Ignore the politically correct lingo—small batch, fresh, organic— who cares, this place makes the best ice cream sundae you will ever eat."

"I remember. Can't believe they're still open year-round. Maybe you could grab us a table and I'll see what I can rustle up."

"Cookie dough, hot fudge, nuts, but hold the whipped cream and the cherry."

"Yes, ma'am," I say, guided by a big white pointy finger and a sign that reads ORDER HERE. There's no one behind the counter, but there is a small brass bell next to the till, the words "ring me" taped to the handle, Alice in Wonderland style. I ring, and from somewhere out back an old woman wearing tortoiseshell glasses, a red felt beret, and black fingerless gloves appears. Ringlets of long gray hair spill around her ears; cavernous laugh lines frame a wide mouth. Her chin may be free of the Kirk Douglas dimple, but she's not fooling me. The genes in this family are as strong as they are distinctive. This has to be the matriarch of the family—the original Mrs. Mike Garvey.

"Yes, dear."

I place our order (I'm going with choco- late chip, and yes to the whipped cream) and watch as Mrs. Garvey flexes her Pop- eye forearms.

"You sort out Ermintrude?" she asks, head down, scooping away at the fluffy in- nards of a stainless steel container. "Saw you out back with Mike and Doc Lewis the other day."

Silly me. Apparently no introduction needed.

"Not yet." But then, thinking about the tragic case of their Jersey cow, "Maybe you can help? Don't suppose you remember where Ermintrude came from?"

"Of course. She was born here. We imported her mother, Clover, from a farm in Canada."

Since Eden Falls is less than twenty miles from the Canadian border, "importing" livestock is just a technicality.

"Clover lived to be fourteen."

"Not a bad age," I say.

"No . . . but now that I think about it, she started acting strange as well. Nuts on both, right?"

"Right. How do you mean, strange?"

"Mike would know better than me, but . . . jumpy . . . ornery. Your father put her out of her misery."

Note to self: check with Doris and see if the late Doc Cobb kept records on Garvey's livestock.

"Do you happen to know if he performed a postmortem?"

"Yes, I do, and no, he didn't," she says, almost sounding offended. "My late husband butchered her himself. Trust me, nothing went to waste. Nothing. There you go."

Mrs. Garvey buries a plastic spoon in

the heart of each sundae and slides the cups my way.

For a second I totally ignore her, lost to bullet points of this new information— Canada; offspring; nothing went to waste. Sadly, the checks keep filling the boxes for my dire diagnosis.

"Did Clover have any other calves?" I ask.

"Sure," she says, telling me how much I owe her.

What if Clover is patient zero?

Distracted, I root around in my pockets for cash and pull out the voucher Charlie Brown gave me—buy nine sundaes get one free.

"This any good?" I ask, sliding it over, followed by a five-dollar bill.

"Certainly," says Mrs. Garvey. "You a friend of Charlie Brown?"

"How did you know that?"

She lets her chin rock back into the fatty wattle of her neck. "This time of year, not many folks fill up one of these cards. Charlie's in here pretty much every day after school. I've tried to push the low-fat yogurt, but she won't listen. Too bad. Lovely girl. Here's your change."

I take it, but drop the coins into the tip jar. Charlie Brown, a pretty but sad teenager finding solace in ice cream. Struggling to deal with her parents' divorce? Is she overweight because her mother wants to abandon her, or does Doc Honey want to abandon her because she's overweight?

"Thanks," I say, picking up the cups and heading for Amy. Then a scary thought crosses my mind and I turn back. "When you said nothing goes to waste, you didn't mean that you actually"—I want to say "ate" but instead go with—"consumed your cow Clover?"

"Sure did. Burgers, steaks, roasts, you name it. A little on the tough side, but nothing a slow cooker can't tenderize."

"Got it," I say, but I'm not thinking about farm life and tough times and making the most of what you have. I'm thinking about Trey, Mike Garvey III, and this improbable but irrefutable link to Ermintrude.

"You took your time. Has my sundae turned into a frappé?"

"Sorry, just chatting with Mrs. Garvey is all."

"Ah, the overpowering allure of another older woman?" she says, taking her first

swallow, savoring the moment before eyeing me (blue eye only). **Another?** Why do
I feel as though this might be a reference
to Doc Honey?

"No, the Garveys asked me to help them
out with a sick cow."

Amy's right, this sundae is unbelievable.

"Farm work? Wow, Bedside Manor **is** in
trouble."

I swallow my mouthful too fast and
wince with the brain freeze.

"Left alone, I think we've got a chance.
But right now our problem is the competition."

"Healthy Paws? Their practice name is
almost as bad as yours."

She scoops another spoonful of frozen
heaven into her mouth. I catch myself
staring.

"That guy you pointed out the other
night," I say. "Their office manager, Dorkin,
you know much about him?"

"The guy with the freaky laugh?"

"Yeah, like a cross between a hyena and
a braying donkey."

"More like a braying ass. He dropped by
the diner a couple of times a few weeks
before your father died."

That must have been when Dorkin was badgering the old man to sell the practice.

"Totally self-absorbed."

"How so?"

"The clothes. The car. The tips. This one time, he claimed he had a lecture to give at some conference in Vegas, wondered if I wanted to join him for the weekend."

I try not to imagine Dorkin's paintbrush whiskers tickling Amy's rosebud lips, but she's already read my agitated features.

"Please, give me some credit. He's like a seventies porn star."

Just then the door swings open and in walks Trey, ignoring the floor mat, work boots stomping a slushy trail toward the counter. Amazing, he's still wearing his **Cool Hand Luke** sunglasses.

"Ma," he screams. "You back there? Ma?"

Grandma Garvey hurries over as best she can, and Trey, clearly aware he's not alone, frantically urges her to come close so he can whisper.

"Does Trey always wear those glasses?" I ask, keeping my voice down.

"No idea," says Amy, leaning in. She's close enough for me to smell the soap on her long, pale neck—lavender. "He's always been, well, different. The mirror sunglasses only add to his mystique. Probably wears them to make you focus on your own reflection and not him."

My spoon hovers in front of my parted lips. **Focus on your own reflection and not him.**

"What?"

I want to kiss her (even more). "You've given me a fantastic idea." I push back in my chair and make to rise. "Just need to find out where he got them."

"Sit. I can tell you. Fancies Convenience Store, this side of the diner. Got a rack full up front near the checkout. Five bucks a pop, but I'm guessing no need to rush. Pretty sure they've only sold one pair."

Amy angles her head back toward Trey.

"Good to know," I say, settling back down.

"That's it? No explanation?"

I smile and scrape my spoon around the inside of my cup, trying to capture every last dreg.

Amy holds her own spoon upside down on her tongue for a second, biding her time. "My friend Mary called. Tells me she brought Gilligan in to see you."

"Oh, yeah. I seem to attract challenging cases."

Amy deposits the spoon in her empty cup. "I believe Fancies also sells earplugs."

I get the reference to the collie's incessant barking. "Gilligan is a little . . . nervous."

"That's the best you can do, 'nervous'? Muzzled by doctor-patient confidentiality?"

This is the Amy I was first attracted to—her sharp wit.

"And I hear you were asking after me the other night," she says.

"Uh . . . yes, well, only because—"

"I'm glad. I'd be disappointed if you hadn't."

It takes all of my willpower not to grin and ask: "You would?"

She sighs. "About the other night, the phone call at the bar. I was in a state of shock. I was distracted, and yes, rude. I'm sorry."

Instead of simply accepting her apology, my socially awkward silence is met with, "Well, what was your excuse?"

Whoa! Amy never gives me any room to hide. Now I've got to articulate my feelings. I'm reminded of a quote from the late Robert Altman's movie **The Player**: **I like**

**words and letters, but I'm not crazy about complete sentences.**

"I guess I'm not used to being around a"—careful, Cyrus—"strong woman."

No physical blow to my body, but her eyes still pack a punch.

"You're going to have to clarify strong, 'cause I'm pretty sure this has nothing to do with what I can bench press."

"I mean confident, assertive."

"And you find this threatening?"

"Different . . . but in a good way." Despite clasping a cup full of ice cream, I run a sweaty hand through my hair. "Professionally and, yes, socially, I've enjoyed a somewhat isolated existence."

"Monastic or hermitic?"

I try not to smile.

"Look," she says, elbows on the table, lips hovering over interlaced fingers. "Most men use their sensitivity as a way to impress, if not seduce. Thankfully you're not one of those men. Your actions speak much louder than your words."

There's an awkward silence. Was that a compliment?

"That phone call. It was someone I haven't heard from in years. Someone . . .

special . . . in my life. Last night was a complete surprise, a big deal. I know it's hard, Cyrus, but please, I'm asking you to leave it at that for now."

Oh dear. How I hate an unsolved mystery.

"I can't help being curious."

"Don't be," she snaps, and then, softening, "Look, I'm happy to take your jealousy as a compliment and not a flaw."

Special. Big deal. These are not "leave it at that" words. She wants me to back off but still be enamored? I stew, my argument for asking further questions building on the back of my tongue.

In my unease she tenses, straightens up, and I catch a crinkle of disappointment ruffling her forehead, as if she might have read the signs all wrong, that I might not be as interested in her as she thought. She shakes it off, perhaps putting on a brave face, and like a fool moving in slow motion, I miss my chance to set her straight.

"Anyway," she says, "my sources tell me **you** were out on a date?"

It's a daring comeback, her timing perfect, less of a deflection and more of a broadside.

"Well . . . I . . . don't think I'd call it a date," I say, my chuckle embarrassingly fake.

"Mary said you were with a strikingly attractive woman who couldn't stop trying to undress you with her eyes."

"Oh no, really, she was . . . no . . . and attractive? Mary exaggerates."

"Drop-dead gorgeous was Mary's actual description. Also head turning and sizzling hot. Don't act so surprised, you're an eligible bachelor. At least you would be if you'd tame that stupid cowlick on the top of your head, relax around the opposite sex, and learn how to use a napkin."

She points to the corner of her own lip, inviting me to attend to a smudge of fudge sauce.

"Eligible bachelor?"

She rocks in her seat, ready with the caveat. "For these parts."

If Mary or some other patron from the diner had recognized Doc Honey, Amy would have used her name. It seems we were both out with people who shall remain anonymous. At least, that is, until Honey gives her lecture at the Knights of Columbus.

"Unlike you, my meeting was not **special** or a **big deal**, definitely more business than pleasure."

She squirms, ever so slightly. Jealousy is making me more snide than quick-witted.

"Huh, will you be seeing her again?"

This may prove disastrous, but I can't help myself. "For someone who doesn't like questions, you're asking an awful lot of them."

She raises a "well, well" eyebrow above her brown eye. "Let's say it's a woman's prerogative."

I crack a smile and, to my relief, so does she. Maybe I haven't totally blown this after all. Maybe now would be a good time to toss out a compliment.

"Last night," I say, "I really wanted to tell you . . . to tell you how much—"

My cell phone rings. I try to press on.

"Coming home to Eden Falls has been, well, eye-opening, but meeting you has been equally—"

"Don't you think you should take that?"

I know I'm staring, and maybe my fixed eyes come across as disturbingly wired, but I want to convey, "No, this is more important."

With a sigh, I pick up, answering in a series of cryptic grunts and yeses, and ending with a weary "on my way."

Amy regards me. "Business or pleasure?"

"Business. Sorry, I'm needed back at Bedside Manor."

"Is everything okay?"

"Yeah, some kind of emergency."

"Oh, with who?"

"Someone called Mrs. Peebles and her dog, Crispin. You know them?"

Amy does a double take, scrapes back in her chair, and gets to her feet.

"Guess I made a mistake," she says.

The tension drops like an invisible curtain between us.

"I'm not with you."

She grabs her coat from the back of her chair and puts it on.

"Like I said, I can pretend the jealousy is a compliment. But not lying. If you're meeting Miss Drop-Dead Gorgeous again, have the decency to tell me to my face. I know for a fact that Crispin died three months ago!"

## 10

I don't know where to begin. Amy was correct, but so was I. Crispin the dog **has** been dead for several months, yet he **is** my emergency patient. How can this be? Sitting in my examination room is a distraught eighty-three-year-old Mavis Peebles, being comforted by her daughter, "Patricia, call me Trish," and a well-behaved, wonderfully silent yellow Labrador that has been stuffed by a taxidermist. Though I'm troubled by the wobbly castor fitted to the dog's left hind paw, I suspect the cause for concern is the small, lifeless creature cradled within the old woman's knotty hands.

"Donny Kutz usually sorts out these little setbacks," says Trish, "only he's wintering in Florida and won't be back until late April."

"Donny Kutz?" I ask, trying not to stare at the way Mrs. Peebles rhythmically strokes what might be the furry exterior of a small pocket pet, like a ferret. It's hard to tell.

"The taxidermist. Lives down near Stowe. We figured you'd be the next best thing."

"But Mrs.—"

"Trish, please."

"Trish . . . with respect, I'm a doctor. I work on living animals." At least I do now.

"Of course," says Trish. "We just . . . well, Mom thought you could try, being as Crispin was a patient here. We understand."

I glance over at the open file on my exam table. Back in October, Crispin was put to sleep for inoperable cancer, the details of the dog's final months documented in my late father's chicken scratch. His writing is almost illegible. Almost. One particular phrase jumps out and snags me— **great dog, great owner**.

Trish bends over her mother, preparing to lift her onto her feet.

"Why don't you show me what's wrong?" I ask.

The younger woman catches herself. She's probably in her fifties despite the standard age-defying tricks—professionally dyed hair cut short, silk scarf to hide the neck, bright red nail polish to draw the eye away from the pronounced veins on the back of the hands. She has chunky diamond studs in her ears. Conversely, Mavis has more gray than dye, more visible scalp than hair. She probably weighs about ninety pounds in her overcoat, her hand-knitted woolen scarf less about providing warmth than reinforcing her frail neck and preventing whiplash. I notice the twisted and gnarled joints of her hands doing all the talking—boutonniere deformity of the thumbs, swan-neck deformity of the fingers—classic signs of end-stage rheumatoid arthritis. She wears skin-colored hearing aids.

"Show him, Mom."

Trish steps aside as Mavis takes the shaggy weasel in one hand and shakes it at me like a lank pom-pom.

"His tail broke off," says Mavis, her voice little and uncertain.

As three pairs of eyes stare at me (one pair particularly unnerving), waiting for a response, I realize that I may want to run screaming from the room, but no part of me wants to laugh. Mavis is trembling, and though the possibility of her suffering from early Parkinson's crosses my mind, she appears genuinely scared. It's obvious Trish feels awkward and embarrassed to be here, but a burden of responsibility to her mother prevails. Why is the daughter indulging a bizarre desire to keep a dead dog—how best to put this?—alive?

"Mind if I take a look?"

I reach forward; Mavis Peebles is reluctant to let go.

**Limber tail syndrome, often seen in out-of-shape Labradors that swim in cold water. Acute inflammation in the muscles of the base of the tail causes the tail to droop. The condition is also known by a particularly apt synonym— "broken wag."**

I study the exposed surface at the base. The tissue could be described as brittle, even "crisp," but that seems insensitive given the dog's name. I'm guessing the break is between the second and third coccygeal vertebrae.

"How did this happen?" The question is aimed at Mavis, but Trish steps forward to huddle.

"He got it caught in a screen door." She's lowered her voice to foil the hearing aids.

"Um . . . this might seem like a stupid question, but that suggests a stuffed dog has been going outside in the middle of winter."

Trish checks over her shoulder and flashes her Mom a fake smile that, as far as I can tell, broadcasts "yes, we're talking about you."

"She takes him out in the backyard three times a day, just like she did when he was alive. It's a ritual, it's comforting. Even if Crispin just stands there. I think his tail must have gotten caught in the door as she wheeled him in this morning."

Maybe senile dementia, not Parkinson's.

"I'll be honest, Dr. Mills." This must be serious because she's whispering now. "I've tolerated this foolish, irrational delusion for far too long. If this . . . injury . . . is the last straw, that would be fine by me and my husband, if you get my meaning."

I peer around Trish and catch a glimpse of poor Mavis. She's looking off in the distance, stroking Crispin's head.

"Crispin meant the world to her, and I know how much she loves canine companionship, always has, but her arthritis is getting to be a serious problem. Simple things—turning door handles, switching on lights, opening the refrigerator—are becoming more and more difficult. She really needs to be in an elderly care facility. But she can't go because the decent ones refuse to take a dog, even a stuffed one. We've got more than enough room at our house, but unfortunately Lionel, my husband, is highly allergic to dog dander. You see my dilemma? As cruel as it may seem, it would be kinder if Crispin turned out to be beyond repair, if you get my meaning."

Trish steps back, pressing her hands together as though the case for the prosecution rests. Mavis looks up at me with the eyes of a frightened child who wants to go home. I never cease to be amazed by how attached people can be to their pets. This yellow Lab has physically remained in her life, yet she's still a wreck at the thought of something **more** debilitating than death causing him harm. Proof positive that this kind of bond can be both dangerous and unhealthy. This woman needs full-time care more than she needs a dead dog. It's normal to outlive our pets. Your dog dies, and you're left with the memories. Unless— unless you can't remember.

Something chirps inside Trish's hand- bag, and she apologizes and fumbles to silence the noise. In that moment, Mavis, unnoticed by her daughter, jerks her head in my direction, eyes coming into fo- cus to meet mine, making me register the subtlest shake of her head. It's over in seconds—Trish awaiting the verdict, the fragile old lady back to patting Crispin's head.

Mavis can only be saying, "No, don't do it," which suggests she knows her daugh- ter's real motive behind this visit. Or am I jumping to conclusions again? What to do? One of Lewis's many mantras pops into my head—**play for time**.

"Why don't you leave Crispin with me," I say to both of them. "I'll see if there's any- thing I can do."

Funny, both women look pleased, as though I've hit upon a solution worthy of King Solomon. For Mavis, it looks like I'm going to fix the tail. For Trish, I'm giving her mother a chance to accept the separation, softening the final blow.

"I appreciate your understanding," says Trish, raising a conspiratorial eyebrow as she shakes my hand, glad to have me on board. Mavis, with her daughter's assistance, eases up and onto her feet, dips low to kiss Crispin on his forehead, and shuffles over to me. Only now do I appreciate her fuzzy white bunny slippers with pink ears.

The arthritic fingers of her right hand beckon for me to come close.

"Thanks, Bobby," she says, and, making sure she's out of her daughter's line of sight, she delivers a sly wink.

Arm in arm they head out to the front desk, leaving me alone with a deceased yellow Labrador on castors. Bobby was my father's name. Physically, aside from our eyes, we look totally different. Is Mavis so senile she's confusing her visit with a time when her dog and her old veterinarian were alive? But what's with the wink?

What if Mavis Peebles is trying to tell me she's really a whole lot smarter than she's letting on?

I trundle Crispin through the work area and park him in an empty run. He's definitely got some mobility issues. Only when I slide home the lock on the run's gate do I catch myself. What's wrong with me? He's not going anywhere. Forget about antibiotics, now I'm the doctor who dispenses WD-40.

I leave Crispin's broken appendage with him. My game of pin the tail on the doggy will have to wait. Time to start working on my backlog of unsolved cases.

First up, Gilligan, the neurotic border collie. Yes, I like the idea of Gillie's owner, Mary, singing my praises to Amy, but more importantly, I have a decent lead to go on—a sample of Gillie's blood.

For the record, I enjoy anatomical or gross pathology, and no, I don't mean disgusting or yucky (I suppose for some all pathology is gross). I mean the inspection of disease with the naked eye. But give me a microscope to find a diagnosis and I'm in heaven.

As I cozy up to the counter of my makeshift lab, everything is at hand, the process of slide preparation so well rehearsed in my memory I can put it on autopilot. Take a drop of blood, place on glass and smear with a deft hand, allow to dry using a warm—not hot—hair dryer, add a drop of stain for just the right amount of time, and voilà—you have a secret cellular story waiting to be read.

I pop my first prepared slide under the microscope and set to work. Four more slides and the result becomes conclusive. Gilligan is anemic, as indicated by his low number of red blood cells. But far more troubling is the fact that the anemia appears to be what's called nonregenerative. Normally if you're losing blood, your body notices and tells your bone marrow to make some more. Either Gillie's bone marrow doesn't want to or it can't. Bad enough to be running on empty, but worse when the only gas station around is closed.

Gilligan's file provides me with Mary's cell number, and I give her a call to explain.

"There's only so much I can discover here at the practice. Ideally I'd like to send off his blood for more tests, and, if you can swing it, we should get an X-ray of Gilligan's abdomen."

Mary's sigh of disappointment hisses in my ear. "Ah, you're killin' me, Doc. Can't afford both. Wish I could. You choose which one will give us the answer."

My turn to sigh. Not only have I got to cut corners to save dollars, but this way, it'll be my fault if I spend her hard-earned money and still don't discover what's wrong.

"Tell you what," I say. "Drop Gilligan off tomorrow morning. No food after midnight in case we need to sedate him. Let's go with the X-ray."

Mary thanks me, but even as I hang up, I'm packaging the vial of Gilligan's blood to send off to the lab. No, of course I can't afford to foot the bill, but somehow I've got to increase my odds of making a diagnosis, for the sake of Gilligan, and hey, if this gets back to Amy as a philanthropic gesture, so much the better.

The novelty of a little sealed envelope icon in the bottom right-hand corner of my laptop screen proves irresistible. Nobody I know (or want to know) would try to reach me by email, which is why I abandon the world of kooky cows and fat cats and peck the digital letter with the arrow of my cursor and wait as two new emails appear in my inbox.

From: Stiles, Gabe
To: Mills, Cyrus
CC: Brown, Charlize
Subject: Sorry!

Hey Doc,
    Sorry if I messed up. I still owe you for not snitching. It was Charlie's idea to hook you up with her mom (yeah, I'm a rat), not mine. If you still need it, here's the link to your profile. My first dog was Jack and we lived on Hoffman Crescent, so you got lucky!
www.lafs.com
Gabe
P.S. Hoping my "covert mission" ;)
will make us even.

I click on the link—purely to research my cover—and I'm incredulous at the depth of the deceit Gabe has created online. Apparently I want to go to Hawaii for my next vacation, the last movie I saw was

**Platoon** (a little dig from Charlize), I have no brothers or sisters, I majored in communications at college, and, it seems, the best part about being single is the hope that "my quest for the perfect soul mate will end with you." Do women really buy cheesy lines like that? Don't ask me how, but Gabe even uncovered a headshot on file with my previous place of employment and photo-shopped it to somehow make me look a whole lot better than I really do.

I close out the link and review the email one more time. He certainly had no problem throwing Charlie under the bus. And what did he mean by the "covert mission"?

The other email has been forwarded via Gabe (from tlovelace@lafs.com). Clearly he's in control of this account and it's no less disturbing.

From: Honey, Winn
To: Lovelace, Thomas
CC:
Subject: Another date?

Hi Tom, Tommy, Thomas,
    I don't know what happened last night. It wasn't like any online date I've ever

been on. It's okay to be nervous. It's okay to be shy. But what I liked best was the way you just wanted to listen, to let our connectivity unfold. Men constantly read me the wrong way. They say (not me) my looks make me unapproachable, out of their league. Either that or they'd prefer to talk with their hands and not their hearts, if you know what I mean. You're different, Tom, Tommy, Thomas, and different is a good thing. Wonder if you're free tomorrow night? Love to continue where we left off. My place? Call me.

Love,

W

XOXO

The L word? Hugs and kisses? My place? What have I done? At best I was confused, jumpy, and totally lost for words. How can Honey interpret my improv performance as sensitive, honest, and even respectful? It's bad enough to deceive her professionally, but manipulating this vulnerable woman's emotions is unforgivable.

I ease back in my chair, clasp my hands behind my head, and stare out the living room window. It's late afternoon, and what little light permeated this grim winter sky has finally given up, submitting to total blackness. With the shadows comes the uncertainty of what I have gotten myself into. Connectivity? There are two things Winn Honey and I have in common: loneliness and, at least on my part, desperation. But here's the difference: hers is rooted in divorce and the need for validation (at least I think so) whereas mine is out of choice and, I could argue, a quest for redemption. Maybe I didn't know quite what I was getting into when I took on Bedside Manor, but it was my choice. I chose to live in a frozen tundra void of humidity. I chose to take on a veterinary conglomerate by fair means or foul. For the greater part of my life I've chosen to be alone. I've learned to embrace the silence, to believe there's a difference between insulation and isolation. Now I'm not so sure. Out here, in the "real world," it seems there isn't a vaccine or nearly enough Purell to stop you getting infected by a truly dangerous contagion—hope. It's the possibility of not being destroyed by Healthy Paws. It's the belief that there's something, I don't know, something unusual, even thrilling, about being around Amy and the chance that she might feel the same way. But now, for all the wrong reasons, I am responsible for inflicting hope on a lonely woman who didn't get to choose.

I press Reply on Gabe's email, insist he owes me nothing more, and ask him to forward this response.

To: Honey, Winn
From: Lovelace, Thomas
CC:
Subject: Friday night

Dear Dr. Honey,
    Yes, Friday night at 8:00 p.m. will work for me. I'd like to explain the real reason for being so nervous.
Sincerely,
Tom

Succinct, formal, and aimed at dampening her anticipation as gently as possible. Dr. Winn Honey deserves to be told the truth, and, though I hate emotional confrontation, an electronic explanation feels wrong. At least at her house I'll be out of the public eye when she comes at me with a can of pepper spray.

I abandon the online research, bundle up, grab my doctor's bag, and decide to head out on an expedition, starting with an important purchase. The plastic bag hanging from the handle of the front door has other ideas. Inside there's a card with my name on it and a Tupperware dish containing a large slice of lemon meringue pie.

I open the card.

> **The diner was all out of humble pie, but I hope this will work. I guess Crispin Peebles lives on! Now you know you're not the only one who jumps to conclusions.**
>
> **Call me soon!**
>
> **A**

Ignoring the absence of "love," I leave the pie on Doris's desk for later and, as I jump into the Silverado, savor the gut-tingling thrill that Amy wants to make up with me.

This evening's version of cold can best be described as fierce. No one uses pleasantries like "crisp" or "brisk" this far north in January. I leave the truck to idle in the Fancies Convenience Store lot—praying the heater will finally kick in—and find what I'm looking for precisely where Amy said it would be. Up front near the check-out, a rack of a dozen minus one **Cool Hand Luke** aviator sunglasses. Make that a dozen minus two. Just as I'm about to pay, another item catches my eye. Next to a six-foot-tall cut-out cardboard primate is a shelf full of Gorilla Glue. It claims to be the toughest glue on the planet. Well, let's see if it's tough enough for Crispin's broken tail.

Purchases paid for, heading back through the center of town en route to an unscheduled but essential house call, I can't help but notice the two figures standing outside the diner. As I slow down, the truck's headlights pick them out, holding them like the flash of a single frame as I trundle past. It's a man and a woman, standing next to an outrageous, brilliant white Humvee. I keep staring as I roll along, but neither of them looks my way. They're facing one another, in each other's arms, wide eyes locked in . . . what . . . joy, mutual adoration. They're oblivious to the nosy curb crawler because they're entranced, their smiles ready to explode. The man is a stranger, but his five seconds in my high beams tells me all I need to know— taller than me and devilishly handsome. Sadly the woman is not a stranger.

Then again, maybe Amy is after all.

## 11

The pitch of the keening horn doppler shifts as the angry car swishes past, and only then do I notice I've been driving the last mile with my high beams blaring. White knuckles fused to the steering wheel, I've been barreling into the night, following the contours of feta cheese snowbanks and chasing the dusty snow-snakes side-winding across the blacktop. I can't shake the man's image, so vivid. I could pick him out of a lineup. But it's the expression on Amy's face that haunts me. I can think of no better way to describe it—besotted.

Maybe I'm being paranoid. What if

Amy's expression was more nurturing than amorous, more maternal than carnal? All I know for sure is, in this sea of love, Amy looked as if she had been saved by the hunky lifeguard, while I looked on, flapping around in water wings, trying not to drown. I am so out of my depth with this woman. I yearn for the gift of the gab, when all I exude is the "gift of the geek." If only this romantic limbo stemmed from a failure to communicate. What if Amy simply needs to understand the intensity of my . . . crush. No, that makes me sound like a horny teenager. Infatuation? No, that makes me sound like a stalker. Devotion. Yes, my earnest desire to get better acquainted. Who am I kidding? How can she feel comfortable around me if I'm still struggling to be comfortable with myself?

Multitasking with a cell phone (actually multitasking in general) is not my strong point, but I dial the phone number from memory, knowing it will ring at least ten times before it's picked up.

Make that twelve.

"Hello, Harry, it's Cyrus, Dr. Cyrus Mills. I'm the guy who helped out with—"

"I may be old, but I'm not senile. I know who you are. How you been?"

Harry Carp is Amy's eightysomething grandfather, the one she's nursing. She lives with Harry and his bizarre mutt, Clint.

"Good," I lie. "How's your dog doing?"

"Never better, thanks to you. You looking for Amy? 'Cause she's out."

"Actually I . . . um . . . wanted to ask you a question about Amy."

Harry pauses. "A bit quick for a marriage proposal, don't you think?"

"No, no, definitely not that. I . . . well . . . there's this other man . . ."

"What about him?"

Harry interjects this so quickly I can't tell whether he's being protective or disinterested.

"Well . . . should I . . . should I—"

"Should I what?"

"Should I be worried?" I blurt out.

I hear Harry catch a few nasal breaths, making me stew.

"I met him the other day. Just for a minute. Seemed nice enough."

Asking if he was a friend or boyfriend seems too direct, so instead I go with something more subtle. "So you've met him before?" Figuring that will at least tell me how long he's been in the picture.

"No, but—"

"But what?" I ask, jumping on the possibility of a flaw—convicted felon, debilitating speech impediment, on the run from the INS.

"I'll say this. Clint didn't warm up to him."

Clint took a while to warm up to me. Or maybe it was the other way around.

Neither of us speak for a full five seconds and then Harry comes back with, "I've got this quote for you."

"From Mr. Eastwood?" I know Harry to be a huge Clint Eastwood fan (every dog he's had throughout his life has been named Clint).

"Of course, but unscripted, from the man himself, not one of his movies. It's about pessimism."

Is it that obvious or does Harry simply see me as a loser?

"'If you think it's going to rain, it will.'"

I come back with a nasal huff. "I thought you might go with, 'If you're waitin' for a woman to make up her mind, you may have a long wait.'"

"**Pale Rider**, right?"

"Impressive, Harry. You take care."

Most people don't use the term **expedition** when describing an unscheduled house call to a sick animal. However, in my defense, this particular creature does merit the adjective **wild**, and besides, after witnessing the scene with Amy and her mystery man outside the diner, I'm grateful for the diversion.

I park around the back of the imposing building and notice a sign that seems tailor-made for me—HOTEL BUSINESS OR DELIVERIES ONLY. In the context of this evening's visit, I certainly mean business and I intend to deliver a cure. Next to the sign, a gridiron of light from a lead-paned window in a door guides me to the top of a short flight of salty steps and a copper doorbell. I press the buzzer but get no buzz. Hopefully it's ringing somewhere deep inside because the cold has already ripped off my ears, chewed away my entire face, and begun to feast on my brain. I'm used to living in Charleston, South Carolina. I don't do freezing, let alone negative digits. Doctorin' bag hugged to my chest, I stamp my feet on a thick rubber doormat, a bad chicken dance that does little to improve the circulation in my toes. Then I notice the mouse, dead and eviscerated, lying where the mat abuts the wooden siding, no doubt the sacrificial offering of a feline version of Hannibal Lecter.

**A census taker once tried to test me. I ate his liver with some fava beans and a nice Chianti.**

The door swings open to reveal the man I came to see—Santa Hemingway.

"Dr. Mills, what a surprise," says George Simms. "You should have used the main entrance for that drink on the house. Come in, come in."

I shuffle inside, the warm air filling my nostrils, every inch of exposed skin prickling as it begins to defrost.

"Actually I came by because I thought I'd have another go at Henry, if he's around."

"He is. This way."

I'm led down a narrow corridor, winding our way between logjams of housekeeping and room service carts, past the drone of washing machines and the aroma of fresh laundry, converging on the hubbub and heat of a hopping restaurant kitchen. Even if I ignore the vintage green-and-white-striped wallpaper, the floor gives away the age of this place. The number over the main entrance, 1853, is not a street address. Based on the subtle inclines and declines of the settled hardwood underfoot, I'm walking on the original flooring of a historic building.

"In here," says George, "though I'm pretty sure Henry's sixth sense about doctors works just as well at home."

George holds open a door marked SECURITY, and I enter a room lit by the flickering glow of closed-circuit TV monitors. Eight LCD flat screens capture crisp black-and-white images of a series of empty corridors, what looks like a bar, a reception desk, the front entrance, and the rear parking lot.

"Fancy setup," I say. "Where's the casino?"

George smiles, grabs an empty swivel chair, and crab walks up to a desk cluttered with computers and keyboards.

"Had it installed a couple of years ago. Expensive, but worth it. Here's why."

George presses a key, and a screen in the middle showing an empty corridor begins fast-forwarding, the digital clock in the bottom right-hand corner whizzing through minutes and hours, people scuttling in and out of the frame, walking at double time, like in a silent movie.

"Half an hour ago, one of our guests claimed a piece of jewelry was stolen from her suite. Naturally she blames housekeeping. Thinks the maid has shifty eyes, a funny accent, insists I call the police. Guarantee, in the next half hour this same guest is going to let the front desk know she found it on a counter in her bathroom or in a drawer under an item of clothing and it was all a big mistake or her husband's fault. But just in case, I have this surveillance video, and I'm going through to make sure no one entered the suite other than the designated housemaid. I'm gonna keep at it, if you don't mind."

"Of course. Where's Henry?"

George spins around an adjacent chair so I can see the seat is actually occupied by a large black comma that slowly uncurls into Henry the predatory, polydactyl cat.

**Cats sleep for two-thirds of every**

**day, so twelve-year-old Henry has only been awake for four years.**

"If you were hoping to jump him in his sleep, I advise against it. Henry prefers to doze, always one eye open, ready to pounce."

**Ready to kill**, I think, remembering the desecrated rodent on the doormat.

"No. I have a different plan." I set my bag down on the desk between George and his cat, extracting a box of glass slides, a pair of old oven mitts from my kitchen, and my secret weapon—**Cool Hand Luke** mirror sunglasses.

**Probably wears them to make you focus on your own reflection and not him.**

When Amy said this about Trey, it seemed like the perfect way to tackle Henry. At least it did at the time. Now that I'm here and Henry's sitting up and watching my every move, I'm not so sure.

As a cat, Henry will not recognize my face. He's more tuned into body shape, body language, and the pitch of my voice. Trying a slow, sneaky approach is doomed. At the very least he'll bolt. Speed and surprise are my only hope.

With my back to him, I apply the mirror sunglasses and the oven mitts and, with the manual dexterity of a lobster, pick up a glass slide in each padded pincer. You know that feeling, the one when you're about to leap out of the plane and trust the parachute on your back? Well, neither do I, but I imagine this is what it's like.

"Do you have any idea how ridiculous you look?"

Ignoring the dissent, I take one step backward, perform a one-hundred-and-eighty-degree spin that may not be worthy of the late Michael Jackson but puts me exactly where I want to be, in the strike zone. It could be the flickering reflective dazzle from the monitors; it could be the two curious black cats that suddenly appear from nowhere, but the sunglasses are the silent equivalent of a SWAT team flashbang, the perfect distractor, allowing me to swipe both slides across the fleshy tip of Henry's nose and step back before he can say, "Ah, Clarice."

"Don't tell me it worked," says George, hitting Pause, freezing the frame, pushing out of his chair, and coming over to see.

Mirrors and mitts off, I inspect the greasy

smears on the glass. I'll have to wait until I get home, but they look like decent touch preps to me.

"We'll see," I say, packing everything away in my bag. "I'll have to stain them up first."

George picks up Henry, or should I say, Henry allows George to pick him up. To be fair, the cat appears stunned, limp, and lost for words, as if I tossed a glass of cold water in his face for no good reason.

"Your father said you were stubborn. Fine by me if you cure my cat's nose."

It seems my father saw a stubborn streak as one of my few virtues.

"I'll let you know what I find. Good luck with your missing jewelry," I say, nodding at the screen. "I'll find my own way out."

"Thanks, Cyrus. Hey, the bar's the other way, if you still want that drink."

I consider hearty St. Nick clutching his black cat with the Karl Malden nose. What an odd but strangely compatible couple. Maybe I should take him up on the offer, especially after gathering inadvertent intelligence on Amy.

"Um . . . no, I really shouldn't but . . ." I can't help myself. "Do you happen to have a guest staying here who drives a brand-new white Humvee?"

Here's my thinking . . . Harry Carp said he only met Amy's . . . friend . . . for a minute, therefore he's not staying at their house. If you drive an expensive SUV and you're visiting Eden Falls, chances are you'll stay at the best guesthouse around.

"Of course," says George. "Mr. Marco Tellucci."

I expected a yes or no, not a name.

"Oh . . . right . . . and is, is he alone?"

"No idea. But I do remember he insisted on a king-size bed. Very specific. Why d'you ask?"

Marco Tellucci. Got to be Italian. Damn! Swarthy, suave, and, no doubt, a sexy accent to boot. Could I hate him any more?

"No reason," I say, backing off down the corridor the way I came. "I'll be in touch."

The word **chill** in **windchill** feels like a cruel joke. I think the local meteorologists meant "windkill" and it came out wrong. Though the drifting snow sparkles in the truck's high beams like fairy dust, there's nothing magical about it. Round these parts the word **chill** is about as useful as the word **warm** in the Sahara Desert.

As I drive, the left, logical side of my brain comes back to my conversation with Harry. Harry said he'd only just met this Marco character. This might suggest someone who's not been in Amy's life for very long, but the phone call at the bar, the one Amy insisted she take, seemed like a conversation with an old friend, and she alluded to the fact that he was someone important from her past. Assuming the caller to be one Marco Tellucci, why did the Italian merit only the briefest of meetings with Amy's favorite relative? Has she been as secretive with Harry as she has been with me? "Seemed nice enough," said Harry. Nice enough for what?

A bend in the road catches me by surprise, sharper than I imagined, and suddenly I'm dazzled by the flash of brilliant blue and red light filling the cab and spilling across the right side of the highway up ahead. Instinctively my foot comes off the gas and I hit the brakes, the back end of the Silverado fishtailing but not enough to lose control. There's time to recognize Chief Matt Devito's police truck parked behind a vehicle that's nose-in down a trail between the trees. **Probably drunk**, I think, looking for telltale skid marks. But I don't see any, and that's when I recognize the vehicle—the windowless double back doors of a dishwater gray minivan—the gaunt man with his faithful labradoodle.

I pull over farther up the road, wishing I had a reverse gear in this stupid truck because now I've got to jog back though the knee-deep snow.

"Doc!" Chief Matt sees me coming, blinding me with his Maglite, the flashlight held at the side of his head, Hollywood-cop style. He's opted for a Cossack hat with earflaps over his standard-issue patrol cap. Less heat loss through his fashionably bald chrome-dome. "I was about to give you a call. Need your skill set to access the victim."

Skill set? Victim?

"What happened? Are they hurt?"

I keep pumping my legs, desperate for traction, trying to get past him, trying to get to the van.

"Doc, stop," says Devito, reaching out to grab me by the arm. "It's too late. The dog's alive, but the guy's gone."

Breathlessness takes me, and for a few seconds I slump, hands on hips, letting the shock and the sadness settle.

"You okay?" asks the chief.

I nod that I am.

"Yeah, it's just . . . I know this guy. Well, I met him. He came in earlier . . . with his dog."

"So who is he?"

The flashlight beam is back in my face.

"I don't know. He wouldn't give a name. I know the dog is Stash."

What I know feels too complicated for right now. Being economical with the truth is still the truth, and if the chief doesn't believe me, he keeps it to himself.

"Follow me and please, watch where you tread. I'm trying to minimize contamination of a potential crime scene."

Crime? What crime?

The van's parked a good twenty yards off the highway, down a narrow trail more suited to ATVs and snowmobiles. It's a whole lot easier to walk in Devito's wake.

"This is one of my spots for a speed trap," he says. "Hide down here with the radar to get myself a DUI from the inn. That's when I saw the van. Didn't look like an accident.

Made me wonder if I might have a lewd and lascivious instead."

First thing I notice about the minivan, the driver's side and passenger side windows are rolled all the way down. No smoke from the muffler, in fact not even a tinkle of cooling metal. The van's engine has not been turned over for some time.

"They're up front," says Devito, waving his beam toward the driver's door, "but the dog means business. You got a blow dart in your truck?"

He backs off as I make the final few feet to the front of the van. Just like that time at the diner, the gaunt man is slumped behind the steering wheel, but this time Stash the labradoodle is lying across his lap. As soon as I go near the open window, Stash lunges, barking with junkyard ferocity. I'm frightened, but more so by the fact that the man doesn't even flinch.

"Shine your light on me," I shout over the barking. "Stash needs to see what I do."

The beam swings into my face, and, staring back at the dog, I call Stash's name while delivering a fake karate chop to my windpipe. It's like pressing the mute button—one gesture and the only sound is the wind in the trees overhead.

Devito pans back to the open window, catching the devil-dog red eyes from the doodle's dilated pupils.

"Stash, sit."

I remember how I was struck by the gaunt man's crisp, confident commands, and I try to mimic them. Again, Stash is on it, backing his haunches up and onto the passenger seat, sitting perfectly square and to attention.

"Stash, stay."

This last one gets a tilt of the head and nothing more. It might be a canine version of "that's redundant, you idiot, I'm not going anywhere."

"Is it safe?" asks Devito.

Sir Lawrence Olivier in **Marathon Man** pops into my head, and you don't know how much I want to say, "Yes, it's safe, it's very safe, so safe you wouldn't believe it." But I just nod, and Devito shoos me back from the vehicle with a gesture he must have learned during Crowd Control 101.

Still wary, the chief opens the driver's side door to reveal a man with no more life in him than a crash dummy. I take in the scene—empty prescription medicine bottle in the well behind the gearstick, half-empty bottle of water, no seat belt, the man's white T-shirt peppered with tiny clumps of black fur. Of course, I already know this is a man with a death wish. I guess when I couldn't help him he decided to find another way. Windows rolled down, T-shirt, January in Vermont. Someone wanted to get cold—real cold—cold enough and sick enough to fall asleep and never wake up.

Eyes fixed on the dog, Devito leans in and pokes under the man's chin to feel for a pulse.

"Oh my God," he shouts. "He's still alive. I could have sworn he was—"

"Step back," I say, pushing the cop aside, squatting down next to the gaunt man, laying my fingers in the jugular furrow below his chin.

In seconds I pick up a pulse, not strong, not weak, but surprisingly regular. I turn to face Devito, shocked, about to agree that he is in fact alive, when I stop and realize something's off. My fingers haven't moved.

"I'll fetch the defibrillator from the truck," says Devito, starting to wade back the way we came, suddenly all animated.

"No wait, hang on a second," I call to him.

Consulting my wristwatch, I count as the hand spins through fifteen seconds, I multiply by four. Precisely seventy-two beats per minute; and that's the important word—precisely. Assuming severe hypothermia and a core temperature less than 82 degrees Fahrenheit, the heart rate should not be more than forty beats per minute. His chest does not move. He's not breathing. I raise the gaunt man's left eyelid. The pupil of his eye is fixed and dilated. He's definitely dead, but his heart keeps beating. Only one possible solution.

"He's gone," I say, standing up. I let the wind slash across my cheeks and allow myself a moment to appreciate the despair in this poor man's demise. What a strange resting place. Even his best friend couldn't save him, though based on the black fluff covering his T-shirt, Stash did everything he could to keep his master warm. Devito won't need forensic testing to discover the dog's saliva all over the man's ice-cold face.

"You're right about the pulse," I say. "But it's too fast for a dead man."

"I'm not with you."

"I'm saying he must have a cardiac pace-maker. The artificial beat doesn't switch off just because you're no longer alive."

To be fair to Devito, he seems genuinely disappointed that we're too late, and for a while the two of us just stand there, uncertain what to do next.

**Like you, I eventually came home, only you got this practice and I got this dog.**

What did the dead man mean?

"Why here?" I wonder out loud.

The chief pans his beam into the darkness beyond the front of the van, but there's nothing to see.

"Another twenty yards out that way and there's an overlook with a view across the valley." And then, as if something makes sense, he adds, "Faces west. Nice sunsets."

"Okay," I say, and start to explain exactly why the man with no name came to see me, and how, sadly, he took his own life because he couldn't wait for nature to take it from him.

Devito waits for me to finish before rifling through the various pockets of the dead man's jeans. Stash does not look pleased. Gingerly, the chief reaches over to open the glove compartment—empty.

"Seems like your client made an effort not to be identified."

The beam flashes on the lower part of the windshield at the dashboard. The thin metal plate with the vehicle identification number is missing.

"Bet I won't find a license plate, either," says Devito, straightening up. "What did you say the dog's name was?"

"Stash."

"Stash? Makes you think our John Doe was a drug dealer. Wonder if he knew Trey Garvey."

And I thought I was the one who leaped to the wrong conclusions. Trey fails a sobriety test, and Devito thinks he's on the trail of a Mexican cartel. Given the apricot fur around the dog's muzzle, my money would be on a nickname, a short version of "Mustache." It may be too dark for Devito to notice, but I keep this to myself.

"The man was terminally ill. I imagine the dog was the only thing making the last few months of his life bearable."

"Then that's how we'll track him down," says Devito, pleased with himself, jabbing a finger in my direction. "The dog will have left a trail. He's obviously been specially trained. So who trained him? And if Bedside Manor wasn't his regular vet, then who was? Your chance to play detective, Dr. Mills."

"I'll see what I can do," I say. "In the meantime, you might want to call a coroner."

I begin trudging back the way I came, careful to follow the trail.

"Whoa, there. What about the dog? I can't take him."

I dip down to see Stash, eyes still focused on his sleeping master, his body fidgeting for the next command.

"Let me try something," I say, coming around the back of the van, "so long as you don't mind me destroying your **crime scene**." In lieu of air quotations I go with a sarcastic rising intonation. Even so, Devito vacillates before waving his permission to go ahead.

The passenger-side door proves difficult to open, buried on the windward side by drifting snow, but as I swing it as wide as I can without a shovel, Stash keeps his back to me, unable or unwilling to escape his responsibility.

"Stash," I call, with the same forceful tone I used before. "Stash, come."

The doodle glances my way, just for a second.

"Stash, come." Firm, not angry.

This time the dog turns his entire body toward the crack in the passenger door, appears to think about it, but turns back.

"Stash, come," I say, unable to keep the regret, the resignation out of my voice, and then, as if against his will, Stash tears free, squeezes through the gap, and jumps down, swallowed by the soft powder as he comes to my side. In the glow of the flash-light, I watch as the dog's head tilts back, ready for his next command—from me.

# Friday

## 12

It seems I have a talent for harboring dogs of mysterious derivation. Last week it was a fugitive golden retriever named Frieda Fuzzypaws. Almost everyone in Eden Falls thought Frieda was missing, everyone except her owner, a guy who wanted this dog out of his life, until he realized she was an integral part of it. In the short time Frieda was with me, I discovered I quite liked canine companionship. Okay, "quite liked" may be an understatement. Oh, she was needy and worshipped my refrigerator, but at least I no longer had to talk to myself.

Stash is an altogether different lodger. I've traded golden tumbleweeds for fur that undergoes a bizarre chemical reaction when combined with powdered snow to form grape-sized, snarly, and intractable balls of ice that cling to Stash's legs and undercarriage. Where Frieda craved physical contact, Stash appears content to be hovering at my side, but he's always by my side, a canine shadow, following me from room to room, including visits to the bathroom—and I don't think this is because he's needy or afraid. If anything, he appears to be on duty. Last night I was getting undressed for bed and he sat in front of me with something stuck in his mouth. My cell phone must have slipped out of my pocket when we were sitting together on the couch. This wasn't about being impressed by a retrieval instinct. This was about being scared by bright brown eyes that might be saying, "Lost something?" Those same brown eyes greeted me the moment I woke up this morning, inches from my face, seemingly chiding me for languishing in bed. And when I offered him breakfast, he wouldn't eat until I was working on my own bowl of granola. It's as though he doesn't quite know how to relax and simply be a pet.

Right now I'm pretty sure Stash is critiquing my attempt to secure Crispin's broken tail back where it belongs. Either that or he thinks I'm a total freak for even trying. Under his watchful eyes, I sit on the floor at the back of Crispin's run, beside me an open pack of surgical instruments, a can of WD-40 (I was serious about fixing that castor), and the bottle of Gorilla Glue.

"Not funny," says Doris, standing over me, trussed up in her downy ski jacket. She's glancing at the card I attached to the gate of the run, a card identifying this patient as "Crispin Peebles, 14-year-old Labrador, Broken Tail, DNR." DNR—do not resuscitate.

"Sorry," I say. "A little gallows humor. Didn't want anyone to not find a pulse and go hunting for a defibrillator." Assuming we've got one.

Doris isn't interested in an explanation, her twiggy index finger flicking back and forth between the two dogs. "Hard to tell which one's stuffed and which one's real."

She's right; Stash possesses an uncanny

stillness and unblinking stare as he waits for my next command.

"Where are my manners? Doris, this is Stash, the labradoodle who—"

"Belonged to that guy found dead in his car last night."

There's no point in asking how. Of course she knows. But she used the word **guy**. Should I infer Doris has discovered the details but not the identity of the man?

"So if he wasn't from Eden Falls, then where?" I ask.

Her only response is to shrug her shoulders, but there's a glint of something that might be pleasure in Doris's eyes, something that tells me she's already on it.

"Well, Stash will be staying with me. At least for now. There, what do you think?" I get to my feet, gesturing to Crispin's tail, ignoring the stainless steel towel clamps holding everything in place until the glue dries.

The snappy upward curl at the margins of her orange lips is faster than a blink.

"It was your father's idea." Doris jerks her hairy chin in Crispin's direction. "Getting him stuffed. Thought it was the best way for Mavis to stay independent."

"I don't get it. Mavis Peebles looks like she's in desperate need of a helping hand."

"Looks can be deceptive," says Doris. "Her daughter, Trish, she means well, but it's her husband, Lionel, who wears the pants and holds the purse strings."

"Lionel—allergic to dogs, right?"

"So he says, though I'd bet the only thing he's allergic to is losing his mother-in-law's inheritance. Trish and Lionel live in a fancy McMansion out toward Patton, but Mavis might spoil the feng shui when friends come over for cocktails, if you get my meaning."

Feng shui. There's clearly far more to Doris than Marlboros and big hair.

"You're saying Trish wants to be rid of Crispin so her mom can either live with her or go into assisted living, whereas Lionel would rather keep Crispin around so that Mavis remains in limbo. Not staying with him because of his so-called allergy, and not eating up her savings in a nursing home."

Doris clucks her tongue like she's encouraging a stubborn horse to move forward and hits me with an unsettling "you got it" wink.

"What do **you** think Mavis wants?" I ask.

"No idea," snaps Doris, visibly insulted. "You do realize the woman's old enough to be my mother?"

"Of course, I never meant to suggest—"

"And given my current pay, I can't afford a nursing home anytime soon."

"That's great, I mean, that I, that we, still get the pleasure of your company, still get the benefit of your . . . expertise."

My detour from salary to corny compliment fails to dent Doris's scowl. I can tell she's jonesing for a cigarette, eyeing a roll of bandage material like it might be worth lighting up.

"Probably wants her dog back in one piece," she says. "And while you're at it, a cure for arthritis. How should I know?"

Doris spins on her heels, nimble and light on her feet, her elaborately teased yellow hair quivering wildly as she marches off.

"I'm practically a spring chicken compared to Mavis Peebles," she shouts without turning back.

And I have to agree. Doris's scrawny legs do share certain characteristics with the domesticated fowl.

With Cripin's tail in a holding pattern (literally), it's time to use Stash for a special assignment—unmasking the identity of the gaunt man. This way I get to bypass the sleuthing incompetence of Chief Matt Devito, and I already have an obvious lead in the investigation—missing testicles. Somewhere along the way Stash has been separated from this part of his manhood. And if he's been neutered, then he's probably been vaccinated, tested for heartworms, treated for ticks, and the list goes on and on. Next clue, though they might not have hailed from Eden Falls, when you're living out your last few days on earth, I'm betting you want to stay close to home. If they're not clients of Bedside Manor, then who better to check out than a certain rival practice across the valley? I pluck Guy Dorkin's crumpled business card from my pocket and dial the number for Healthy Paws.

The phone is answered by a recording that insists I pay particular attention because their menu has changed. I'm asked if I have an emergency, need a prescription filled, want to leave a message for a doctor, need to make an appointment. Eventually I meet the criteria of "for all other calls, press 0" and get placed on hold, forced to listen to a sycophantic female voice asking if I knew that fleas could jump up to eight inches high. Yes!

"Hey, hello, howayya, this is Healthy Paws and I'm Popcorn, how can I be of service?"

Whoa there, what kind of a greeting was that? I'm exhausted. Did she really say her name was Popcorn?

"Hello . . . Popcorn, this is Dr. Mills, I work at Bedside Manor, over in Eden Falls."

There's silence on the other end of the line, not an "Uh-huh, I know it, yes, Bedside Manor," just total silence. I press on. "I have a dog, a black labradoodle, that answers to the name of Stash, and I wondered if it belonged to a client of yours."

Another silence and then with her mouth she hits me with a burst of "yeah, sure, okay, please hold" and the fawning female recording comes back, telling me how vital it is for me to get my senior dog examined every six months. Where's the elevator music?

"Looking to poach another case, Doc?"

It's Dorkin, the question direct, not a trace of levity.

"Um, no, not at all . . . I picked up a dog—"

"Does it make you feel better, asking my permission? Help you sleep at night?"

"What are you talking—?"

"You as good as accuse us of malpractice with Sox Sauer, so what's next? Animal experimentation? Operating a Ponzi scheme?"

What's got into him? I guess the gloves are officially off.

"I'm, well, I'm simply trying to find out if a dog by the name of Stash is a patient of—"

"No. No, it's not. Have at it. You're desperate for business. It's not one of ours. Knock yourself out."

I don't do snappy ripostes, and normally the option to hang up would trump my typical bumbling weak comeback. But when I made this call, I had Doc Honey on my mind.

"So that lecture you've set up in Eden Falls is . . . what? You feeling civic minded?"

An insolent huff hisses down the line.

"If you're that worried, come along. In fact we'd love nothing more than to hear you defend your particular brand of veterinary medicine. I'm sure you could enlighten us about the discovery of X-rays or the benefits of a thing called"—he splits the syllables for maximal debasement—"pen-i-cill-in."

"Brag all you like about your flashy equipment, Dorkin, but believe me, people pay attention to what lies behind the curtain."

"Good. I'll save you a seat, and we'll let the pet owners of Eden Falls decide where they can get the best care and the best value. How's that sound?"

He hangs up before I can say another word. Suddenly all I can think about is my upcoming rendezvous with Doc Honey. Like it or not, I have to come clean, to confess my sins to an enemy combatant, an enemy with a ready-made public forum in which to air my double life as the nefarious Tommy Lovelace. I'm doomed. At best, I'm a deceitful creep. More likely, around here I'm that hillbilly trying to exploit a sad and lonely doctor for kinky sex and insider information. Either way, it's not good for me or Bedside Manor.

Sitting at the microscope with Henry the cat's slides, I'm reminded of the old days, simpler times, as the scientist who kept his head down, kept the rest of the world at bay, and lived his life with pain-free objectivity. The old Cyrus would have run screaming from a confrontation with Doc Honey. The old Cyrus would have been turned to stone by Amy's heterogeneous eyes, let alone her confidence. But it's taken Bedside Manor and less than two weeks in frigid Vermont to make me want to change. Sure, being cold and isolated (welcome to Eden Falls) ensures self-preservation and protects against humiliation, but inside, I realize now, I was as dead as most of my patients. Sometimes I think it might be easier to shake off this state of dreamy weakness, to put up my guard and retrieve a sharper, harsher focus. But for all my financial and emotional troubles, I can't and won't go back. These days, the comforting armor of the introvert, the second skin that fit me so well, is nowhere near as snug. And, for now, it can hang in my closet with the mothballs.

More often than not, as a pathologist, I'm given a slide, a biopsy, or a chunk of tissue, together with a note from the clinician telling me what he or she suspects I'll find. It's like being a wedding DJ—even if you have a great sound system, it helps to know the kind of music you'd like me to play. The thing is, if I can't deliver a diagnosis, it's the clinician's problem, not mine. Blame your own crappy technique, your inability to get me a decent and representative sample, but don't blame the pathologist. Now, forced to wear both hats, faced with this particular pair of slides, failure to make a diagnosis means another round of mortal combat with Henry, or, worse still, losing a client to Dorkin and Healthy Paws.

Though the cause of Henry's nasal horror may lie within these greasy smudges, it needs to be cajoled, carefully deciphered, and with only two samples available, there's no margin for error.

**Calm, Cyrus, be logical. Think about what you know.** I know George Simms said he tried antibiotics, antifungals, and steroids, all to no avail. Conclusion—the nasal lesion is not caused by a bacterial infection, a fungal infection, or an inflammatory process. Why? Because there's still a big fat tumor on the end of poor Henry's snout. Let's prove it with a Diff Quik stain.

I hold on to the first glass slide by my

fingertips and dip it in tiny vats of blue and red dyes. Quick rinse, dry, and it's under the lens, my fingers tweaking the knobs that control the coarse and fine focus on the microscope, the prepared slide zipping back and forth, and in less than a minute I have my diagnosis—or, that is, I have **no** diagnosis. It's not cancer. It's not a tumor. All I see is cellular schmutz. That's what you get when you're reduced to little more than a snot-wipe sampling technique. Damn.

One down, one to go. One slide stands between me and cat scratch fever, a rabies booster, stitches, and a course of intravenous antibiotics. The mirrored-sunglasses trick will never work a second time.

There are plenty of staining options used to enhance and identify certain microbes, but pick the wrong stain and it's over. Think. Henry had no response to antibiotics. Why? What if the bacteria were resistant?

There's a pile of files next to me on the counter, and I dig out Henry's, flicking my way through the pages of messy notes until I discover which antibiotics Doc Cobb used. The world is full of bacteria, but my father chose well, starting out with a sawed-off shotgun approach, hitting a broad target before working his way to a more specific antibiotic, the pharmacological equivalent of a sniper's rifle. Still, nothing appeared to work. Why not? Common bacteria would have been wiped out. There's only one possible reason—Henry is not afflicted by a common bacteria.

This time I go to the cupboard. Stash, now seated, keeps an eye on the action. Maybe he's hoping for an Old Mother Hubbard moment. Instead, I'm face-to-face with remnants of my late mother's life, in the form of her meticulously organized collection of lab equipment—rare stains, a mechanical stop-clock, and a classic piece of school chemistry memorabilia, the Bunsen burner.

It's like following a Martha Stewart cookbook recipe. Fire up the burner, flood the last remaining slide with a crimson liquid, place in flame and steam for five minutes, take care not to flambé with the acid-alcohol and presto—feast with your eyes. Fingers twitch, the slide zips, and in less than a minute I have my diagnosis, scooching my chair back from the microscope and over to Stash.

"High five," I say with uncharacteristic sporty machismo, and, as if we'd spent years together perfecting the trick, Stash instantly raises a black paw and we connect. Without thinking, I pull his whole body into me, up and onto my lap, like he's a kid ready for a picture book story, and I bury my face in the soft, sweet-smelling fur of his neck as I whisper, "Good dog." It's over in seconds, but I catch myself—no, **we** catch ourselves, like that moment in the movie **Grease**, where Danny Zuko and Kenickie share a spontaneous bromantic hug, realize it's not cool, and separate like it never happened. There's a split second of direct eye contact, the shift from mutual affection to mutual embarrassment, and Stash leaps gazelle style from my lap as I glide back to my microscope and the bright red chains of tiny bacteria floating in clouds of seafoam blue.

Henry is the victim of an uncommon bacterium, a bacterium belonging to the same family of organisms that provides us with such delights as tuberculosis and leprosy. It's known as a mycobacterium, and it won't respond to your typical antibiotics. You need a special Ziehl-Neelsen stain (thanks,

Mom) to unmask it. Now that I know what I'm dealing with, I can even pin it down to a particular species—**Mycobacterium microti**—the vole bacillus. And when I say vole, I mean rodents, as in the prey of a cat regarded as an excellent mouser. Now it makes perfect sense. Where's an infected, cornered mouse going to bite a cat? Right on the end of his nose.

There's a Walgreens pharmacy in Patton. It turns out they carry the 2% isoniazid ointment Henry needs to treat his nose. I can pick it up, drive over to The Inn at Falls View, and deliver the Holy Grail—diagnosis and cure. I'm almost tempted to perform a self-congratulatory fist-pump while releasing a protracted "yessssss." Almost.

"Doris, I'm just going to run over to . . ."

But Doris is outside, wading through a cloud of cigarette smoke, and the only person standing at the front desk is none other than the computer geek himself, Gabe.

"Hey, Doc, you got a minute?"

The Napoleon Dynamite look-alike seems pleased to see me.

"Um . . . sure . . . shouldn't you be at school?"

"Free study time," he says, as though I should know. He's still wearing his gray Unabomber sweatshirt (hood down, thankfully), but strapped across his chest and shoulder, he carries a laptop bag.

"Tell me this isn't about that dating thing again?"

"No, no way, Doc. That was Charlie, not me. This you're going to love. But we should go somewhere private. You know that dog's loose, right?"

Stash looks up at me, checks out Gabe, and comes back with what I might best describe as a withering stare.

"Yep. He's with me. Come on through."

I close the exam room door behind us, and Gabe's already pulling out pages of computer printouts and organizing them in piles on the stainless steel table. Straight away one unifying, striking, and disturbing feature jumps out at me—at the top and center of each page sits the Healthy Paws logo.

"What have you done, Gabe?"

Somehow Gabe manages to look more confused than I do. Oh no, now I remember his email—**P.S. Hoping my "covert mission" ;) will make us even.**

"What you asked me to do."

"I didn't ask for anything."

"Doc Lewis said you did. He said nothing dangerous, just a little creative snooping around, that's all. Help give you a leg up with the competition." He lovingly double pats the nearest sheet of paper.

"Hold on." My eyes race across the pages. They're spreadsheets, production numbers, undoubtedly confidential. "Stop right there, Gabe. This is totally illegal."

"Maybe."

"No, it is."

"Maybe, but only if you got caught and only if you were stupid enough to leave an electronic footprint."

I don't know much about Gabe, but one thing seems clear: when it comes to computers, he is far from stupid. Dorkin's sarcastic tone rings in my ears—**Let the pet owners of Eden Falls decide where they can get the best pet care.**

"Explain to me how you did this?"

"Too technical, too boring," says Gabe, "except the password stuff, which is always cool."

"It is?"

"Of course. It's key. Cracking the password is the best. You like puzzles? Of course you like puzzles. See, most passwords are logical, personal, and rarely random."

"Password," I offer. "123456. Trustno1."

"I said logical or personal, not stupid. It's the only way we remember them without writing them down. I've been to Healthy Paws lots of times with Mom for Tallulah's checkups. I've seen what kind of software and hardware they use."

"But how do you know Dorkin, assuming he's the one who sets the password?"

Gabe grins, loving his advantage. "I pay attention. I've watched the way Dorkin handles owners when they pay their bills. He plays favorites. If you're wearing lipstick and a short skirt, he's all, 'Sure, we can work something out,' otherwise, he's hauling you off to collections. Guy's a dick."

Neither Stash nor I disagree.

"Normally I start with the pet name angle, but the unrestricted part of the system told me Dorkin doesn't have any pets registered with Healthy Paws. Weird for someone running an animal hospital, right?"

This comment makes me wonder whether I'd best adopt Stash as soon as possible.

"So I get more creative. Personal dates—birthdays, his own, his kids', wedding anniversary, that sort of thing. Dorkin's divorced, never had kids, and his date of birth didn't work."

Gabe reads my alarmed expression. "Don't ask. Anyways, next up, the man himself. What do I know? I know he loves himself. I know he wears nice clothes, nice watch. Vanity and wealth. Naturally I check with the DMV and bingo, Dorkin bought a vanity plate for his Mercedes. I type in six letters—T-O-P-D-O-G—and, open sesame, I'm in."

I don't know if I should be impressed or patting him down to see if he's wired as part of an FBI sting operation.

"For a while I snoop around, mainly boring numbers, but then I think, why not check out Tallulah's record, calculate their markup, see how badly we were being ripped off. That's when I noticed things didn't add up."

Gabe has set up his evidence such that anyone with a little business savvy should be able to compare the master spreadsheet that Dorkin generates for himself with the individual monthly totals each doctor gets to see. All I can say for sure is that Doc Honey is significantly underperforming compared to her colleagues.

"I'm still not with you. Looks like rows of boring numbers to me."

"That's what you're meant to see. But if, like me, you love numbers, it starts to unravel. Here," he picks up one of Dr. Honey's monthly Excel sheets, "the doctor gets a percentage of everything he or she does, stuff like vaccinations, dispensing medication, running blood tests. If they don't bill, they don't get a paycheck. Dorkin, on the other hand, is on salary, but if you notice, he takes a percentage of all the nonclinical stuff the hospital has to offer, like boarding, grooming, pet food, chew toys, dog beds, dog outfits, you name it. Nothing leaps out until you compare the monthly figure each doctor actually gets to see with the number on Dorkin's master spreadsheet."

Gabe's index finger bounces between the figures for different months and different doctors and the pattern floats to the surface. He's terribly excited, in a zone, and I notice because I know exactly how it feels. Math nerd meets science nerd.

"The doctor's production figure is always

less than they actually generate. So Dorkin's skimming?"

"Essentially," says Gabe. "Where he
can, he's weighting the bills in his favor.
Nothing big, nothing greedy, just a steady
couple of hundred here and there from every doctor, enough to make a difference,
not enough for them to notice. Over a year,
even after taxes, he's got a sizeable increase in his personal revenue."

I look back at the figures again, and this
time the fraud is obvious. No one gets
harder hit than Winn Honey. I can't help
but wonder whether he's punishing her.
Personal vendetta?

"How many people know about this?"

"Me, you, and Fido."

"You didn't say anything to Charlie, did
you?"

"No."

"Gabe?"

"Okay, yeah. But you can trust her."

My thoughts become sidetracked by
the smart, funny, but ultimately unhappy
sundae-loving daughter of my online girlfriend. I deliberate, stew a little, but have
to ask. "Does Charlie ever talk about her
home life?"

"You mean why she's fat?"

I'm not good at acting appalled so I don't even try.

"Her dad moved out a couple of years ago. Went to live with a twenty-three-year-old he met online. Now they're married, have two boys, twins. Charlie and her mom dealt with it in their own ways. The Doc went on the nerve diet, got in shape, and started dating younger men, maybe to prove a point. That left Charlie to feel abandoned by both parents. Dad's got his new family, and Mom doesn't want a teen-age daughter cramping her dating options. I think Charlie eats to annoy as much as to forget."

"That's too bad. They've had a tough time," I say. "But you really shouldn't have gotten me involved."

Gabe looks more impartial than contrite.

"And it was wrong to hack into Dorkin's computer."

"Ah, c'mon, Doc, this is epic."

I hate to admit it, but he's right (or even righteous). The best I can do is to keep quiet.

"Face it, Guy Dorkin's totally screwed. Forget a little illicit porn or online gambling, this info can send him to the Big House. So why look so worried?"

Standing there, slack jawed, and, to be honest, a little afraid, I have what I can only describe as an out-of-body experience. It's as though I'm watching myself in the third person as I do three unusual (for me) things. Firstly, I realize my hand has been resting on Stash's head, and, unlike his previous master, it's not because I need the support. Secondly, though I am equal parts grateful and furious with Lewis for commissioning this damning little project, I sweep Gabe's proof into a pile. Lastly, and most troubling of all, I turn to Gabe and say, "I wonder if you might do one more thing for me."

## 13

It is time to admit it—I'm forming a dangerous attachment to this funky-looking doodle. My revelation occurs the moment we
turn left out of the parking lot. Stash sits in
the Silverado's passenger seat, one eye
on me, one eye on the road, and into my
head pops an awareness of . . . concern.
I'm concerned that I can't provide this animal with a seat belt or some other dog-
appropriate safety device in the unlikely
event of an accident. Is feeling a burden of
responsibility part of falling in love?

We're heading into town, my phone already against my ear, calling Lewis.

"Where are you?"

"Sitting with my wife, having a coffee. Busy appointments? Need me to come in and give you a hand?"

Damn. How does Lewis do that? I want to be angry at him for mobilizing the computer geek behind my back, but he's the dutiful husband, spending time with his dying wife, happy to hop to if I need bailing out.

"No, no, it's slow."

I glance over at Stash. I'm getting less creeped out by the constant scrutiny, though his look might be more "hang up and drive already."

"Sorry to hear about the guy with his labradoodle. You taking on another lost dog, Mr. Patron Saint?"

Lewis is referring to the moniker, the lasting tribute, my father acquired—the Patron Saint of Lost Dogs. When someone came across a stray dog or if a dog needed to be adopted because its owner was relocating or lost a job or died, the late Bobby Cobb posted its picture on a wall in the waiting room and made sure it found a good home.

"We'll see," I say, wanting to get back on

topic. "Gabe dropped by. The kid who's good with computers."

"Really? Find anything?"

Amazing. No apology, no backpedaling for sending a minor on a counterintelligence mission. I press on as best I can, explaining Dorkin's little scam.

"What were you thinking, asking a kid to go cyber-snooping? What if he got caught?"

"He said he owed you. Asked if we wanted help setting up a practice web page and he'd do the work for free."

"So you suggested the veterinary equivalent of Wikileaks?"

"He was the one who mentioned hacking. Took me a while to realize this had nothing to do with horses. I thought it might give us some ideas about how Bedside Manor might compete. Know your enemy. Never imagined he'd find anything useful. Believe me, Dorkin's playing dirtier than us. You catch this morning's **Gazette**?"

"No."

"Grab a copy. And be sure to thank Peter Greer next time you see him. Dorkin must be furious."

What has Greer done now?

"Let me think about what to do with

Gabe's information," says Lewis. "I'll be in shortly."

We hang up, and since I'm passing the gas station, I pull over, eager to grab a copy of the newspaper to see what the fuss is about.

The one gas station in Eden Falls is the sort that only offers full-service pumping. A kid bundled up like Shackleton darts around, popping gas tanks, topping off, running back and forth with credit cards.

I find what remains of a parking space next to their Himalayan snow pile, get out, and order Stash to stay. Beyond the pumps and the forecourt is a one-story building divided into two parts. To the right, a mini-mart where, in addition to jumbo bags of Doritos, two-liter bottles of soda, and all the ice-melt, antifreeze, and snow shovels I could ever need, I'm hoping to find a copy of this morning's **Gazette**. To the left, bays of jacked-up cars and trucks float above men in dark blue jumpsuits. Country music plays in the background, accompanied by the rev of an engine, the rattle and hum of a torque wrench, and the echo of expletives. The place exudes a heady mix of oil, exhaust fumes, and testosterone. That's when I recognize one of the mechanics coming my way.

"Doc, everything all right?"

It's Drew, Mary's husband. He's wringing some sort of pale cloth in his hands and it's hard to tell where the oil ends and his fingers begin. But hey, the guy can actually speak.

"Thought you were seeing Gillie this morning. Something about an X-ray?"

"Right," I reply. "Of course." Of course I totally forgot that Gilligan the neurotic collie was coming in for an abdominal X-ray. And of course Drew can tell I forgot. "Doc Lewis is expecting him," I lie. "Just picking up a **Gazette**."

Drew gives me the slow-nod treatment, and for a second we both study the fascinating scuff marks on his steel toe—capped boots.

"Sorry about the advertising," he says.

"That's why I'm getting the paper."

Drew looks confused and points toward the gas pumps. "Those ads."

At each of the four pumps, above the price of gas, are glossy posters of adorable and painfully cute dogs and cats imploring their supermodel owners to take them to the best vets around, to Healthy Paws, "For those on all fours." Their Patton phone number is prominently displayed.

"Tried telling my boss . . ."

Though Drew natters on about the merits of supporting local businesses, I'm not really listening because an enormous, brilliant white Humvee has rolled into the lot. The tinted driver's side window powers down, and a voice orders, "Fill her up with premium." I can see two men inside and there's a lot of hand gesturing going on, direct eye contact and flying spittle. The man in the passenger seat is a stranger. The man in the driver's seat is the same handsome devil who held a limp and smitten Amy in his powerful arms the previous night.

". . . anyway, I tried. So we'll hear from you later?"

The guy driving the Humvee certainly could be Italian, in a stereotypical perfect-stubble, man-whore, Lamborghini-driving, **"bellisimo bambini"** kind of way. Is Drew waiting for an answer?

"Right. Yes. Speak to you later."

The mechanic ambles away, shaking

his head, probably thinking he should have gone straight to Healthy Paws.

I'm frozen to the spot, unable to resist the allure of the ugly white whale of an SUV. Obviously the two men inside are fighting, and I'm reminded of something Doc Honey mentioned in her email: real men speak with their hearts, not their hands.

In order to eavesdrop and gather some useful intelligence I start to cross the court, closing in on the Humvee, only to be yanked through one hundred and eighty degrees by the long arm of the law.

"Thought it was you," says Chief Devito, steaming coffee cup in his free hand. "You get anywhere with that trick dog, Hash, or whatever it's called?"

About to correct him, I think better of it.

"No. Nothing. How about the owner?"

The chief puffs out a plume of condensation in disgust. "It's like the guy never existed."

I try not to smile, but Devito reads my pleasure. Then he looks past me, noticing the white Humvee.

"Hey, isn't that the guy I saw out with Amy from the diner?"

I turn around, attempting to look like I don't know what he's suggesting, as the monstrous SUV drives away.

"Funny, 'cause someone told me you two were dating."

The chief raises his cup to me, savoring the last word as he heads back to his truck.

Nothing left but to buy a copy of the **Gazette**, join Stash in the Silverado, and discover what the fuss is about together. I find it on page seven, flashing back to my conversation with a tetchy, combative Dorkin. This explains everything.

Healthy Paws invites you to our Open
House and Free Clinic.
Come see the fucture of veterinary medicine.
Whether you've got a pocket pet or a Great
Dame, your satisfaction is our guarantee.
Free lice and tick shampoo for all our
pet-loving pubic.

The Germans coined the word **schadenfreude**, which means pleasure derived from someone else's misfortune. No one ever said schadenfreude leads to good karma. That's why I shouldn't be smiling, but I am, all the way to The Inn at Falls View.

During my recent nocturnal visit, I never appreciated how classy the hotel looks in watery winter daylight. Elegant might be a better word, the front of the historic building defined by a façade of seven ornate two-story colonnades to create a classic New England porch and deck with views of what was once a spectacular series of waterfalls. Thanks to a rock slide eighty years ago, the "fall" is little more than a trickle of its former self, a forgettable sightseeing opportunity. The inn, however, has clearly put some work into landscaping. If global warming ever kicks in, I could imagine myself in a rocking chair on the deck, sipping on a sweet iced tea, surveying their beautiful gardens. For now, I'll have to make do with spying a row of bright red poinsettias in hanging baskets.

Having noticed a PETS WELCOME sign, Stash and I park the Silverado, and this time the two of us stroll through a dark, expansive foyer, ignoring the wood-beamed ceiling and the cozy allure of a crackling log fire. We cross a football field–sized oriental rug and walk up to the reception desk.

"Cyrus, here again so soon. Need a Bloody Mary?"

Santa Hemingway seems to think I've got a drinking problem.

"No, sir. Stash and I thought we'd bring you a present. And by present, I mean a cure for Henry's nose. By Stash and I, I mean the dog I'm . . . fostering . . . for now."

"Wait. Cure?"

I explain my findings from the slide, the theory about the mouse bites, the reason why the previous treatments failed, and why this one will work. George listens in rapt silence, like there's going to be a test afterward.

"Unbelievable. Un—"

Just as he's about to split the word with what I fear might be a celebratory expletive, a couple of guests walk by and Santa doffs an imaginary cap before wishing them a pleasant day of . . . what? Igloo building? Ice sculpting?

Depositing the package containing the ointment on the reception counter, my hand is snapped up before I can have it back and subjected to a vigorous pumping. Then, as if this level of gratitude simply won't do, George comes around, pinning me in a bear hug, ignoring my stiffness and refusal to offer more than a halfhearted back pat. Stash stares up at me. I wonder if he knows an attack word that might allow me to escape.

"Can't thank you enough," says George, holding on to me at arm's length, his eyes glistening with tears. "Seriously. Hey, that reminds me, you got a minute? There's something I want to show you."

George leads the way through a door behind the reception desk, down another corridor, and into the same room as before, the one with the bank of video monitors.

"The other night you asked me about a white Humvee."

George starts playing with a mouse, pulling up images, consulting a handwritten note on a piece of paper.

"Did your guest find her missing jewelry?" I ask.

"About five minutes after you left. Here it is."

I look at the screen, at a still image from a ceiling camera obviously placed at one end of a corridor.

"I wouldn't normally do this sort of thing,

and I don't need to know what this is about, but you've gone out of your way for Henry, so here goes."

George clicks the mouse, and a couple in conversation emerges from a room. The door is checked to make sure it is locked, and then the man offers the woman his arm, the gesture theatrical, formal, like a father offering to walk a daughter down the aisle. The woman takes his arm, the man, looking straight ahead, says something, and the woman's head snaps backward before she doubles over. It's more than laughing—she's breathless: she's cracking up. She's Amy.

"This is the owner of the Humvee. This is Marco Tellucci."

George freezes the image, Tellucci caught in an Armani-handsome pose— almost dashing—wearing a closed-lip smile as though he's so subtle, so amusing, he doesn't need to laugh at his own jokes. In the still, I catch a glint of light from a tear next to Amy's right eye, her brown eye, from laughing so hard.

"They came from room 21, a suite, nice king-size bed. And that's Amy, from the diner in town."

I struggle to make my sharp intake of breath not sound like a gasp. "Looks like they know each other pretty well," I say, striving for disinterest, knowing I come across as aggrieved.

We bid George farewell, and I manage to keep my mouth shut until we're back on the highway.

"I can be witty," I tell Stash. "I may not have his looks or money, but I'm pretty sure there are some women who think I'm amusing."

I glance over at the dog riding next to me. Stash keeps his eyes straight ahead and locked on the road, a gesture I, in my vulnerable state, interpret as him saying, "Dream on, buddy" or "Some women, but not the one you **really** want."

I shudder. What's gotten into me? I'm seeking advice on a floundering love life from a dog. Is it possible my relationship with Amy is over even before it got started? Or, once again, am I simply jumping to the wrong conclusion? Snap out of it. I've come too far to click my heels and mutate back to being a cloistered introvert. There has to be a logical explanation.

I flash to Leonardo DiCaprio in **The**

**Beach**, falling in love with the French girl who already has a serious boyfriend. **When you develop an infatuation for someone, you always find a reason to believe that this is exactly the person for you.**

I mean, it makes perfect sense that Amy might have a suitor or two waiting in the wings, poised to snap her up. As far as I know I'm still a contender.

Maybe it's time to step out of my comfort zone. If this is the kind of man Amy usually prefers, then she needs to know that there's more to me than meets the eye.

Hanging on to the steering wheel, I fumble for my cell and dial her number.

"Hey, it's Cyrus, where are you?" Careful, too probing. "I mean, **how** are you this fine day?"

"I'm . . . good. What's going on?"

"Nothing. Just driving back from a house call. Hideous nasal deformity in a cat. I . . . I . . . was thinking about you."

"Really. You see a hideous nasal deformity and think about me. You saying I should get a nose job?"

"What? No. Of course—"

"So when are we going to graduate from ice cream to something slightly more . . . romantic?"

What? Is she asking me on a date? And if so, what's with Tellucci?

"You mean no jimmies with rum and raisin?"

"Exactly, but maybe we could keep the rum."

Forward **and** flirtatious.

"Um, that sounds great. How about finally grabbing something to eat at The Inn at Falls View?"

This is where I had originally planned to take Amy on our first date, but the offer gets away from me before I realize this is Tellucci's home base.

She hesitates, eventually stretching out the word **sure** and sounding anything but. It's enough to make me **not** ask, "When?"

I can't help but notice how Stash has his head down and neck outstretched. His abdominal muscles appear to ripple. Either he's getting motion sickness or my side of the conversation is making him nauseated.

"You know, I bumped into our resident detective this morning. He says he's seen you out and about with a male model."

Okay, so I made that bit up, but I need to gauge her response.

"Devito's an idiot. Like I said, this was all in the past. Time to stop being so inquisitive, Cyrus, and let it go. I'm serious. It meant nothing."

**It meant nothing.** Isn't that what adulterers say about casual sex?

"Besides, I hear I'm not the only one working on a new relationship."

It didn't take long for the gossips of Eden Falls to have me sleeping with Winn Honey.

"You still there?"

"Please, relationship is too strong a word," I counter, "and only applicable if prefaced with the word **business**."

I count five Mississippi's.

"I meant the black dog, the one belonging to that John Doe. Who did **you** think I meant?"

The laugh on the other end of the line tells me two can play at this game.

"Did you know that in the Australian version of Monopoly, they've replaced the little metal Scottish terrier with a little metal labradoodle?"

"Wow, someone's fallen in love."

I hear a voice in the background.

"Sorry, Cyrus, got to go. Harry's calling. Promise I'll be free one of these nights. So make this dinner date happen, okay?"

She's gone before I can clarify whether "free" means available or liberated. Either way, I'm certain Amy wouldn't want me to ask.

The detour back to Bedside Manor adds fifteen minutes to our ride. Let's call it clinical research, for there's a particular piece of property I need to check out.

The house stands alone, set way back from the road, and appears to be a fine Frank Lloyd Wright reproduction. This is the home of Trish, daughter to Mavis Peebles, sister (so to speak) of Crispin, the stuffed Labrador.

For half a minute, Stash and I survey the property. Amy's right. I am inquisitive. I'll even accept stubborn and relentless. But there are times when this approach to life can come in handy. And maybe this is one of them.

Back inside the truck, I dig around for two vital pieces of equipment—a snow brush with ice scraper (widely unavailable in South Carolina) and an empty plastic grocery bag.

"Time to test a certain somebody's immune system."

The passenger seat of the Silverado is proof positive that my late father transported a large number of pets. The upholstery resembles a calico seat cover of assorted colors of canine and feline fur. Thick nylon bristles make quick work of gathering a sizeable **CSI** pile of hair and dander that I bag and stuff inside the pocket of my pants.

"And from you, I need a little saliva." I hold out my hand in front of Stash's mouth. "Stash, lick." Nothing. "Stash, lick." Not a flicker in his eyes. Either this is not in his repertoire or, more likely, I'm using the wrong language.

"Stash, pucker up."

No dice.

"Stash, kiss."

The world goes black as sixty pounds of dog leap onto my chest and begin coating every exposed surface of my skin with a shellac of saliva from a serpentine tongue.

"Stash, sit, Stash, sit."

It's as if the feeding frenzy never happened, Stash calm and distant, me dripping drool and panting.

"Good boy," I say, pulling myself together, scraping saliva from my cheek, and rubbing it into both my hands like Purell. "Okay, let's go see who's home."

With a truck lacking a reverse gear, you've got to love a circular driveway. I park, order Stash to stay, stuff a sticky right hand into the bag-o'-fur in my pocket, and head for the front door. It's open before I can find the bell.

"Can I help you?"

This has to be Lionel—turtleneck sweater, thinning black hair swept back and slick, brown corduroy pants, and plaid slippers. Very cozy. Where's the smoking jacket and the pipe?

Squeezing some fur into my gluey palm, I extend my right hand and rush forward.

"Dr. Cyrus Mills," I say, giving him little choice but to shake, clasping my left hand on top, preventing the quick getaway. "I was in the neighborhood and hoped I might have a word with either yourself or Trisha. Lionel, right?"

"Right," says Lionel, his welcome smile more like a wince of revulsion as he tries to wipe off his hands without me noticing and him seeming impolite. "Is this about my mother-in-law's dead dog?"

"It is."

He seems quite happy for me to state my business while shivering on his stoop. "Perhaps I could come in?"

Lionel still seems unsure, as though he might want to see some sort of veterinary ID or guide me through some radioactive decontamination chamber. In the end he beckons me into a stark mudroom.

"Appreciate you removing your shoes. There's a selection of guest slippers on the shelf behind the coat rack. What are you, size eleven?"

"Ten and a half," I say, stumbling sideways, one boot dangling off my ankle, grabbing his left wrist as I pretend to fall, imparting another snail trail. I make my apologies for being klutzy and find a suitable blue suede pair. Snazzy.

"Do you need to wash your hands?"

I shake my head and offer a manic smile as I wipe my hands down the front of my overcoat. What's gotten into me? Lionel's discomfort is almost invigorating as I follow him into a living room that looks totally unlived in. Two enormous white leather couches face one another, separated by a bare glass coffee table sitting atop a plush black-and-white-striped rug. Three of the walls are an oppressive flat slate gray, void of pictures or photographs, but the entire fourth wall is not a wall. It's a window of sorts, no frame, no curtains, just a single massive pane of glass offering a spectacular wintry view of forests and mountains to the north. It's like staring at a humongous Vermont postcard.

"Nice room," I say, plopping down into the couch, rocking all the way back, wiping my hands back and forth to appreciate the quality of the leather and to spread my allergenic payload.

Lionel is visibly uncomfortable. He sits down on the couch opposite.

"Sorry, Patricia is out. I happen to work from home."

I think I'm meant to notice his wife's proper moniker.

"That's nice. What's your line of work?"

"Marketing. But I'm, well, between jobs for right now. There was something you wanted to discuss?"

I give him the knowing nod, the one that

says, "Don't you mean laid off and currently unemployed?"

"Yes, that's right, Crispin. Sorry, but there's something on your face."

I make a motion toward my own right eye, to better direct him toward this imaginary fuzz. Let's see if those allergies to dogs are real.

Lionel's right index finger works the corner of his right eye, depositing a sample dangerously close to the sensitive mucous membranes of his conjunctiva. This is too easy. It's totally unprofessional and possibly murderous (though what would the police charge me with—assault with a deadly hair? I doubt it) but this thing with Amy is making me bold, if not reckless.

"It's gone, it's gone. Must have been a piece of fluff. Yes, I wanted to discuss Crispin, your mother-in-law's stuffed Labrador."

Lionel composes himself, passes a saluting hand through his cultivated but failing crop of hair, and once more tries to sit. I note no hives on his hands or wrists, and he's not scratching.

"What about it?"

"Well, by mending the broken tail I'm

worried I'm only achieving a temporary fix."

"Temporary. You think it will break again?"

"I mean it feels like we're not addressing the bigger problem. I know I'm just the veterinarian, my involvement is peripheral at best, but it seems obvious that Mrs. Peebles requires assistance in her daily life. A stuffed dog may offer low-maintenance companionship, but what she really needs is physical, if not professional, help."

"Mavis won't be parted from that dog. We've tried. This house has a separate apartment out back, less contemporary but nice all the same. It's hers if she wants it, but sadly, that dog and I can't be in the same house together, let alone the same room."

Lionel pauses for dramatic effect, and I can tell this is a well-rehearsed vignette. "Deathly allergic to canine dander. I have to carry an EpiPen every time I go out." He sighs, resigned to his sad lot in life.

"Wow, a sensitivity capable of inducing anaphylactic shock. Scary." No puffiness, not a welt, swelling, or hint of a wheeze. I note the corner of his right eye—normal blink, no edema, and no excessive tearing.

"Then, between you and me, maybe it would be best if I tell Mrs. Peebles I **can't** fix Crispin's tail. Tell her it's time to say goodbye, once and for all."

"No, no, I don't think that's such a good idea."

"But then she could live here. Without an allergy-inducing dog."

"Yes, but think of the emotional up-heaval. My mother-in-law is a fragile and sensitive soul. She's very attached to Crispin, and that kind of shock might be dangerous to her health."

"I see. I just thought that . . . well . . . given her physical limitations, this might be as good a time as any to cut the cord. Perhaps she could discover the benefits of a nursing home?"

This time Lionel pretends to ponder the suggestion.

"I'm led to believe they can be pricey," he says, straining to sound cursory, as though he hasn't researched it down to the last penny.

"Extremely. Though my colleague, Doc Lewis, prefers to call it financially crippling.

Sold his veterinary practice so his ailing wife could be cared for in a decent facility. All gone. Seventy-three years old and he's having to work for me."

I'll take the recoil of his head on his shoulders as a sign of genuine surprise or concern.

"But what do I know? Ms. Peebles's finances are none of my business."

"Right," says Lionel, though I seem to have lost a part of him, no doubt the "what's going to become of my wife's inheritance" part. "Well"—he gets to his feet—"thanks for keeping me in the loop. I'll be sure to discuss this with Patricia, but for now, anything you can do to keep old Crispin limping along will be much appreciated."

He tops off his cloying smile by folding his arms across his chest, fingers tight and immovable under his pits, as though he's pretending to be cold to avoid further contact.

We exchange our goodbyes, and I traipse back to the Silverado. Though Lionel has stopped short of tattooing DNR on his mother-in-law's forehead and warning every eager paramedic "you save her life, you take her home," his sentiment feels

pretty much the same. Mavis's bunny slippers are not welcome in his sterile lair. I
may not know how much he needs her
savings, but I do know this—Lionel is definitely not allergic to dogs.

## 14

Gilligan's abdominal X-rays are hanging on a white light-viewing box in the work area; Lewis is sizing them up as if he's trying to appreciate a piece of modern art that could have been painted by a kindergartener.

"You just missed them," he says. "I told Mary you'd give her a call once you looked at the films. This your new sidekick?"

I introduce Stash, who sits politely by my side, accepting a pat but otherwise remaining passive. He's like one of the Queen's Guard at Buckingham Palace, stoic and unwavering when on duty.

"He's staying with me till Devito figures out who he belongs to."

Lewis considers Stash, steps over to a nearby cabinet, brushes aside a half-empty box of bandage material, and pulls out what appears to be an old Polaroid camera.

"What you doin'?" I ask.

"Just a minute," says Lewis, framing Stash while the dog keeps his eyes on me. There's a click, a flash of light, and the buzz of fresh film emerging shiny and wet from the camera's base. Lewis grabs the undeveloped image by its matte-white border and begins wafting it back and forth like a fan.

"Put him up on the Wall of Fame. See if anyone recognizes him. If not, someone might want to adopt him. Here you go."

He hands over the Polaroid. Somehow Stash manages to look uncomfortable, awkward, like it's a photo for a mug shot or a school yearbook.

I put it in the breast pocket of my shirt but feel the need to come clean.

"To be honest, I was thinking about keeping him myself. I know he's a ragamuffin, what with the dreads and the weird clip job around his face. But there's something . . . pathetic . . . about him. The way he's always . . . I don't know . . . on. It's as if he can't relax."

"Huh," says Lewis. "Who does that sound like?"

"I'm serious. He's very smart and responsive to verbal commands. I've tried 'at ease' and 're-lax,' but nothing works."

"I heard you met with his owner."

I finally tell Lewis about the gaunt man's sad request for help. "When I asked what was going to happen to Stash, he said it was up to me. I've no idea what that meant, but this feels like the right thing to do."

Lewis seems to brighten whenever I start getting sentimental. I take it as a cue to clear my throat and get back on task.

"Thanks for taking these." I nod at the black-and-white images of Gilligan on the viewing box.

"No problem, but I'm not sure I've been much help."

The three of us gang up on the X-rays. We're looking at a side shot and a front-on view of a canine belly with all its shades of gray.

"Maybe some more contrast will help," I think out loud. "You want to turn off the overhead lights?"

"Do what?" says Lewis.

"The lights," I say, pointing to the switch, just out of Lewis's reach.

Whether it was the gesture, the phrase, the insistence in my voice, or Lewis's hesitation, Stash trots over to the wall, stands up on his back legs, and with a practiced downward jerk of his snout, we are plunged into darkness.

Though my eyes are adjusting, our silhouettes turn to one another, sharing a tacit moment of appreciation for a talented animal before we turn back to the films.

It's a bizarre pattern of white commas, curlicues, and cedillas littering the film from the collie's stomach all the way through to his colon.

"Dimming the lights doesn't make it any less weird," says Lewis. "I've certainly never seen anything like it before."

I catch Stash turning back and forth between us, following our words like they're a verbal tennis match and he's the ball boy, poised and eager to help out.

"Let's back up. This . . . stuff . . . whatever it is, has to be inside Gillie's guts. And if it's white on an X-ray, it has to be dense enough to impede radiation."

"It could be bone. Chewed up, cracked, and splintered bone."

"Could be, and that might explain why he's losing weight and off his food, but how do you tie in the trembling and the seizures?"

"That's why they came to you, my boy. And now you've got carte blanche to find out."

I'm confused.

"Amy dropped by to see you," says Lewis. "She saw me working on Gillie and insisted I bill her, not Mary."

"She can't afford to do that."

"That's what I thought, but I used a little more tact. She promises Mary will pay her back, but she knows money's tight right now and, more importantly, she knows how much the dog means to her. I'm telling you, that girl's a keeper."

I let my head rock all the way back, eyes reaching upward for heavenly inspiration.

"Do I want to know?" asks Lewis.

"Probably not. See there's this other guy in the picture and—"

"Stop right there." Lewis's hand parachutes down and settles on my shoulder. "You know the most important thing I've learned in fifty years of marriage: honesty—with each other, but also with yourself. So, answer the question—why do you like this girl so much?"

Lewis gives me "the stare." I've seen it before. It's like being injected with truth serum, the way its kind intent makes you want to find the right answer.

"Okay. I've spent the better part of my adult years avoiding emotional risk, making sure I wasn't vulnerable to—"

"Heartache?"

". . . the allure of a beguiling woman. Look, Amy's unpredictable, pigheaded, and dangerously outspoken. But no other woman has ever made me feel that way."

"Then make sure she knows exactly that. If she prefers someone else, she's not the girl for you."

When Lewis shifts into paternal mode, I'm always gripped by trepidation, but here's the thing, these conversations always leave me with a certain calm.

Lewis beams. Lesson delivered, he shouts, "Stash, lights."

I don't know who's the quicker study, the labradoodle or Lewis.

"That really is a neat trick. But to more

serious matters. Where are you with Garvey's cow, Ermintrude?"

"I'm working on it."

"And?"

"It could be bad. Real bad. But I'm still not a hundred percent certain."

"Then make sure you are and, no disrespect, I hope you're wrong. What are we going to do about tomorrow's lecture at the Knights of Columbus? Best if we go together. Form a united front."

The thought of having to defend Bedside Manor's antiquated ways to a room full of strangers while I'm getting the third degree from Dorkin fills me with dread. Give me a root canal or a colonoscopy any day. And let's not forget the guest speaker, Dr. Winn Honey, eager to broadcast how her professional rival hides behind a porn star pseudonym so he can exploit lonely women through online dating.

"You really think I need to be there? I mean, you're the one who packs the waiting room. Eden Falls will be there to see you, not me."

Lewis eases back in his stance, begins to worry his lower lip with that chipped upper incisor.

"Is there something you're not telling me?"

**Plenty**, I think, feeling myself being seduced by the coward's way out. I could bail on this evening's date with Dr. Honey, drop her an apologetic email and claim I tried but never really felt a vital connection. Which is true. Then, if Lewis flies solo at the K of C, Winn is none the wiser and I get to focus on sorting things out with Amy.

Lewis steps around Stash, the statuesque lion by my side, drifting into my personal space.

"If you're worried about this turning into some sort of confrontation, don't. We're starting to build something special here at Bedside Manor, something authentic. We're not going there to defend—we're going there to flaunt."

His hands reach out to squeeze my triceps while his eyes reach out to squeeze my conscience. What's with the sorcery of a wise old man?

"You're absolutely right. I'll be there." Though I may have a black eye, a red handprint embossed on my cheek, and an ice pack held to my loins by the time I arrive. "What d'you think we should do with the stuff Gabe filched?"

Lewis gives me his best Cheshire cat impression.

"You're not to worry. Think of it as our weapon of last resort."

"Now you sound like Truman."

"Trust me," says Lewis. "I have a cunning plan."

"I mean, the kid hacked into their computer system. That's a felony."

Lewis releases his grip, the letting go almost as dramatic as the latching on. "Which part of 'trust me' don't you understand?"

I smile and excuse myself to call Mary at home, mumbling my way through an unhelpful description of Gilligan's bizarre X-rays, suggesting I drop by to take another look at him in his home environment. I follow up with a call to one of the few people in my phone's contact list.

"Hey, Doc, what up? All excited for your hot date?"

It's Charlie Brown, and I thought, given this time of day, that she'd be in class and I'd leave a message.

"Don't tell me, another gym class."

"You got it. If you're calling for advice, ditch the cologne—it makes her sneeze.

And don't laugh when she says she loves Rod Stewart or that her favorite movie is **Pretty Woman**, and don't ask to see her photo albums."

"Actually I was hoping you could gauge her mood for me."

"Hmm . . . okay . . . different. Definitely different."

"That's not helpful."

"But she is. Sure she's nervous and excited and stressing over every last detail, but there's something . . . different."

"Like what?"

"Like, like she had me check out what she planned to wear, and she puts on this short skirt 'cause she's got, like, great legs, and I tell her it looks too slutty. Instead of reaming me out, she actually listens to me and goes with nice pants. It's like she wants to do this right. It's cute."

This revelation is bad enough, but then Charlie finishes me off with: "I'm really glad. Different for my mom is a good thing."

Perfect, another dilemma to further complicate my love life.

"Will I see you this evening?" I ask.

"God no, I've been told to make myself

scarce. I'm hanging out at Gabe's. Pretty cool nailing Dorkin, yeah?"

Gabe, what a blabbermouth.

"Look, you keep quiet about Dorkin, and I'll tell your mom the Loveatfirstsite.com scam was my doing."

"Why would you do that?"

"Because she needs to know who I really am."

"The big reveal? So soon. Come on, play along for a while, just see what happens. I know you'd be good for her."

But in this phrase I think I hear an unspoken "you'd be good for **us**."

"This is the first date in forever where she's actually planning on wearing underwear."

Whoa, way too much information. "Look, Charlie. I don't want to upset you, or her, but it's not fair to deceive your mother."

Charlie waits a beat. "I totally get it. If this is going to work, you want things to be right from the start."

As far as I can tell, the only thing Charlie "gets" is the misguided and heartbreaking concept of "if my mom is happy, she will be happy with me." Unbelievable. I'm supposed to be dealing with patients who can't (or won't) tell me where it hurts. Instead I spend just as much time helping those on two legs as I do those on four.

"What's happening with Marmalade?" I ask, making a point of changing the subject.

"Not much. Fat as ever but still just as loved by my doting mother."

And there it is, the bitterness in her words stinging my ear. Fat cats retain unconditional love. But not fat daughters.

"Anything you want to tell me about this, Charlie?"

"Nope. Except in my next life, I'm coming back as a cat."

She hangs up, and I decide the best way to prevent a panic attack over my upcoming revelation to the smitten Dr. Honey is to bury myself in some heavy-duty research.

Whichever way I come at her case, Ermintrude is a disaster. My number one pick for the poor Jersey cow is a disease that still has no blood test and, more importantly, no cure. One quote jumps out at me—"diagnosis means certain death." I think about Trey Garvey's mood swings, clumsiness, light sensitivity, and craving for sunglasses. It all makes sense. If only the connection between Trey and Ermintrude were a leap, a stretch—instead it feels like a logical step, and a short one at that.

In need of a distraction, I switch over to a series of articles on the weird metallic objects dogs swallow (guitar strings, pincushions, razor blades, tinsel, none of which look quite the same as Gilligan's X-rays) and then, during a lull in my attention span, pay a visit to the so-called Wall of Fame.

It's no wonder the Polaroid camera fell out of favor. The wall is a crowded hodgepodge of regular photos and homemade missing posters (I notice the one from last week—Frieda Fuzzypaws, the fugitive golden retriever). But it's the faded Polaroids that draw the eye. Despite the lack of direct sunlight, every canine in question appears to suffer from a severe case of jaundice. With no dates anywhere I can't tell how long the wall has been around, but in the absence of a serial dog snatcher, and given Eden Falls's population of little more than two thousand people, it's been a while.

The photos are arranged in neat rows, right to left. I retrieve Stash's photo and think about clearing a space for him in the middle, at eye level, but it doesn't feel right, altering my father's legacy. Each dog has a number printed on the white space at the bottom of the Polaroid. I guess that makes sense when you don't know the dog's name. I look at the last photo—a miniature pinscher, Lost Dog #41. Even as a still image, Stash comes across as anxious and a little too tightly wound. The man said, "It's up to you," and therefore #42 is staying with me. No need for a Sharpie or a piece of tape to put it on the wall. The Polaroid feels very much at home, back in my pocket.

About to turn away, my eyes settle on an object that's both out of place and eerily familiar. Hand-cut, roughly shaped like a dog bone, it is made from cardboard, with two small holes at each end to accommodate a long piece of string. I flip it over, flip it back, sigh, and smile. It's a sign (possibly in more ways than one) and I knew exactly what it would say, a bold font declaring "OPEN" on one side, and on the reverse: "DOG GONE, BACK SOON" (a witty alternative to "closed," or so I thought). I made it for Dad when I was ten, Mom providing the materials and scissors, and then proudly hanging it in the front door of the clinic. I'm amazed that he kept it, let alone put it on display. Maybe he liked its sentiment, the optimism, the lack of finality. Maybe it was his hope for a lost son. Whatever the reason, I unpin the sign from the wall and put it back where it belongs on the front door.

When I return to my laptop, a gnawing sense of guilt and regret guides me toward my email. This concerns Gabe. Who knew the kid would be such an accomplished hacker? When I asked for his help I was simply gathering information, doing a background check, perfectly reasonable. Now it feels more like an invasion of privacy and, worse still, a betrayal of trust.

I begin typing.

Subject: Abort Mission

Hi, Gabe,

Please cancel my request for further information as discussed. It will not be necessary. Appreciate your discretion.

C

I press Send and have time to wipe my palms down my face and breathe a sigh of relief before a reply arrives in my inbox.

Subject: Too late!

Hey Doc,
   Already done. See attachment. Otherwise hit delete. Good luck this evening. Don't forget your sildenafil citrate!!!!!
G

Sildenafil citrate—the active ingredient in Viagra (hey, I'm a scientist, I know these things). Not funny, Gabe, not least because of that pixilated paper clip and what lies within its 124KB file.

Click on Delete or double-click the attachment?

Open it up and I'm not just jealous, I'm despicable, insecure. Amy's invasion of privacy is reprehensible. Delete it and I'm naïve, myopic, and deserve to look like a fool. After all, information is power, and, for a scientist, irresistible.

The email sits open, the arrow of my mouse hovering in no-man's-land. In the end, the interpretation of objective data wins over moral willpower and I click on the paper clip.

It's from the Vermont State Archives and Records Administration. It's a digitized copy of a legal document. It bears a notarized stamp, it hails from nearby Burlington, and, based on the date, it was registered some thirteen years ago.

I've stopped breathing, the vacuum inside my lungs amplifying the pounding of my heart.

There are details of witnesses, names I don't recognize, someone claiming to be a justice of the peace, but all I see is the two names at the bottom of the page that are very familiar.

An enormous corkscrew twists around my guts.

**Mr. Marco Tellucci in one column, Amy Carp in the other. Groom and Bride. Bride and Groom.**

It's a marriage certificate, and even though my index finger keeps clicking the Delete button, the image in my mind refuses to go away.

## 15

Let's skip the denial phase and get straight to the anger.

"Do I look gullible?"

I like to think I'm simply airing the question, not asking the black canine in the passenger seat for his opinion.

"God damn it," I yell, slamming the steering wheel with my palm for effect. This time Stash glances my way. Though his raised eyebrows are probably the result of being startled, it's easier to interpret their message—"Yes, you look gullible to me."

**Calm, Cyrus, calm. Consider the facts.** The devil's advocate to my immediate right stares back, my shock, disappointment, and blossoming insecurity eager to give Stash a voice.

"Amy doesn't wear a wedding band."

**It's called cheating.**

"Amy lives with her grandfather, a man who, by his own admission, barely knows her . . . husband."

**Maybe Amy was ostracized, their marriage a rebellious act driven by an irrepressible love.**

"Now you're just being combative."

**Thank you, I try.**

"But what kind of a man ignores a wife nursing a sick relative, a wife forced to work all hours while he stays in a fancy hotel, cruising around in a gas-guzzling tank? Why not help her out, at least financially?"

**If she's as independent as you think, she might not want his money. Better yet, she might choose to be his love slave.**

A shiver courses through my body.

"Wait a minute. The phone call in the bar, the call Amy **had** to take. I witnessed her reactions and noted her body language. She was genuinely surprised. Marco

Tellucci may be her husband, but she hasn't heard from him for quite some time. Yes, and that's why it was important, that's why they've been catching up. The bigger question is where has he been?"

**Easy. Serving time in a federal penitentiary for what he did to the last man who went after his wife.**

My inner monologue may be on to something, but it's time to ditch all this unproductive speculation. Like my mother, Ruth, used to say when she first got me interested in looking down a microscope: **Keep your mind open; weigh all the possibilities. Let the facts speak for themselves**.

Back at Bedside Manor, I had clung to the most obvious explanation until a computer ping announced a follow-up message from Gabe:

Subject: One more thing!

Hey Doc. Before you ask, I already searched for documentation of a divorce. Nothing out there.
G

I'm not sure whether I was more disturbed by this news or the fact that Gabe, a kid I barely knew, correctly anticipated that I would find his attachment irresistible. Do I really come across as shallow, impetuous, and, worst of all, entirely predictable? What has this thing with Amy done to me?

This leaves me with two other possibilities: "separated" or "getting a divorce." Either way, based on the video footage from The Inn, the relationship between Tellucci and Amy appears entirely amicable. The question I keep circling back to is why would Amy warn me off? Why would she want to test my faith in her, to challenge my ability to trust? She must know how much I struggle with these abstract concepts. And I'm not buying reverse psychology, begging me to let it go while secretly wanting me to find out. This may sound painfully naïve, but my best guess is Amy is trying to protect me. But from what? Did she marry into the Mob? Was the guy Tellucci screamed at in his Humvee a hit man?

My hand drifts over to the passenger

seat and I watch it go, like it belongs to someone else, an **Addams Family** "Thing" mussing up Stash's poufy haircut. Now I see why some people turn to these silent creatures for comfort and support in times of crisis. No head games, no lies, no pain. I pull back my hand. Is this dog turning me into "some people"?

I glance over at the clock and see it's almost two. I am going to be late for a house call, to check out Gilligan the neurotic border collie. If I keep busy, keep moving, my mind cannot be caught, and there can be no reckoning, no obsessing. This revelation about Amy makes me want to revert to my old ways. Who needs all this . . . mess? Maybe it's time to shut the world out, box up my feelings for Amy, and focus solely on Bedside Manor. Hey, a little flirtation with Dr. Honey tonight may be the perfect antidote. If only Tommy Lovelace knew how to flirt.

We pull up to the driveway of an isolated ranch house—set back among junk trees, plaques of black mold on rotten white siding, ice patches on a roof in need of insulation. Off to one side there's a rusty car on breeze-blocks and next to it, under a tailor-made tarp, what can only be a snow-mobile.

"Stash, stay." About to turn the engine off, I change my mind. Can't have the doodle getting cold.

Halfway up the driveway, the collie emerges from somewhere out back, barking, zipping through the snow, darting forward and leaping around.

"Do I look like a lost sheep?"

Someone might benefit from a little attitude adjustment. I'm referring to myself, not the dog.

"Gillie, no, stop that. Sorry, Doc. He'll be fine in a minute. Come on in."

Unlike my visit to Lionel's house, no blue suede slippers for me. I stomp on the doormat and step inside. I never had grandparents growing up, but if I had, this is how I imagine their house would have smelled— a potent mix of boiled cabbage and BEN-GAY. It's more distinctive than unpleasant, and I remember how this house was once Grandma's house. Mary's traded the riding hood for a red sweatshirt.

"Come on through to the back. Didn't think you'd be by so soon."

Gilligan leads us down a central hallway,

and I take note of a formal dining room to my left (six Shaker chairs around a table, Tiffany-style lamp dangling from the ceiling) and a bedroom to my right (queen-sized bed, pink duvet, yellowing floral wallpaper). I enter a galley kitchen with a den and breakfast nook.

I note the peeling linoleum, chipped Formica, avocado-colored appliances. Curious about this retro style, I wonder where they're hiding the orange shag carpet.

"We've got big plans for the place," says Mary, making me feel awful and judgmental.

"Hey, you should see my apartment." As soon as the words get away from me, I realize, in the shock written on Mary's face, I might as well have said, "Don't worry, I live in a dump as well."

"I mean, this place has . . . great bones."

Mary looks as unconvinced as I sound.

"I hope there won't be a charge for this," she says. "It's not like it's my fault you weren't at the clinic when you said."

Back to money. Perhaps I should have just driven around for a while, taken my mind off Amy that way. Besides, impressing her friend seems unlikely to make a difference at this point.

"Sure. Let me palpate Gilligan's belly one more time."

To be fair, Gilligan is much better behaved at home. Oh, he's still squirrelly, running figure eights in and out of Mary's legs before I can latch on, but at least this time I get to maintain the integrity of my eardrums.

"Any more seizures?" I ask as I run my hands front to back, top to bottom, trying to trace the path of the mysterious metallic material lurking in his guts. I should be poking something sharp, something that makes me pull back my hand to discover a bloody fingertip, but Gillie and the divining power of my palpation give me nothing.

"No," says Mary.

"He's been vaccinated for rabies, distemper, right?"

"Of course."

Of course, that would be too easy. Then I notice his teeth, the way the incisors are worn down.

"Is he a rock chewer?"

"Not so as I've noticed," she replies.

**Stop staring at me, Mary. I'm trying my best here.**

"Did he defecate this morning?"

She hesitates, and I'm not sure if she's searching her memory or confused by the language.

"Bowel movement? Did he go to the bathroom this morning?"

"Yes. Why?"

"Could you please show me where?"

Mary opens the screen door out back and points vaguely in the direction of the tree line.

I excuse myself (as if I'm the one who needs to use the bathroom) and wade out into the snow until I discover a collection of excrement (or maybe I should say an archipelago of frozen tootsie rolls). I'm no expert on dog poop, but it looks pretty normal to me. I bag a sample and slowly head back, running out of options.

"Anything?" Mary asks.

"No."

"Not a clue?"

"No, I have plenty of clues. My problem is interpreting these clues on a shoestring budget. In my world, disease doesn't offer a friendly wave while shouting, 'Hey, check out this clue. It's pathognomonic.'"

"Patho-what?"

"It's a tell, a sign, a revelation that says find me and you will have your answer. Mystery solved. It's great when you find it, but it's rare. Gilligan needs more blood work, urinalysis, abdominal ultrasound. His clinical picture fits nicely with hepatitis, inflammation of his liver, but what's the cause—viral, bacterial, toxic, copper, idiopathic?"

"Idio-what?"

"Idiopathic, it's a fancy way of saying I haven't got a clue."

"Yeah," she says, letting me see the frustration in her eyes. "That's what it sounds like."

I tilt my head to the ceiling, close my eyes, and suck down a lungful of air. She's right. This woman needs an answer that I don't have. She's looking on as her dog refuses to eat, as his ribs stick out, as his waist sucks in, as he thrashes around on his side, helpless and afraid as an electrical storm sweeps across his brain.

"I'm sorry, Mary. I'm not having a very

good day, and that's no excuse, but maybe Gillie needs to see a doctor who's a hell of a lot smarter than me."

The sensation is like bile rising to the back of my throat, but I must fight back the nausea and swallow it down.

"I'd be happy to give you a referral. No doubt Healthy Paws in Patton will be able to sort him out."

"That's it," says Mary, hands on hips. "You're giving up?"

I squeeze my lips into a bloodless gray line and nod, avoiding eye contact.

The Clint Eastwood quote crosses my mind. **A man's got to know his limitations.**

"I'll be sure to fax over all Gillie's information, and I'll mail out his X-rays from today. Make sure they don't waste money by repeating what's already done."

I make to leave, glance back, and see Mary busy cradling her dog's head in her hands, whispering the same mantra as me in his ear.

"Sorry, I'm sorry."

Through an oily cloud of smog I make out Stash, face pressed into the Silverado's windshield as soon as he sees me marching down the driveway.

"Get back on your seat," I say, hopping up into the warm cab. I've probably used about a quarter of a tank idling, but it was worth it for a fast getaway. I let up on the clutch and begin to roll forward. Suddenly Stash begins barking his head off. I slam on the brakes, thinking I've run something over.

**Don't tell me Gilligan got loose.**

But when I turn to Stash to see what the fuss is about, I can see he's barking at the border collie standing in the window. Gilligan must be up on his back legs, front paws on the sill, his rooting snout sweeping heavy curtains off to one side. It's the room to the left of the front door, the dining room.

**He stays in the exact same spot where I left him. Standing at the dining room window, waiting for us to come home.**

**The exact same spot.**

I lean over, plant a kiss on the top of Stash's head, and I don't care who sees me.

"Stash, stay. Mary, Mary," I scream, charging up the driveway. "There's something I forgot."

Mary opens the front door, and I rush right past her, ignoring the mat, traipsing snow across the floor, entering the dining room uninvited while she's fumbling for curse words.

This time, in true **Wizard of Oz** fashion, I pull back the curtain. Concealed behind the heavy drape, I discover the answer to my prayers. The elusive pathognomonic clue—the windowsill has been thoroughly gnawed and gnarled by canine teeth.

"What is it?"

**The worn teeth—not a rock chewer, Gilligan's a windowsill chewer.**

I can't speak, the smile on my face interfering with my ability to form words. Instead I do something wholly out of character for me. Blame the emotional upheaval of the day or the thrill of **not** sending a case to the evil empire. Maybe, most of all, blame the realization, the certainty, that I can do this. There's something tangible about how good this moment can feel. Impulsively I reach my arms around Mary, hugging her so tightly her feet leave the ground as we spin like a whirling dervish.

"What the—"

"It's the paint, Mary. The paint."

"I can see that. The dog's ruined that sill. I told you he gets separation anxiety."

I check out the adjacent window—same thing.

"Old house, you said."

"Yeah, so?"

Suddenly I can see it, the case unraveling, so obvious now.

"Those white flecks on his abdominal X-ray. They're flecks of paint."

Mary tilts her head to one side. "Wait. You said Gillie swallowed something metallic."

"He did," I say. "It's lead paint. Common in an older house. It would have been picked up on a home inspection if you'd gone through a Realtor."

I watch as the wheels begin turning behind Mary's eyes.

"But Grandma left it to us. No inspection needed. I never even—"

"Why would you? It hit me when my dog started barking at Gillie standing in the window."

**My** dog. How easily that rolled off the tongue.

"Chronic lead poisoning will make you lose weight and lose interest in food. Changes in mentation are common."

Mary frowns. I really need to rein in my lexicon, I mean vocabulary.

"I'm saying it'll make him act weird. Even cause seizures. He waits at the window, gets anxious, chews on the sill like an infant sucks on a security blanket, and gets his daily fix of lead. Gilligan is obviously in the forty percent of lead poisoning cases that don't show basophilic stippling in their blood." I continue to explain. "Little blue dots on his red blood cells—classic for lead poisoning. When you see them on a slide, you've got your diagnosis. But I didn't see them. I ruled out lead when I should have kept an open mind. It was a stupid mistake. I'm sorry."

"Don't be silly. How do we treat it?"

Damn, and I was doing so well.

"I can't remember. Something to do with thiamine injections. I'll look it up. No point in making Gillie vomit. Keep him away from the paint for now, but you need to get rid of it. All of it."

Gilligan has backed up in a corner, watching the show. I can't tell if he's expecting praise for his oral woodworking skills or denying culpability.

"You're incredible," says Mary, smiling before lunging at me with her own version of a celebratory hug. "Amy promised you'd fix him."

This time around I bristle, but mercifully Mary makes it brief.

"I'm calling her," she says, jabbing a finger in my direction. "Amy needs to know she's on to something special."

"I wish, Mary," I say, faking a smile. "I wish."

« **16** »

My heart is skipping beats, my mouth refuses to generate saliva, and there are butterflies the size of bats flapping around inside my stomach. And please, before you label this as cute, nervous excitement regarding my rebound date with Dr. Honey, this is all about dread—tongue-tied, knee-knocking, "I think I'm going to be sick" dread—at the thought of unmasking Tommy Lovelace as her pesky rival from Bedside Manor.

There's a bottle of red wine in the passenger seat where a labradoodle should be. So weird, the relationship between appreciation and loss, the "only realize what you've got when it's gone" syndrome. In part I'm referring to Stash after leaving him home alone tonight. I'm sure he's seated behind the apartment door, head angled up, waiting for my return (okay, I confess, I went back to check and he hadn't moved). But I am also talking about two-timing Amy and the way we never had a chance to see if our sparks could catch fire.

This time there's no pink Jeep parked in Dr. Winn Honey's driveway. Charlie Brown took her marching orders and hopefully went over to Gabe's without the need for a hot fudge sundae detour.

I turn off the truck's engine, reach over to grab the wine, and catch myself in the rearview mirror. Can the man in the reflection go through with this? Maybe a little romance is a good thing: a much-needed escape from Amy and a way of softening the blow for being a vet and not a porn star. According to Charlie, her mother is usually more than willing and able when it comes to dating the opposite sex. I can practically guarantee the patrons of the Miss Eden Falls diner will know I spent the night long before I sip my mug of morning coffee. Dr. Honey is a beautiful woman (the word **hot** should be restricted to temperature). She's intelligent and spirited, but let's face it, I'm struggling for the superlatives that count because compared to Amy, she doesn't have it. She simply doesn't wow me, and I'm pretty sure she never will.

"Be gentle but be clear."

I watch as my reflection winces. "Be gentle?" Please. This woman will go postal the moment I tell her who I really am.

"Okay. Get her drunk, slip it into the conversation, and run."

"Is that you, Tom?" asks the slim silhouette standing at the open front door.

"Yes," I shout, dropping down from the cab and making my way up the driveway. "Parked on the street because my truck has a problem with reverse. Didn't know if you preferred red or white?"

"Someone hasn't been doing his homework," says Dr. Honey with a pout and a little offended shimmy of her head before smiling, reaching for the wine, and planting a kiss on my right cheek. "It's on my profile. Good to see you again."

I'm slow to let go of the pinot noir for so

many reasons. Clearly Dr. Honey's been listening to her daughter's fashion advice— Levi's that show off a waspish waist and long legs, a white cotton shirt, ironed into submission, open at the neck, drawing the eye to an ornate gold necklace and not her cleavage. The effect is conservative yet classy, and it's disarming. No vamp or tramp. Why did I bring wine? It only adds to my deceit. **Confess, Cyrus, here and now, on the stoop.** At the very least I should hold on to the bottle in case I need something to defend myself.

"You okay?" she asks, ultimately snagging the bottle from my hand. "Looks like someone needs a drink. We're in the kitchen."

I follow, wondering if I'm meant to notice the Marilyn Monroe wiggle to her hips, and we arrive at the island soapstone counter. There's a sweating bottle of Chablis, a breathing bottle of Bordeaux, and an assortment of cheeses, crackers, grapes, and cured meats on a Provençal platter.

"Lovely house," I say, remembering this is supposed to be my first visit.

"Thanks. The only good thing my ex had going for him was money. I got to keep it, but the mortgage is a killer on one salary."

**Ninety percent of pet owners fight more passionately for pets than money in a divorce.**

Dr. Honey shrugs, raises the uncorked bottle of white in my direction, and I nod my approval.

"Your email the other day," she says, beginning to pour, the bottle steeply angled, quickly filling the glass to the brim. I notice the pale lipstick smudge on the rim of her glass—clearly not her first. "You always so . . . formal?"

Stop wringing your hands and cut to the chase.

"Uh . . . I should . . . There's something I have to explain."

Dr. Honey passes me my drink.

"Yes, there is," she says, chinking her glass against mine, a little yellow liquid slipping over the side, before taking a sip (make that guzzle). "The reason I make you nervous."

I begin to mumble, proof positive of her effect on me.

"So . . . um . . ."

In her narrowing green eyes I sense

concern tinged with vulnerability. It's too cruel too soon. Better to wait for her blood alcohol content to rise to a more soporific level.

"Do you . . . model?"

She throws back her head, dazzles me with teeth, the muscles in her face relaxing with relief. Maybe I should have hit myself over the head with the wine bottle.

"The photos on the way in? Very observant. No, but that's nice of you. They were part of a motivational plan after the divorce. Weight Watchers and six months with a personal trainer, proof of a before and after."

She leans back against the island, rocking her pelvis forward.

"Before?" I stammer.

Dr. Honey laughs through her nose. "Oh, those are locked away in a safe deposit box."

"And your daughter? No pictures?"

She takes another swig. The glass is half-empty.

"No recent pictures. Let's just say the divorce and adolescence have taken a toll. My daughter's a beautiful girl, but she's not looking her best and refuses to have her photo taken. Please, try the prosciutto. It's from this little Italian deli across the street from work. Really good."

Dr. Honey pops a slice into her mouth and hands me a napkin. I act as though I didn't notice her trying to change the subject.

"So there **is** an upside to working at Healthy Paws," I say, cutting a slice of gorgonzola and thinking, **Hey, if she wants to vent, relieved to unload what might be another useful tidbit of negative information, who am I to stop her before I make my announcement?**

"Hardly. Though, assuming I keep my job, I'm supposed to be in Miami next weekend on the company's dime."

"Wow. Guess they can't be that bad."

"Yeah they can. It's a conference for Healthy Paws veterinarians from all across the country. Held twice a year. Attendance is mandatory."

"What is it, CE?"

She rocks back in her stance, puzzled by my understanding. How would a guy who reviews movies for a living know about continuing education?

I freeze, pretending to wait expectantly for an answer.

"No, it's more like a cult. Total immersion and indoctrination, twelve hours a day for two days. Lectures on how to read the client, how to improve the client experience, how to project empathy, not just sympathy."

"Sounds like psychobabble."

Dr. Honey puts her glass down.

"Shake my hand," she says, "like you're meeting me for the first time."

I surreptitiously wipe my palm across the back of my jeans, and we shake. She seems pleased.

"What?"

"Palm sideways, in the neutral position, eye contact, and a smile. Mutual respect and genuine friendship."

Clearly these classes are a waste of time. And why is she still holding my hand?

"Watch out if I roll my palm on top. It says I'm a control freak. That's why they call it the upper hand."

I flash back to my first encounter with Dorkin, but manage to catch myself before using him as an example.

Finally she trades my hand for the wineglass.

"The main focus is how to squeeze more

dollars out of every office visit. It's brain-washing."

"Will your daughter go with you?"

Dr. Honey flashes me a tight smile.

"Right now, I'm not sure she'd feel comfortable poolside in a bathing suit."

Instead of a response, I tease a grape from its stem and think about Charlize and what really motivates her to overeat.

"Part of me envies those vets in Eden Falls."

I jerk to attention. "Really?"

"Sometimes," she says, crunching into a cracker and washing it down with the last of her wine. I wonder where her tolerance lies and whether she can be an angry drunk. "I'd kill not to have to milk my clients for every last dollar, to not have to see a new patient every seventeen minutes or else. What a concept, taking your time, really getting to know the animals and their owners. Probably end up making just as much money by earning trust and confidence."

Amazing, she's starting to sound like Lewis.

As she's freshening her glass, I notice the reason behind my first visit to this house.

"What on earth is that?"

My performance may be wooden and hammy, but Dr. Honey follows my pointy finger in the direction of the recumbent feline next to the refrigerator. It's hard to tell where the cat's love handles end and the folds in her beany-bed begin.

"This is my soul mate, the one true love of my life." She clip-clops over and scoops up the panther-sized creature, careful to bend at the knees. "This is my Marmalade."

In her cradling arms, Marmalade's high lipid content seems to take on a liquid state, her dimensions spilling in all directions, impossible to contain.

"Wow. Would it be impolite to ask how much he weighs?"

"Careful, Tom," says Dr. Honey, nuzzling into Marmalade's face but keeping her eyes on me. "You're talking to a woman who used to be 'big boned.' All I'll say is **she's** closer to thirty pounds than forty."

"Slow metabolism? Glandular problem?" I keep the phrase **that's a relief** to myself.

"I wish I knew," says Honey, putting Marmalade back down (I noticed her arms were starting to tremble from the effort). "I've spent a fortune on tests and everything has come back completely normal." Her eyes begin to glisten, necessitating a reviving hand waft to settle her emotions. "What kind of a doctor can't sort out her own cat?"

In the world of real dating this would be deemed a perfect opportunity to put a comforting arm around her. Naturally, I freeze.

"Based on what you just said, the problem can only be too much food and too little exercise."

"Go on," she says, clearly pleased that I'm taking an interest. "But keep in mind I'm the only one who feeds her. I know exactly how much she gets, down to the ounce." Dr. Honey knocks twice on the closed pantry door. "No way she's eating too much food." She steps in close enough for me to smell the alcohol on her breath. "I'm fed up with talking shop. I want to hear something about you and those movies you get to watch for a living."

"Well, it's not really all that exciting."

"Ah, come on now." She loops a stray lock of hair behind her left ear, places her right hand flat on my chest. "Tell me about your last review."

I remember what Charlie said and think about describing the plot of **Pretty Woman**. How far can I get before she figures it out? What if she's amused, embarrassed but thrilled that I made the effort to find out her favorite movie? Once again, I'm still leading her on.

The clock's ticking, and the cougar seems ready to pounce. Without preamble or plan, total desperation has me launching into a perilous stream of consciousness.

"Okay. It was a low-budget, independent film. First-time director working with what was essentially an improvised script."

I drain my glass of wine in two big gulps, Dr. Honey encouraging me with "keep going" eyes.

"There's this . . . single mom, and she's a good person, you know, but she's lonely and she's been hurt. Her teenage daughter has some . . . issues. The kid binges on ice cream because it numbs the pain of abandonment."

"Ugh, this sounds really depressing."

"No, no. It's more like a morality tale. See, there's this unique allegorical character in the mix, a pet cat, and this cat is morbidly obese, yet her mother doesn't care, because no matter what, she will love this creature unconditionally."

She slams her empty glass down on the counter, and I'm amazed that it doesn't shatter.

"Thomas, what's going on here?"

Suddenly, I feel the shift from blurting out thoughts to genuine brainstorming, as the pieces of the puzzle fall into place.

"Please, just give me a minute. It all makes sense. This mother's been hurt, she's in denial, but she knows there's a Prince Charming somewhere out in the world, happy to make her pain go away, a knight in shining armor more accepting of a cute, fat cat than he ever would be of a weak-willed, fat kid."

Flat palm on the chest tightens into a firm grip of my shirt.

"What's this about?"

"I'm getting to it," I plead, trying to back up as I spew sentences. "The plot gets really contrived when this stranger . . . truly, a well-intentioned man . . . gets caught up in the relationship, but by the time the credits roll, it's all good . . . everything gets resolved."

I'm buzzing with the excitement of the discovery I've just made.

"I don't know what you're up to, but you're freaking me out and you should go. Now."

It was the way Marmalade sat patiently in front of the pantry door when Charlie was around, as though the cat knew it would be worth the wait. Not so with her doting mom.

Dr. Honey's furious and visibly creeped out by my performance (who could blame her?).

"Please, I'm leaving and I'm sorry, sorry in more ways than I can say. But the solution lies with why the cat was fat."

"Get out," she snaps.

My upper body makes to leave, but my feet haven't moved.

"Because it was the daughter's fault."

"What?"

"It was Charlie. I suspect she's been overfeeding Marmalade."

"But why?" she whispers.

I take a deep breath because this is way out of my comfort zone.

"I'm guessing she wanted to prove a point. No matter how much she overfed Marmalade, no matter how bloated and slovenly the cat got, you never stopped loving her. Could you say the same about your daughter?"

By the look on Dr. Honey's face, that was as uncomfortable for her as it was for me. She turns away and takes a moment before grabbing a napkin as a makeshift handkerchief. Head down, a subtle rhythmic shudder of her shoulders is the only outward sign of her crying.

"It was Charlie who got me into this," I say, ready to explain everything.

Dr. Honey spins around to face me, tears running down her cheeks, napkin balled up in a clenched fist.

"Charlie?" she says in disbelief.

"I know she meant you no harm. I think she thought I could help."

"I don't understand. Who are you?"

I try to stand up straight, firing-squad stiff, bracing for my punishment.

"I'm Cyrus Mills. Dr. Cyrus Mills. Actually we spoke on the phone the other—"

That's as far as I get. Whatever made me think I'd be the victim of a well-deserved slap across my cheek? Had I known Winn Honey's personal trainer was big into martial arts and kick-boxing I would have delivered my explanation in an email. Instead I'm dropped, laid out flat by a roundhouse kick to the side of my temple.

# Saturday

« **17** »

The weatherman warned of a "dusting" of snow in the afternoon, which around these parts means anything less than a foot. That's why I'm hitting the road early, eager to escape a personal forecast that promises lengthy spells of anxiety, bursts of loneliness, and a deluge of self-pity. Rather than brood over last night's thorny encounter with the veterinary equivalent of Bruce Lee and my pending comeuppance at the Knights of Columbus, it's time to make a house call I've been trying to avoid for far too long.

It's not easy steering and changing

gears when you've got a bag of frozen peas pressed into your left temple. Still, the swelling from Dr. Honey's karate chop is beginning to subside. I wish the same could be said for the tension between us. Before midnight I received a text from Charlie.

Mom's really mad!

I waited for more, but that was all she wrote. Maybe Charlie's phone was confiscated or maybe she sided with her mom, making me their common enemy.

Stash comes along for the ride. Thanks to Chief Matt Devito, our mystery man with the pacemaker is still John Doe and Stash's provenance remains unknown. Fine by me, and not just because I'm more than happy to look after a homeless Australian labradoodle. It's also that, in light of my recent emotional . . . challenges . . . I am appreciating a straightforward, transparent relationship with a dog.

I pull into Garvey's Nursery and Garden Center and park in the same spot as before, up by the farmhouse, but this time Stash and I walk the trail that leads to the

main barn alone. No need of my doctorin'
bag. There's no remedy for the message
I'm about to deliver.

Before heading out I sat down with Lewis
to discuss what I was going to say. I reviewed the facts of the case and tied them
to the scientific data I had unearthed, and
by the end of my presentation, not only did
Lewis buy my argument, he agreed that
we had an obligation to go public. Though
he offered to join me, I told him this one
was mine.

"If there are going to be fireworks," I
said, "might as well blame the guy who lit
the fuse."

Stash and I pass the outlying greenhouses and the petting zoo, dormant until
spring, the clearing where they hope to
groom a tubing park, and the snowy silhouette of the mini-golf's windmill. I feel
like the heartless demolition man, here to
erase the soul of three generations and an
Eden Falls institution. Worse still, there's a
second unsuspecting victim in this case.
That's why I set up a date with the psy-
chotic bovine, Ermintrude, her owner, Mike,
and her ailing caregiver, Trey.

As soon as we enter the barn, my nostrils

are overcome by the earthy, methane-laden steam heat of tightly clustered animals, my ears are assaulted by a command that reverberates in the post-and-beam heavens overhead.

"Get that dog on a leash."

It's a while before I see the man in the olive green jumpsuit, black beanie on his head, and familiar mirror sunglasses climbing down from a ziggurat of small, square, neatly stacked hay bales, lugging a pair toward one of the stalls. It's a perfectly reasonable request, until you appreciate that I don't have a leash on me and Stash walks to heel like he's the best of show. The doodle hasn't flinched once at the scurrying sheep or the hawking llamas. It's obvious he's totally unconcerned—eyes front, steady gait. Either aloof or bored stiff; it's hard to tell.

"Stash, stay," I command, and, without missing a beat, without turning to check, I keep walking, eyes on Mike Garvey the Third, watching him stop in his tracks, impressed enough to drop his bales and stare in awe.

"Ignore the dog, Mr. Garvey, and the dog will ignore you and your livestock. He's a highly trained dog. He won't be a bother, I promise. Your father on his way?"

Stash stands in the middle of the barn's central aisle, staring at me with perfect tunnel vision. You've got to love this dog. Trey is clearly impressed, and, truth be told, I am too.

Garvey grunts (at least I think it was Garvey and not the Gloucester old spot pig behind him) and marches over to Ermintrude's stall, cutting the orange nylon cord that binds the hay with a penknife and teasing it into mouth-sized wads to scatter in the trough on the other side of the railing. The Jersey stands in the shadows, head in the corner, trembling and disinterested.

"Something came up. He's not coming, and I'm busy," says Trey, brushing past me, nostrils flaring with disdain, returning to the haystack, climbing up and picking off the next layer. Does he hate me, veterinarians, or all human life-forms?

"But Mr. Garvey, you and your father suggested this time, not me."

He hesitates, inhales deeply, releases a throaty growl, and carries on distributing a bale to the goats, another to the sheep, before stomping back to grab more. Trey appears as focused as Stash, but unlike the disciplined labradoodle, obsessive-compulsive demons are at play. It seems this task must be completed before he can chat, and, from the looks of things, the bales are picked off in a precise order to whittle down the stack. No doubt the fodder is delivered in exactly the same order to each of the different livestock every day of the week. Clearly, Trey is a creature of habit.

I wait at Ermintrude's stall, the one nearest the haystack, serenaded by the repetitive coo of squatter pigeons, and try to get a read on the patient.

Cows perform over forty thousand jaw movements every day, but not this cow. She spooks and shudders sideways when I clap my hands. It's heartbreaking to see her xylophone rib cage, her spine craggy and sharp, slack muscle slung across bone, her sunken eyes, feral and beseeching. Then something moves in the shadows next to her, a bird maybe. She flinches, backs up, and I notice a small amount of green discharge forming a crusty halo around her left nostril.

"You still here," says Trey, marching over, palm clasped to his forehead like he's either forgotten something or his headache is back with a vengeance. "Speak to Dad, not me."

"But this concerns you, Mr. Garvey, as much as it concerns Ermintrude."

Trey straightens up, works a grubby index finger into his chin dimple (how does he angle a razor into that cleft?), and then, dipping his head enough to study me over the top of his sunglasses, says, "I ain't no cow."

"Actually cows are eighty percent genetically similar to humans."

Trey gives me a look like that figure might be on the low side.

"Hey, got anything for a migraine?"

"No," I reply, ignoring the déjà vu. "How long has the cow had a nasal discharge?"

Trey says nothing.

I try again. "A snotty nose."

It's hard to tell whether his silence is based on ignorance or irritation.

"Look, I'm no expert on farm animals, but your father asked me to find out what's wrong with Ermintrude. I have a diagnosis, and it concerns you too."

"Why me? I just look after her."

"I realize that, but your diseases are inextricably linked. You have what she has, and vice versa."

"So she's contagious?"

"Not in the way you're thinking. I'm not talking about a bacteria or a virus, I'm talking about an infectious protein, something called a prion."

"Sounds like a type of foreign car."

I'm pretty sure Trey's not trying to be funny. Jaw twitching, hands constantly on the move, shuffling side to side like a boxer waiting for the fight to begin—he's a nervous wreck.

"Prions are tough, really tough, can't be killed by disinfectants, can't be destroyed by normal cooking techniques. You know what scientists call prions?"

I'm not planning on waiting for an answer, but Trey shakes his head all the same.

"Immortal."

He takes a step back, and I know I have his attention. Now, how best to explain?

"I did a lot of research and tried not to come up with this answer. I took my time, weighed the history, the signs, the available diagnostic evidence. But I kept returning to the clinical similarities between you and the cow."

I want to rip off his sunglasses so I can get some kind of visual feedback. Watching my own awkwardness in the mirrors is not helping.

"You both dislike sunlight. Ermintrude presses her head into corners because, like you, she suffers from migraines, and according to your father you've both been acting a little . . ." **Careful, Cyrus**. "A little different. Not yourself."

His stillness has me more worried than his silence.

"You deserve to be the first to know, and either I can talk to your family or you can, whatever you think best, but when I leave here, I will be calling the State Veterinary Board. In a matter of hours, your parking lot will be full of camera crews, reporters, and network helicopters circling the skies overhead."

"Am I about to be famous?"

He seems to have brightened.

"In a way, yes. See there's only been one other case like this in the entire United States and that was over a decade ago. It cost the American Beef Industry billions in lost exports. And that case originated in Canada as well."

"Canada?"

"Ermintrude's mother. She was imported from Canada, right? Started acting strange, slaughtered on the farm, and, as your grandma told me, 'Nothing went to waste, nothing.' Ermintrude's mother was patient zero, the source of the prions, the infected proteins. Some of her tainted body parts must have gotten into the food chain, a chain thankfully confined to your family and your livestock. I don't know whether your juvenile diabetes put you at greater risk, and I'm not sure why you would be immunocompromised, but you and Ermintrude must have consumed contaminated beef. Nothing would have happened for years, the prions lying dormant in your brains, waiting for their moment, taking their time, starting off slowly, causing a little depression, mood swings, a little clumsiness, working their way up to relentless migraines that laugh in the face of Advil. But they're immortal, remember, they cannot be stopped, and in a little over a year from the time of diagnosis, they'll . . ."

"They'll what?"

I swallow. For all the tens of thousands of cancers I've diagnosed during my career I've never been the doctor who delivers the bad news, forced to witness the crippling power of a few well-chosen words. I'm led to believe there's an art to it, a need to cut to the chase.

"They'll kill you. You might live with the disease for a year or so, but it's always fatal."

He should be hearing this from his family physician, not the new vet in town.

"Enough already, what have I got?"

"Trey, I'm sorry, but I'm pretty sure, not one hundred percent, but high nineties—"

"What?" he screams.

"Mad cow disease," I blurt out, causing him to rock on his heels.

"Whoa, whoa, wait a minute." Trey appears lost in a recollection, his face hardening into a frown. "You're a hundred percent certain that the only way I could have gotten this disease was by eating Clover?"

"Correct," I reply. "I'm afraid so."

The guffaw he releases comes from deep within; uncoiling from a titter to a boom, hearty and genuine, causing him to double over, stagger backward, and pick himself up.

This is not the reaction I was expecting.

He removes his glasses, and for the first time I see his eyes—hazel, bloodshot, and wet. Catching his breath, Trey wipes away tears with the backs of his hands.

"I'm a vegetarian, Doc. Have been since my freshman year at college, a year before Clover died. Never ate beef since. I can't speak for Ermintrude, but if she and me have the same thing, it ain't mad cow."

As I stand there, feeling as dumb as I must look, watching his eyes transition from relief to indignation, an enormous bird poop, sloppy and flecked with green, splashes on the center of my forehead, a milky bindi dribbling down my face.

Trey loses it, gasping for air, at risk of peeing his jumpsuit.

Fortunately I'm carrying a handkerchief.

"Should have worn a hat, Doc. Still, supposed to be good luck." Then he winces, driving his fingertips deep into the bridge of his nose, as if stabbed by another round of sinus pain. The Trey that comes back is exasperated and ready to explode.

"You'd best go before I start to think

about how my dad's spending good money on an animal doctor who wants to give his son a fatal brain-eating disease."

"Now, Mr. Garvey, I never meant to—"

Spittle hits my face before the shriek reaches my ears. "I said go."

I take a step backward, determined not to wipe off the spritzed saliva on my chin, and look over at Stash. He's not moved, but he has changed his focus. His head angles up, checking out the birds perched on the rafters above. I follow his gaze up to the hundreds of pigeons roosting in the beams.

The Gloucester old spot pig waddles over to the railing—**white with big black spots**. The black dog in the aisle—**not a single white splotch anywhere.**

**Pigeons. Pooping pigeons. But where, exactly, are they pooping?**

Without saying a word I march down to the other end of the barn and slowly work my way back, checking out the stalls and the flooring for traces of avian fecal matter. And then, though I'm a little slower than Stash, I see what's been going on.

"Please, Mr. Garvey, just answer this question and then I promise I'll leave. When you feed Ermintrude, do you follow the exact same routine as I witnessed today?"

Trey growls but his reluctant shrug makes me press on.

"You feed Ermintrude first, right? She always gets the top, outer layer of hay?"

"Yeah."

"And the other livestock gets the deeper layers, not outer bales, always deeper."

"What's your point? I like to keep things neat."

"My point is you're feeding Ermintrude hay that's covered in pigeon droppings. The bales from underneath are protected by the top layer that always gets fed to Ermintrude because she gets fed first."

"And what, there's a Prius in the bird poop?"

"No, not a prion, a fungus. Coccidioidomycosis. You can inhale it into your lungs or your sinuses, and then, if you're unlucky, it can work its way into your brain. Damn! That's why she's got the snotty nose. That's why you've got the migraines, the sensitivity to light, and that's why you're a little clumsy."

Trey appears taken aback.

"That's why you failed a sobriety test

even though you tested negative for alcohol."

"I told Devito I never smoke pot, but he wouldn't believe me."

In the moment it takes Trey to relive his encounter with the chief, I glance over at the cow, meeting her big brown eyes and wanting to apologize. This is not about my failings as a farm animal vet. This is about manipulating the signs to fit a concept floating inside my head. This is about humility, my misdiagnosis as stupid as my correct one was inspired.

"This cocci-whatever, it's not going to kill me, is it?"

"No, but you need to be on the right medications. Get over to the emergency room in Patton, tell them you want to be tested for . . . Forget it, I'll write it down. Here, if you're positive, we'll treat Ermintrude the same way. Oh, and you're going to need to get rid of your pigeon problem. No more photo ops with the bird feed, okay?"

If I'm expecting a smile or a grateful handshake, it never comes. Hopefully those social miscues can be corrected. Then again, who am I to talk?

"How much?" asks Trey, suddenly dead serious, sunglasses back in place like he's ready to play poker.

"Forget it. I'm sorry I screwed up. After the mental anguish I put you through, there's no charge for the visit."

Garvey twists his lips off to one side. "No, no," he says, shoving a thumb over his shoulder in the direction of Stash. "I'm asking about the dog. How much do you want for her?"

Stash held his ground the whole time. Twenty yards away and we still have direct eye contact. He's like a diagnostic talisman—first a collie, now a cow.

"Sorry, Mr. Garvey, but you couldn't pay me enough. The dog is not for sale."

« **18** »

As I roll into the packed parking lot of the Knights of Columbus Banquet and Reception Hall I'm greeted by an illuminated sign that claims this facility is PERFECT FOR PARTIES, WEDDING ANNIVERSARIES, AND FUNERAL LUNCHEONS. Given my present state of mind, all three options sound anything but "perfect." Obviously I'm not in a party mood (okay, I rarely am), and if Amy's celebrating thirteen years of marriage to her Italian lover (it's lace and yes, I looked it up) you can count me out. Also, two forty-five in the afternoon seems a little late for lunch. So what does that leave me with? That's right, a funeral, and though I'm sure Dr. Honey would love to bury me alive, the only practice headed for that big clinic in the sky is Healthy Paws.

I park next to a miniature version of the Andes plowed into the back of the lot (turns out the forecast was right—just a dusting) and watch as the new converts to the Church of Healthy Paws stream from their vehicles and march to the main entrance, eager to hear the gospel from the new testament of veterinary medicine. To be honest, I hope Winn Honey can deliver a decent sermon. Yes, I know this sounds strange for a man who still winces when he probes the swelling above his left eye, but the way she's handled her daughter since the divorce seems more misguided than heartless. Born of hurt, it's no better than me abandoning my late father. I can do penance, but I can never truly achieve forgiveness. Winn Honey has a chance, and I wish her well (which is not the same as wanting to get within range of her hands or feet). I did my bit solving Marmalade's weight issues. Everything else—parenting techniques, abandonment issues, a quest for redemption—is **way** beyond my job description (and comfort zone). If I started a conversation, Charlie and her mom can finish it on their own.

I didn't know what to wear for this event, but I went with one of my father's tweed jackets and matching wool ties. It feels a little forced, a little too gentleman farmer, but at least I look presentable.

Once outside the truck I'm assaulted by a whipping wind that cuts and slices like a scalpel, drawing tears as I head for the door. The last thing I need is to look like I've been crying. Fortunately I don't recognize anyone as I dab my lids with a handkerchief until the infamous Ethel Silverman rounds the corner with her husky, Kai, in tow. I flash to the poster for this event, the one outside the diner—"Dogs Allowed*." I never did find out what that asterisk meant—behaves well with others, vocally restrained, unlikely to defecate indoors? Perhaps I should have brought the labradoodle. It's obvious Stash hates being alone. His parting expression, indelible, caught in the split second before I shut the apartment door between us, was more than sadness, it was disbelief, unable to accept the fact that he's out of a job, that I, the master he serves, don't need him.

I slow down, giving Ethel and Kai a chance to make their entrance, and then, heart pounding, on a deep breath worthy of a free diver, I step inside.

The hall is just that, a grim, airplane hangar of a room with weak fluorescent lighting struggling to permeate the gloom of windowless, wood-paneled walls. It's deceptively crowded because everyone has gathered at this end, so as soon as the door closes behind me I'm forced to bump, squeeze, and apologize as I try to move forward and get my bearings. The steady drone of conversation never wavers in the tight circles of talking heads, and I notice the occasional dog on a leash or cradled in an arm. It seems the congregation has been corralled to make room for neat rows of metal chairs in front of a podium and projector screen at the far end of the hall. No one seems keen to take a seat.

Scanning left and right, striving for curious not furtive, I catch a glimpse of Doris's yellow beehive, bemoan the fact that this is my best (only) social option, and then, to my relief, spot Peter Greer, the editor of the **Eden Falls Gazette**. At six-five, Greer is a skyscraper of a man, head and shoulders above the masses. I can't see who he's with, but since he's a proven Bedside Manor ally, that's where I'm headed.

Then she comes at me as a neon pink blur, a girl in a gaudy scrub shirt sporting hair bleached to the point of whiteness and gelled into a stiff crown of daggers.

"Canine, feline, or exotic?" She smiles (sincere but manic), and shakes three gift bags in my face.

"I beg your pardon?"

"You got a dog, a cat, or somethin' fun like a sugar glider or a chinchilla?"

I take in the Healthy Paws logo on her breast pocket and the plastic name tag above it—Popcorn—ah, their perky receptionist. If I were going to name a girl Popcorn, and I never will, this is precisely how I would hope she'd turn out. Her eyes are poached-egg-white wild, lips twitching with anticipation, effervescent to the point of bursting. She must have Red Bull for blood. Right about now, Doris is looking pretty good.

"A dog," I say, and with that moment of

acknowledgment comes a surprising awareness, best described as delight. This brief
warm-and-fuzzy sensation is quickly ex-
tinguished as a gift bag bearing the picture of a frolicking Lab puppy gets shoved
in my direction. I peek inside and glimpse
a bottle of flea shampoo, a Healthy Paws
refrigerator magnet and bandana, and bio-
degradable poop bags in a bone-shaped
dispenser.

"Thanks," I say with a polite smile, "but I'll
pick it up on the way out." I have no intention of doing so.

Popcorn offers me a "suit yourself" shrug
and zips off, presumably for a double
espresso refill.

As Greer sees me coming, the crowd
parts, and in the shadow of his eclipse I
see he's in conversation with none other
than Lewis.

"Ah, ready to do battle, Dr. Mills?"

Greer reaches out and crushes my hand
(I'm sure this is not meant to be intimidat-
ing), while Lewis takes control of my free
shoulder with his usual death grip.

"Bring it on," whispers Lewis. "We can
give as good as we get, and besides, we
have home-field advantage."

I try to smile back, to be buoyed by Lewis's confidence, but the muscles around my lips and eyes betray me, twisting into a silent plea for mercy.

"Ladies and gentlemen, time to take a seat and let the fun begin."

I recognize the voice, the authoritative yet chummy tone, like he's introducing a fairground attraction. Over on the far side of the room, I make out the man himself, Dorkin, and next to him, in a smart business suit, none other than the Jackie Chan of Patton, Dr. Winn Honey. Fortunately neither of them seems to have noticed my presence.

"Excuse me, gentlemen," says Greer. "Mr. Dorkin has asked me to join him down at the front. Seems he has a bone to pick with me over the ad we ran the other day. Don't know what to tell him. Either my copy editor is an imbecile or a japesome wag." He raises his eyebrows at me, but to Lewis he conspicuously double-pats the breast pocket of his overcoat before drifting away.

"Do I want to know what that was about?" I ask.

Lewis grins. Today's bow tie is blue with a repeating pattern of playing cards and sharks. The symbolism is obvious—a card shark—a person who uses skill and deception to win. What has he done now?

I get the full upper-arm-squeeze, pep-talk treatment. "Dorkin found me before you arrived. He's going to give you a chance to say a few words, but I can tell he'd rather put you on the spot. If he tries to push your buttons in front of this audience, be yourself, be the doctor who has a passion for animals."

"Yes, but strictly speaking my passion is for the diagnosis, the thrill of solving a medical mystery. I mean, the pets are okay but, well, the owners, they just tend to get in the way of—"

His fingers find the ulna nerve as it crosses my elbow, their squeeze triggering my "funny bone." "Easy, Cyrus. Best leave the passion for pets and people to me, but Dorkin's sure to pick on you because Bedside Manor is your business. Don't waffle. Keep it brief. No one remembers a drawn-out, complicated response. Only brevity can deliver a knockout punch."

Why do I feel more scolded than inspired?

"You really think Bedside Manor can go

head-to-head with Healthy Paws? Handle this level of scrutiny?" I wonder, suddenly unsure.

"Absolutely," says Lewis, but I pick up on the subtle quaver hidden in his vowels.

I'm reminded of **The English Patient**, the sandstorm scene where Kristin Scott Thomas asks Ralph Fiennes if he thinks they will be all right.

**Yes. Yes. Absolutely.**

**Yes is a comfort. Absolutely is not.**

"I'll be up front, with Greer," says Lewis. "You and I sitting together, not right, looks weak."

I could argue that together we demonstrate solidarity, but he's gone before I get the chance. I'm guessing there must be a hundred and fifty people in attendance, a good showing for a Saturday afternoon, with most folks drawn to the front. I notice a guy in a camo jacket on the aisle seat of the last row, a German short-haired pointer on one side, and at least four goody bags stockpiled on the other. Something tells me he won't be staying for long. I come around, slink into an empty back row via the side, and settle into a seat, nice and low. With plenty of space up front I'm a little surprised when someone plops down next to me.

"Hell-o," says Amy, bumping my elbow, acting all—dare I say—chipper to see me.

Involuntarily, I develop an acute case of tetanus, the muscles of my body stiffening, my spine turning rigid. I grunt a reciprocal hello.

"What's wrong with you?"

My mind jams with our last conversation, Amy shutting me down for being, oh, I don't know, a little curious about a man who turned out to be her husband.

"Nervous for your girlfriend's speech? You think she'll get annoyed if I sit here?"

Though she makes the question sound serious enough, mischief sparkles in her blue and brown eyes.

"What happened to the side of your head?" She prods an index finger into my temple before I can speak, causing me to flinch and suck saliva between clenched teeth.

"I slipped in the shower."

She stifles a laugh. "That's the best you've got? 'Cause I'm leaning toward lover's spat."

"We are not lovers," I snap, loud, insistent, and, unfortunately, the only voice in a room that suddenly went quiet. Everyone turns in our direction, Amy managing to join the masses with an overplayed look of surprise. From the podium, Dorkin picks me out, and, keeping his eyes on me, says something to Honey, who's standing by his side.

"Someone's in trouble," Amy says, barely moving her lips.

"She's not my . . . girlfriend," I whisper, facing forward, my cheeks still radiating atomic heat.

"Hmm, you might be right. Her death glare is clearly aimed at you, not me. I'm sensing animosity, not jealousy."

I turn and take in Amy's profile as she fakes anticipation, like a kid eager for the show to start. Such long eyelashes. Why is she here and acting all . . . frisky?

Time to shut her down.

"Shouldn't you be brushing up on your Italian?" I ask.

She jerks back to face me, aghast.

"What do you know, Cyrus?"

"Nothing much. A name. A country of origin."

"Best keep it that way," she says, adding,

"**non essere un cretino**," in a perfect Italian accent.

Dorkin interrupts before I can get any more information out of Amy. "Wow, what a fantastic turnout. Obviously the pet lovers of Eden Falls know the value of veterinary care, and at Healthy Paws, our veterinary care is remarkable. State of the art, open twenty-four/seven—fantastic value."

"If he keeps this up I'm going to puke," says Amy behind a cupped hand.

"But I'll get my turn later. Right now, it's my great pleasure to introduce Dr. Winn Honey, one of **four** veterinarians working at our **conveniently** located Patton office. Dr. Honey graduated from the University of . . ."

Honey bows her head, hands clasped together in front as Dorkin proudly rattles off her credits and achievements.

". . . and, last but not least, compared to Doc Lewis and Doc Mills, she's a whole lot easier on the eyes, am I right, gentlemen?"

If the gentlemen of the room agree, they keep it to themselves, and though Honey smiles, like no doubt she's had to so many times before, the sexist shot garners an indignant murmur, not a receptive laugh.

She must have spurned Dorkin's advances in the past. That's why he's got it out for her.

There's a round of applause as Honey takes the podium and Dorkin settles into his seat on the front row, Lewis on his left, Greer on his right. The overhead lights dim, and up pops the first slide of a PowerPoint presentation: **Practical First Aid for Your Pets**.

"Thanks, Guy, for that . . . generous . . . introduction. And for all the women in the room, be grateful you didn't have to work with him **before** he completed his sexual harassment training."

"Whoa, snap," says Amy, over pockets of applause. "I can see why you like this girl."

But I'm not clapping; I'm staring at Dorkin. Lewis and Greer might have to hold him down. Why would Honey go straight off script and defy her boss?

"So, what follows is meant to be practical and easy to remember. Don't worry, there's no quiz at the end. Here are some of the most common emergencies you might face."

The audience oohs and ahhs over the

picture of a forlorn basset hound puppy with a fiberglass cast on his front leg adjacent to a bulleted list that includes: fractures, open wounds, choking, heatstroke (not much chance in these parts), insect bites and stings, household poisons, and seizures.

Three more slides in, and it's clear that Dr. Honey is a gifted and effective orator. Nice pace, informative but entertaining slides, lots of direct eye contact. She's everything I am not in a public speaker. The audience is receptive, and I can see Dorkin relax and settle back into his seat as though he might be able to forgive her earlier indiscretion.

Twenty minutes later, my eyes slide over to Amy and she reciprocates, smiles, and goes back to the talk. But I keep staring. She seems so at ease, the . . . wife . . . who capsized my world. What a fool I've been to think that this funny, edgy, beautiful woman would be interested in me. Her choice of a man—no, husband—with his vanities, should tell me all I need to know. If this is her taste, she was always going to spit me out.

"What?" asks Amy, eyes forward, locked on the next slide.

"I, um, wanted you to know I didn't mean to find out about Marco Tellucci," I mumble. "It was an accident. George from the inn was reviewing some security video and—"

Amy raises a hand to silence me, leans in, her lips brushing my ear. "Cyrus, you can be the smartest person in the world—and the dumbest. You of all people should know everyone has baggage."

She takes my hand, gives it a squeeze, and leans back in her seat.

I'm speechless. Do all women speak this cryptic language that men like me cannot understand no matter how much they wish to learn? I've been wallowing in self-pity about having been one-upped by the Italian. I've seen the marriage certificate. It's fair to say a marriage is a little bit more than "baggage." What am I missing here?

Ten minutes later, as Honey gets to her conclusions slide, she has her first moment of hesitation, fumbling through her notes as though she's lost her place. It takes me a moment before I realize what's happened. Charlie Brown tiptoes down the row to take the empty seat on the other side of me.

"Hey, Doc, thought I'd come for the fireworks. Offer some moral support."

I introduce Charlize to "my friend" Amy and make a point of clarifying that Charlie is Dr. Honey's daughter.

"That's quite a shiner," Charlie whispers.

"I'll live," I say. "How are things between you and your mom?"

Charlie frowns, rolls her hand from side to side. "Better. She made me come home, and we talked till two in the morning."

"You should know the evidence for the cause of Marmalade's obesity was entirely circumstantial and . . . well . . . postulating why it happened was . . . just a guess and . . . very unprofessional. I'm sorry if I—"

"I'm glad. It was time she knew. I wanted her to solve the problem; I wanted her to see what was staring her in the face. It's too bad you and mom didn't hook up."

I can tell Amy's listening.

"I should never have gone along with your dating scam. I only did it to get the inside scoop on Healthy Paws. That's all." And then, to test my theory, I add, "Besides, your mom's too attractive for me. I prefer a woman who's more plain, even homely."

The pain in my left shin tells me I was right.

"But guess who's going to Miami next weekend?"

I turn full on to Charlie. She's genuinely excited, and more than I might expect for a girl hoping to get a tan or sneak an alcoholic drink poolside. I reckon she's thrilled to be getting a chance to bond. Good for her. I wish I'd been smart enough to take the same chance when my father was still alive.

Dr. Honey puts down her laser pointer and says, "So . . . yes, I think, yes, that's the final slide."

Dorkin steps forward, clapping his hands as he heads to the podium, encouraging the audience to join him in a show of appreciation.

"If we could have the lights up, Dr. Honey will be happy to take questions, and I encourage our colleagues from Bedside Manor to join in the discussion." And then as a calculated afterthought, "Assuming they wish to do so."

Dorkin directs his most insincere gap-toothed smile at Lewis and then me.

Almost immediately, Ethel Silverman is up on her feet.

"Thank you, Doc, for all . . . that . . . but what I want to know is why you and your fancy hospital are trawling for business considering Eden Falls already has a perfectly good veterinary practice."

I don't know whether to hug Ethel or scream at her. Talk about cutting to the chase.

"Well," says Dorkin, lighting up, "perhaps Dr. Honey would be kind enough to start us off."

It's as though Dorkin just downed Popcorn's stash of speed, virtually salivating at this gift. It's the perfect opportunity for Honey to deliver a coup de grâce, to make her audience bask in the tender caress of Healthy Paws while spurning Bedside Manor as they would spurn a rabid dog.

Winn Honey takes her time, looking not at Dorkin or Ethel, but out, to the back, to Charlie and me.

"Great question, and one that could only come from a client who's incredibly loyal to Bedside Manor. See, we can try to compete, bully it, or buy it, but that kind of loyalty is about connections, personalities, a gut feeling between people and between people and animals. Healthy Paws has the toys, the fancy bells and whistles, we can run every test and provide every treatment option, but at the end of the day, what matters is how your practice makes you feel. Do they listen? Do they care?"

She waits a beat, but then her eyes target Charlie.

"As a doctor and as a mom, for far too long I've been guilty of valuing appearance over substance. It's bad enough to look and not really see, but it's far worse not bothering to look at all."

I catch the glint of a fat tear rolling down Charlie's left cheek.

"So let me answer this way. The reason we're here is to let you know you have a choice, and choice is a good thing, but choose to look, to ask, to dig, and please, dig deep, because what counts, what really counts, you won't find floating near the surface."

Ethel looks perturbed, whereas Dorkin looks like his head is about to explode.

"Yes, but to your point about choice," says Dorkin. "By definition you are making a comparison. Shouldn't we talk about what's on offer? Dr. Mills, perhaps you'd like to say a few words. Dr. Mills?"

Everyone turns my way, and the moment I have been dreading has finally arrived. I get to my feet, say, "No, I think Dr. Honey summed it up perfectly," and sit right back down. From the front, Lewis nods his approval—not exactly a knockout, but definitely brief.

All eyes turn back to Dorkin.

"Well . . . okay . . . but I'm sure Dr. Honey would love to tell us about some of the—"

"Actually I'm good. So, if that's all the questions, Healthy Paws thanks you for coming, wishes you and your pets the very best of health, and please, grab all the freebies you can on the way out."

There's another round of applause, the audience stands, and it's hard for me to see what's going on up front.

"What have you been up to, Dr. Mills?"

The question comes from Amy, who, like me, waits in the back row, letting the room clear enough to watch the action unfold. It's not exactly a silent movie, given that the melodramatic piano soundtrack has been replaced by the babble of people and the occasional canine yip, but it's obvious who's the villain and who's the heroine.

"I'm not sure," I reply as Dorkin jabs an index finger in Honey's face before pointing toward the exit. That's when Lewis steps between them, his habit of close talking finally coming in handy, as Dorkin is accosted by Greer and served with a mysterious document.

"Oh no he didn't—"

"Didn't what?" asks Amy.

I don't reply, imagining Lewis in his card shark bow tie, prepared to use skill and deception to win, handing over the confidential spreadsheets to Greer. I see Greer's double pat over his breast pocket, their unspoken exchange that said, "Only if things get ugly."

"Didn't what?" Amy insists.

I shush her even though I can't hear a thing as Dorkin shoves the papers away, turning to leave as they flutter to the floor. Greer ignores them, reaches out with a big hand, and yanks, Dorkin spinning around, visibly shocked by the assault. For a second I think we might be in for a skirmish, but Greer has him by the lapels of his suit, lifting up, forcing Dorkin onto his tiptoes. I watch as the manager's body goes limp, hands thrown wide open in surrender.

Greer releases his grip, rounds up his evidence, and hands it over.

The English editor has his back to me (I hope he's saying something facetious like, "Someone's in a spot of bother"), but I have a great view of Dorkin, eyes flitting back and forth, the recognition of being caught in his deceptions causing him to buckle at the knees. The Dorkin who addresses Greer is quite different—grievously wounded, submissive, and possibly begging for his life.

"If you don't tell me what's going on I'll—"

"I'm not entirely sure," I maintain, distracted by the way Greer whispers in Dorkin's ear, producing vigorous acquiescent nods from the Healthy Paws office manager. Whatever passed between them, Dorkin appears inordinately grateful and in a hurry to leave, storming up the aisle and past us toward the exit. "But it looks like it's all good."

A fist pummels my left upper arm.

"You are the most annoying, cryptic man I've ever—"

"He is, isn't he?" says Greer to Amy, suddenly next to us and looking pleased with himself.

"What did you do?" I ask, sotto voce, pulling him aside.

"All fine and dandy, old boy. Lewis insisted I only use your . . . discovery . . . as an insurance policy, just in case. When Honey went off message, I couldn't stand by and watch her career go into free fall. I made Dorkin an offer—to make **this** go away, **you** go away. No one knows about the embezzling of funds, Healthy Paws backs off Eden Falls, and Doc Honey gets to run the Patton office the way she wants it run."

"And Dorkin agreed?"

"What choice did he have? The only person who lost out is me. First decent scoop in years."

Greer winks at me, nods a chivalrous "good afternoon" to Amy, and follows the stragglers out of the hall.

Amy has her arms folded across her chest. I jump in before she can say, "Well?"

"We blackmailed Dorkin to make sure Doc Honey kept her job."

She appears totally unfazed by this revelation.

"Huh, see, wasn't so hard. But then you've still got competition?"

"What?"

I'm not really listening, preoccupied by the action up front: Doc Honey, arms wide open, rushing over to embrace Charlie Brown. They bury their faces in each other's shoulder, their grips tight.

"You're smiling, Dr. Mills."

"Sorry?"

I turn to face Amy, and she's looking up at me with those hypnotic heterochromic eyes. The rest of the room—and all its intrigue—falls away.

"Perhaps I've misjudged your Dr. Honey," she says, a smile toying with her lips, "but sometimes it's easy to bark up the wrong tree, if you know what I mean."

I can't tell if she's talking about herself or me. Is this flirting or taunting? What married person acts this way? This whole thing doesn't sit right because there's obviously something between us. I can tell I still have a chance.

"So, this might be a little last minute for a woman with your hectic social life, but how's tomorrow night for . . ."

My sentence trails off as soon as I see the change in her eyes.

"Look, Cyrus . . . right now . . . I can't," she starts.

I don't even let her finish. I raise my hand in defeat; it's time for this roller coaster to stop because I need to get off.

I turn and head for the exit, trying to extinguish the hope that Amy will call my name.

No need to worry. She never does.

# Sunday

# « 19 »

There are twenty states in the union, including Vermont, where there are no regulations regarding dogs riding loose in the back of your truck. If the dog falls out on a fast corner, you might get a ticket for failure to secure a load, but for the most part, legislation hasn't caught up to children, let alone pets. That's why I'm not too worried about Crispin, snug under a fluttering nylon tarp secured by bungee cords to the flatbed. Not that he's going to bark or complain about the cold.

My cell phone rings.

"His name's Seth Pickrell," says Lewis, sounding mighty pleased with himself.

"Your mystery man. Stash's owner."

"How?" I ask. "And more importantly, does Devito know?"

I can't hide the element of panic in my voice. Does this mean I'm going to have to return Stash?

"Don't think so," says Lewis. "And I'm pretty sure I've covered my tracks. I got to thinking about what your doodle can do and came across this nonprofit called NEADS that offers assistance dogs for combat veterans, the hearing impaired, children with autism, people with physical disabilities. I called them up, asked them if they ever trained a dog named Stash. Turns out they did, only Stash has been missing for the past three years. Dropped out of their system."

"I don't get it."

"Your doodle was partnered with a fellow named Al Pickrell. Al lived alone, a little nothing place in the woods outside of Patton. Poor guy had Lou Gehrig's disease, and Stash was by his side to the end."

"And Seth is Al's son?"

"Bingo. A son who left home at sixteen,

a son who, decades later, only returned to pick up his late father's dog. Seth wasn't a sick man when he took Stash. He didn't need a service dog. He needed a link to his dad. I guess it's just a little extra bit of grace that Stash could also help Seth when he got sick."

"Wait a minute. You couldn't have gotten all this from one phone call. Is Gabe helping out again?"

"Please." Lewis scoffs. "Even though the family's from across the valley, I have a far better grassroots source."

Ah, Doris.

"I told the folks at NEADS we got suspicious when a service dog named Stash showed up with a guy who refused to give us a name or address."

"So they want him back?"

The line goes quiet for a few seconds. "That's up to you. They asked me to describe him, and, well, I might have left out the bit about his orange mustache. I figured you could call them back and correct my mistake or . . . maybe invest in a little hair dye to keep him all black. Either way, I told Devito we'd had no luck tracking down John Doe's service dog."

**I eventually came home, only you got this practice and I got this dog.**

Was Seth like me, another lost son looking for redemption? Was Stash his only and best connection to a father he never knew, a living link to a past he wished he could do over?

"And one more thing," says Lewis. "NEADS told me the magic words."

"I'm not with you."

"The command that will finally give that poor dog a chance to relax and let his hair down."

Lewis repeats the phrase, and I swear Stash glances my way as though he's heard what was said.

**What a human hears at twenty feet, a dog can hear at eighty feet.**

I hang up, pull off Eden Falls's main strip, and locate my destination, a goldenrod yellow doll's house with a wraparound farmer's porch. Looks like Trish came from humble roots. If she married up, I'm betting Lionel needs the inheritance money because they're overextended.

Snow-encrusted cars line both sides of the narrow street, but Mavis Peebles's driveway is a short, steep slope, so I pull straight in, praying a neutral gear and gravity will let me roll my way back onto the road when I'm ready to leave.

"Stash, come," I say, inviting him to exit on my side. He's coming with me because the flicker of a small orange dot on the dashboard tells me I need more gas. If I leave him in the warm cab with the engine idling, the Silverado won't make it to the nearest station.

The "toughest glue on Planet Earth" appears to be living up to its name. Crispin's tail is restored to its horizontal former glory, and with a little comb-over, you can barely see the join. I grab the back feet and associated castors, ready to pull the faithful Labrador off the back of the bed when I think back to my one and only meeting with Mavis Peebles.

"Thanks, Bobby," she said, accompanied by a conspiratorial wink. A senior moment or a secret communiqué?

For now I leave Crispin to guard the truck. Time to find out what my late father was up to.

Following a snow-blown path I take two steps onto the wooden porch, where a sturdy wrought-iron door knocker allows me to announce my arrival. Stash stands by my side, attentive but patient, doing a fine impersonation of Crispin sans castors.

I hear a TV being muted, a rustling movement inside, and the creak of floorboards.

I knock again.

"Just a minute," says a soft female voice as though from the other side of a powder room, attending to last-minute details in order to appear presentable.

The door swings open, and Mavis Peebles lurches forward in sturdy sheepskin slippers and a hand-knit woolen cardigan over a minty blue nylon housecoat.

"That's not Crispin," she says, pointing with her knotty arthritic index finger.

"No, Mrs. Peebles. This is my dog." I hesitate, the "my" still feeling conspicuous but pleasantly invigorating. "This is Stash." I look down and do a double take. Stash's perfect impersonation of the dead dog himself has been spoiled by an aberrant behavior new to this particular labradoodle—he's wagging his tail.

"I didn't want to leave him alone, if that's okay with you."

Mrs. Peebles looks more flustered than confused.

"Where's Crispin?" she asks.

I glance back at the truck, feeling guilty, tempted to allay her fears, but this is about far more than fixing her dog's broken wag. "Maybe we could come in?"

Mavis swivels around, full body, not just neck, like she's taking stock, making sure the coast is clear prior to opening the door wide.

Before I can say thank you and step inside, a certain canine has barged past me in order to nuzzle and methodically lick Mavis's right hand as though saliva might be the breakthrough cure for rheumatism.

"Friendly, isn't she?" says Mavis, hobbling over toward a couple of straight-backed wooden chairs gathered around the heat from an old cast-iron radiator. Her gait is a side-to-side rocking motion, like an Emperor penguin's. "Can she have a cookie?"

"Of course," I say, taking in a small sitting room that's clearly been converted into a bedroom. Aside from the high twin bed underneath the window, there's an armoire, a series of built-in bookshelves, and a small TV. The sound has been turned off, but based on the overacting and the plethora of beautiful people this has to be a soap opera. The handsome stubbly face of a swarthy Casanova pops up, and unfortunately I'm reminded of Mr. Marco Tellucci.

On a table next to her chair (at least I assume it's hers because it's the only one covered with thick cushions) Mavis decapitates a ceramic yellow Labrador cookie jar, reaches in (accompanied by the sound of an electronic yap), and removes a small Milk Bone. Stash meets her eyes, waits for a nod of approval, gently takes it on his tongue, trots off to the other side of the room, and eats it slowly and methodically, lying down.

"Tea? Coffee?"

"No thanks," I say, as Mavis waddles off through an open door that appears to lead into a kitchen.

"Can I help?"

"No," snaps Mavis. "Sit," she commands, and I wonder if Stash's presence has made the old woman flash back to her days of training Crispin.

Dutifully I take the matching chair without the cushions. Now I see why Mavis chose them—rigid, upright, easier to get in and out when your joints are trying to rust stiff.

The items on the table next to the Lab cookie jar tell me how Mavis must spend her days: two balls of wool tangled around knitting needles (remarkable given the deformity of her hands), the remote control, and, surprisingly, a Kindle reader.

Stash, having finished his treat, races past me to see what's going on in the kitchen. What's gotten into him? In his hurry, he broadsides one of the cushions on Mavis's seat, exposing the edge of a small book. I reach over to tuck it back in, but the cover title gives me pause—**Wicked Hard Sudoku**. It's not the Boston slang that strikes me as strange; it's the notion of a senile geriatric having the mental capacity for complex mathematical games.

Leaning back in my chair I glimpse part of a galley kitchen, red cabinets, white appliances, and, disturbingly, Stash with his front feet up on a counter as though he's begging for more to eat. I hear the whistle of an electric kettle coming to a boil and the chink of mugs (guess I'm having tea).

There's still time. I adjust the cushions to hide the Sudoku and turn on the Kindle. I don't have an electronic reading device and sometimes I wonder if they're only good for curious men to read **Fifty Shades of Grey** in total anonymity, but up pops Tolstoy's **Anna Karenina**. Not exactly mindless pulp. And then there's the "last" button on the remote—a travel show on PBS. Quickly I flick back to . . . whatever they call this show—**Days of Our Guiding Hospital**—apparently television for the mentally infirm.

"Thanks," I say as Mavis returns, handing me a trembling mug.

She carefully places hers on a coaster on the side table prior to easing down into her chair. Stash stands off to her side but out of reach for petting. Strange, I think, him keeping his distance, until I notice the four circular depressions in the plush blue carpet, spaced at the corners of a dog-sized rectangle. It's as if he's showing deference to the senior dog, not wanting to stand in Crispin's spot.

"You fix the tail?" asks Mavis, her focus on my lips, avoiding eye contact, as though she needs to prove how mentally infirm she has become. I am convinced it's an act, or at the very least, an exaggeration. Lewis would be all over me, insisting I tread cautiously, but the clinician in me needs the backstory while the movie geek can't help but think about David Mamet's **House of Games**, Joe Mantegna saying, **It's called a confidence game. Why? Because you give me your confidence? No. Because I give you mine.**

"What if I said no, Mrs. Peebles?"

Slowly her eyes ascend my face.

"Do you have doctor-patient confidentiality?"

"But you're not my . . ." I hesitate. "Sure," I say, "nothing leaves this room."

Mavis sighs, eases back in her chair, hands flopping down on the rests. "This was your father's idea. He knew I'd rather be crippled here at home than trapped in some hospital bed or my daughter's . . . space station."

"Idea? You mean having Crispin stuffed?"

Mavis leans over and picks up her mug with both hands, relishing the warmth.

"I'm not crazy or senile, but how can I care for a new dog? Most of the time I'm too sore to walk to the kitchen, let alone out of the house. I'm eighty-three years old. Who'd look after my dog once I'm gone? It wouldn't be fair."

"Hold on, Mrs. Peebles. You're saying my father told you to act a little . . . kooky?"

"No. I just improvise every now and then. It's not hard. Stare off into space, say something senseless or based on a childhood memory. Just enough to keep them guessing. No, Doc Cobb suggested taxidermy—low maintenance, quiet company, and guaranteed to look scary mad. The ban on pets at local nursing homes was a bonus."

"But what about your daughter? I got the impression she wouldn't mind whether it's a nursing home or her own home, she just wants you to get the care you need."

"Have you seen her home?"

"Yes, I have."

"You met Lionel?"

I take a sip of my tea, trying not to wince. It's acrid from stewing too long.

"Exactly," she says. "He might swear up and down how he'll make a nice apartment out back, but Lionel's always quick to chime in about his allergy. He'd love it if I croaked."

I should argue with her, suggest her son-in-law might find it hard to show his true feelings, but I reckon she's right. That's why I have no problem throwing Lionel under the bus.

"The allergy thing is a lie. When I visited, I made sure he came into contact with fur and canine saliva, the most common dog-related allergens. He never sneezed, scratched, or sniffed once."

Mavis's lips peel back to reveal her beaming dentures.

"Your dad told me I'd like you. So apart from trying to kill him, why would you visit his house?"

I flash my eyebrows and let a breath of exhaled air fill my cheeks. "Well . . . I, I don't know . . . Look, I managed to fix Crispin's tail. You want me to fetch him from the—"

"Sit back down. Why'd you visit his house?"

I shrug and wonder how Amy might reply. "Some people say I'm nosy. I prefer curious. I've always liked solving any kind of puzzle."

"I like puzzles," says Mavis, digging under her cushion to show me her "incredibly challenging" Sudoku. "But there's more to it than that."

"Not really," I say, working on an awkward smile.

The concavity afflicting her spine cinches a little tighter, a finger henpecking in my direction. "Yes really." Her grin captures every wrinkle of her face like the barometric lines of a low-pressure system. "Just like your father. Easily hooked, all in, and duty bound to do what is right."

"Please, he was the saint, not me. I just wanted to make sure you considered all your options. This way you know you can keep Crispin **and** live with your daughter, assuming you want to."

Mavis narrows her eyes but lets me appreciate a glint of satisfaction.

"Some might say you're meddling in matters that don't concern you."

I nod. "Fair enough, but they obviously mattered to my father. Think of it as carrying on where he left off."

"It's more than that," she says, taking a sip. "You're trying to finish the job." Mavis studies me, lowers the mug, and adds, "You're an odd one, Dr. Mills. Take it from someone who's pretty good at pretending to be someone she's not, it feels good to open up every now and then, let the world see what's on the inside."

I feel myself relax. Doctor-patient confidentiality works both ways. "Not me, Mrs. Peebles."

"Just like your father. Well, not quite."

"What do you mean?"

"Bobby Cobb was a lot smoother round the edges. He talked a lot about you."

"He did?"

"All the time. Worried about you being alone."

I let the word "alone" settle and then shiver from its emotional chill. Amazing. My father can still reach out and touch me through his devoted clients.

"But the lengths to which you've gone for me, it says a lot. You should let it show."

"I am who I am, Mrs. Peebles."

She reaches over to Stash, who shimmies sideways and leans in for a scratch. Even when he's getting attention he's intent on making it as easy as possible.

"Tell me," Mavis says. "When you and this dog are alone, how do you act?"

I think about it. "I don't act. But it's different with a dog."

"Is it?" Her lobster-claw hand makes gentle pincer movements behind Stash's left ear that have him transfixed. "You keep things simple, let the dog know how you really feel. It's not complicated. It's honest. Alone with a dog you're allowed to shine. Be the person your dog expects you to be. I got to see that side. Bet most folks aren't so lucky."

Now I'm getting pep talks from a crazy lady with a stuffed dead dog.

"Let me grab Crispin," I say, getting to my feet, Stash making no move to follow me. I head out to the truck. **Be the person your dog expects you to be.** Where did she get that phrase?

Poor Crispin slides out the back of the flatbed, and, hugging him to my chest, I carry him back to the house. He's incredibly light, literally a husk of his former self, but his importance is a weight that will never change.

"Shall I put him in his usual spot?" I ask, carefully docking his castors with the reciprocal depressions in the carpet.

In her excitement and the struggle to put down her tea and get to her feet, Mavis loses her grip on the mug, the spill pooling toward her Kindle.

"I'll get that," I say, heading toward the kitchen, but the black blur is already back, clean white tea towel in his mouth, plopped down in the center of the milky brown puddle. Obviously Stash wasn't just scouting the kitchen for food, he was getting the lay of the land, a helpful recon mission.

"Good dog," says Mavis, mopping up the spill, glancing my way, truly impressed.

I say nothing, not because I don't have something to say, but because I'm afraid of what needs to be said. It's so obvious. This is what Stash was trained to do, loves to do, needs to do. His raison d'être is to be of service. That's why he follows me everywhere, why he hates to be left alone. Everything that makes me incredulous, in awe of this creature, is nothing but a trick, but to someone like Mavis Peebles, someone who needs him, it's the difference between opening a door or staying shut in behind it, the difference between light and dark, between leaving something lying on the floor or picking it up. Independence or a kind of imprisonment. It's as obvious as it is painful.

But what of Mavis's fears about adopting a new dog? Easy. I'd love to take Stash for daily walks, and, if ever there came a time, I'd have him back in a heartbeat.

That leaves the daughter, "Patricia, call me Trish," and her faux-allergic husband. Though Stash is inherently hypoallergenic, I can confirm that in Lionel's case, my "laying on of hands" met with no adverse reaction. Whether Trish approves, wants her mother to move right in, or stay put, that's none of my business. Again, if Stash needs a home, I'll be first in line.

"Mrs. Peebles . . ."

Twenty minutes later, my phone call made, I drop to one knee and take Stash's head in my hands. For all his loyalty, devotion, and unwavering service, it's time for me to give him something in return. We lock eyes, and finally I get to deliver the magic words.

"Stash. **Free time**."

Part of me imagined it would be like hitting a switch, turning him off, the doodle slumping to the floor relieved to be off duty. It shows how much I know about dogs. Instead Stash lights up, spins on his back legs, charges off into the kitchen, and sprints back with a tea towel in his mouth, goading me into playing a game of tug-o'-war.

"Call me if you need anything," I tell Mavis, reining in the crazy doodle with a "Stash, sit" while tying the towel to the handle of the front door. Some time ago Trish had made sure the round knobs were traded for long handles to ensure better leverage. Now, with "Stash, door" (it wasn't hard to figure out), life is even easier.

"You're sure about this?" asks Mavis.

I'm trying to keep in the moment, to make the logical, practical choice, but with a newfound spirit of honesty, I say, "No, I'm not. I'm going to miss him. But somehow I know Stash is sure, and that's what counts."

Mavis escorts me to the front door, and I can't help but feel stung by the way Stash has already chosen to be at her side, not mine. Without saying a word, she gestures with a hand, encouraging me to leave, as though she's well versed in the art of difficult goodbyes—best to make them quick, clean, and final. What is it about people who've done some serious living? Instinctively, Mavis knows not to reach out, not to touch me, not to say more.

Shuffling down the icy incline to the truck—the man who came with two dogs, leaving with none—I resolve not to look back. Maybe the arctic air helps the blanket of cold objectivity settle in around me. It's not meant to make me feel normal; it's meant to make me feel less. I need to think of it this way: Stash gets to utilize his many talents and Mavis gets a new beginning. I pat the Polaroid memento I've been carrying around in my breast pocket.

Cautious of the slope and the possibility of black ice, I slip-slide my way to the truck, hop inside, and turn on the engine. Foot on the brake, gear in neutral, I'm about to roll back when the rustle of a lace curtain in an upstairs window catches my eye and I see a figure staring down at me—it's Stash.

He's only there for a few seconds—scruffy, intense, and unfailingly determined to make things better—but it is more than enough to feel good about my decision. I witnessed how Stash's training gave him purpose, but the cynic in me got to feel his gift. If he can lift me up, then for someone like Mavis, this dog is a life preserver.

# ≪ 20 ≫

I'd like to think the decision came down to my training as a pathologist, but I can't ignore the phrase **be the person your dog expects you to be**. My life coach swami, Mavis Peebles, had a point about deconstructing my feelings and venting my inner monologue. Around Stash I was unguarded. I was the real me, and like it or not, this real me continues to gravitate toward a baffling and demoralizing waitress. In my old job, when something was dead or dying, I had to know why. If Amy refuses to come clean about the man who, on paper, is her husband, and there's still something to salvage in our floundering (hopefully not dead or dying) relationship, then I must uncover the truth by another route, by asking Marco Tellucci himself.

Figuring out the where and when was easy. A guy called Liam, working the front desk, took my call.

"Hi, Liam, I'm supposed to be meeting my friend for dinner tonight at the inn, and I can't remember whether Mr. Tellucci booked for seven thirty or eight."

"Just a moment." A pause. "That's eight o'clock, sir."

So, still around and with limited dining options in Eden Falls.

"Thanks. And it's just the two of us, right?"

"That's what it says, sir."

The "who" is a little more tricky because in this context it's about who Tellucci has invited to join him. Yesterday, at the K of C, Amy shot me down for trying to set up a date for tonight. If she's the one dining with her husband, I'd have to lure him away from their table to face him, **mano a mano**. Or, I could storm in there, play the part of the rejected lover, and demand an explanation in front of the other diners. Or, I think as I stand under the hot shower with just over an hour to go before eight, perhaps it would be easier (and safer) to simply call his room.

I imagine myself as the high school geek (not much of a leap), the one with the crush on the popular cheerleader, the one who let her copy his homework because she said hello to him in class, the one who plucked up the courage to ask her to the senior prom, watching her laugh, gag, and recoil because she already had a date with the handsome quarterback. If only this meeting were a twenty-year reunion, and Marco Tellucci turned out to be an alcoholic, abusive womanizer, recently terminated from his place of employment and the victim of a senseless random acid attack to the face.

I step out of the tub, towel off, and watch my reflection appear in the steamy bathroom vanity mirror above the sink. Since there's a good chance Amy will be there I want to look my best, which means shaving for the second time today. I'm hoping for contrast with Tellucci, who probably prefers to show off a five o'clock shadow that grows out by eleven most mornings.

Rummaging through my father's medicine cabinet door, I discover a bottle of Old Spice aftershave and an ancient tub of Brylcreem for men. I splash a few drops into my palms and slap my bare cheeks. Hardly the pheromone I was hoping for, and dipping my fingers into the sticky white gel, I'm not convinced "just a little dab'll do ya!" In order to overpower that pesky cowlick, my hair congeals into a greasy, slick helmet. What an idiot. I turn on the shower and start over.

Ten minutes later and I've moved from personal grooming to fashion. If this turns into an altercation I might do well to wear something substantial like chain mail or a Kevlar vest. But what if there's a dress code or I have to hang out in the restaurant waiting to pounce? Still out of my comfort zone but having learned my lesson, I iron a plain white cotton shirt. Though my father's old blue blazer feels a little too nautical to me, complete with tiny anchors embossed on the gold-colored buttons on the cuffs, it fits well enough. That leaves me with one more decision—wear a tie or sport an open neck. Part of me wishes I had a silk ascot or a thick gold medallion and a bounty of bushy chest hair, hoping to see Amy's reaction. But this is Vermont, and I'm only there for a reckoning. I tuck the tie (my one and only) inside my breast pocket, just in case.

First order of business is gasoline for the Silverado, and as I roll up to the pumps, a figure in a black ski mask suddenly appears at my window. I'm halfway into the passenger seat thinking I'm about to get carjacked when I remember the gas station is full service.

"Forty dollars of regular," I shout, squeezing two twenties through a crack in the glass just in case, and the would-be assailant disappears, leaving me with an unwelcome reminder of Healthy Paws—an ad, a glossy conspicuous banner strung over the pump. Only this one has been defiled. Oh, there's the familiar logo, the smiling faces on the pet and human models, but the last seven digits of the telephone number have been covered over with a strip of duct tape and replaced by different numbers handwritten in black Sharpie.

I check out the other pumps on the lot, each vandalized in the same manner. I could blame another round of bad luck for

Guy Dorkin, a printing error with the advertising company. But something tells me this correction comes courtesy of Gilligan the collie, Drew's silent way of saying thanks. I'm not sure how he explained it away to his boss, but dialing the phone number for "the best veterinary practice around" puts you straight through to Bedside Manor.

On the drive to The Inn at Falls View, I finalize my strategy. Catching Tellucci alone will be preferable—more civilized, less dramatic. There could be an opportunity to accost him on a bathroom visit. He might receive an anonymous tip that a man in a blue blazer appears to be keying his Humvee. Either way, a confrontation **away** from Amy will avoid—no, minimize—her outrage (or at least I won't have to witness it), and I won't be subjected to a humiliating bout of comparison-shopping with her husband. Let's face it, I can't compete with the Italian when it comes to looks and money, leaving me with what—character? According to the Internet (which never lies), the top three winning traits men should exude around women are confidence, wit, and sensitivity. This explains everything. Intelligence, arguably my greatest strength, appears to be optional. Though the Italian may be smart **and** successful, I'm hoping his opulence comes courtesy of a trust fund, lifelong mooching, or some illicit activity that I can report to our hotshot detective, Chief Devito.

Ironically I park next to the white Humvee (pleased to see that salt and slush have soiled its showroom dazzle), jog up the steps of the main entrance and through the lobby, and head for the bar and restaurant.

"Hey, Doc, finally," says George, dressed in what appears to be a uniform of black pants, black shirt, and narrow black tie. "Here for dinner?"

"Yes, I'm meeting some . . . people I know."

"Excellent. And look at this."

He pulls out his smartphone and begins swiping his index finger across the greasy surface.

"See: before . . . after."

He's flicking between two photographs showing close-ups of Henry the cat's nasal deformity. It's been two days since I dropped off the medication. I wouldn't expect visible signs of improvement for at least a week, which is why they look identical to me.

"That's great," I say, remembering a scientific article describing how nearly forty percent of pet owners thought their dog's lameness got better despite being given sugar pills. If George is happy, I'm happy. Placebo effect or not, like Lewis says, "The owner's always right."

"Can't thank you enough," says George. "You want to wait at the bar? Grab that drink?"

It's at this point I realize my plan is riddled with holes. What am I going to do, spy on them? And what am I going to say? "Excuse me, but you seem to be married to the woman of my dreams."

"Why not," I reply, and George gestures for me to follow.

It turns out the bar is perfect—empty, dark, and offering a view into a romantically lit dining room dominated by an elaborate plaster ceiling from which hangs a monster of a chandelier. There's a round table for eight directly below and it's empty. Given the context of why I'm here, it's hardly surprising that I'm reminded of the movie **The War of the Roses. If love**

**is blind, marriage is like having a stroke.**

I position myself on a corner stool where I can hide behind a floor-to-ceiling wooden support beam. Overhead, the sound of a string quartet on the speaker system stifles the murmur of diners in discreet conversation. It's a slow Sunday night in winter, but even so, George has strategically placed his patrons to fool new guests into thinking the place is far from dead. I half envy a bearded man, picking at his food, head buried in a book, and I notice the couple I saw the other day in the hotel lobby. I wondered whether they were on their way to some sort of winter sporting activity. Thanks to sunglasses and inadequate sunblock, their raccoon impersonations suggest the answer was yes.

"What can I get you?" asks George, coming around the bar.

Keep a clear head or loosen up?

"Maker's Mark, up."

While George fixes my drink they walk in, the Telluccis, arm in arm, headed toward a table for four. **Strange**, I think, **four, not two**. But the gods are on my side. Amy takes the chair with her back to me.

That's when I notice, tucked into the far left-hand corner of the room, another woman with her back to me, her hair carefully pinned up into a bun; the young man facing me leaning in, animated and vaguely familiar.

"There you go," says George, sliding over a glass containing at least a double measure.

I nod, take a sip, and relish the burn in my throat as I spy Amy's hand resting on his, giving it a squeeze before letting go.

"I'll be in the kitchen. Let me know when your friends arrive and you need a table."

"Actually, George," I say, knocking back the entire drink like a shot, "I wonder if you could do me a favor."

A minute later and Mr. Marco Tellucci is headed my way, the recipient of a mystery phone call at the bar. George has been kind enough to give us a moment alone.

The Italian brushes past me, picks up the hand piece, and says hello to a dead line as I get down from my stool.

"Mr. Tellucci, I wonder if I might have a word in private."

He hangs up in slow motion, looks confused—no, it's more than that, maybe wary or even afraid.

"Who are you?"

"My name is Cyrus Mills and I don't want to disturb your evening, but I'd like to—"

"Cyrus," he exclaims, clutching his chest like he's relieved when I was hoping for a heart attack. Without hesitation he steps over, hugs me, and plants a kiss on both of my cheeks.

"Amy has told me a great many things about you," he says with only a trace of an accent but more than enough to catch your ear, especially, I imagine, if you're female.

I consider speaking too slowly, cranking up the volume, and overenunciating as I say, "Amy told me nothing about you."

All I've got is a whispered, "Really?"

"But this is wonderful. Come, come, you must join us. I insist."

At this point he begins strong-arming me toward his table, and I reckon I've got about twenty seconds in which to tear free of his grip and run. I didn't bank on him shouting across the room, "Amy, look who I found."

Suddenly a moment of uncomfortable camaraderie must look more like a citizen's arrest and I freeze, the busted bad boy.

Amy spins around, gets out of her chair, and before I can soften the blow with a hasty compliment about how gorgeous she looks in a long-sleeved silky black dress, her eyes have dropped to the floor and she's shaking her head.

"Just couldn't let it go, could you," she says.

Part of me wants to come back with "when something's worth fighting for." But remember, I'm standing next to her husband, so I say nothing and let my crimson cheeks do the talking.

"Sit," says Tellucci, pulling back a chair for me opposite Amy, "let me pour you a glass of Prosecco."

He reaches for a bottle in an ice bucket before I can refuse, filling my glass with a practiced, deliberate hand and topping up two more. Though this is a table for four, it's set for three. Who else are they expecting?

"Here's to Cyrus," says Marco, "a man after my own heart."

We chink glasses and sip in unison as Marco signals to a waiter for another bottle. What's he up to? **A man after my own heart?** I have nothing in common with this man.

"You made poor George lie about a phone call," says Amy, "just to get Marco alone?"

I nod, sheepish, guilty as charged.

Amy shakes her head again.

"Then be my guest. Pretend I'm not here. But don't forget, I was the one who tried to keep you out of this."

She makes this sound slightly threatening. Maybe I should be concerned about the Cosa Nostra after all.

Marco stares at me, apparently riveted by my curiosity.

"Okay . . . well . . . to be clear, you, Marco, are Amy's . . ."

"Life partner" and "soul mate" flash through my mind, but Amy gets there first.

"Marco is my husband."

Despite having seen the certificate with my own eyes, from her lips the phrase pierces me like a steel blade, shockingly cold and deep. I fumble for my glass and knock back a healthy swig of the fizzy wine, hoping to numb the pain as Amy turns to the Italian to add, "**Tecnicamente parlando**."

Tellucci frowns but arches an eyebrow in agreement. What's that about? I want to ask but he's leaning into the table, eager for his next question.

"And . . . you've been . . . away . . . for quite some time."

"Away?" Marco parrots, making me want to suggest, "Kabul? The International Space Station? Leavenworth prison?"

"Yes, I live in San Francisco. Pac Heights. You know it?"

"Just the movie; Melanie Griffith, Michael Keaton. But you're not **from** California?"

"No, no. **Monterosso al Mare**. It's a small town in the—"

"**Cinque Terre**," I interject. "Never been, but I've read about it. Supposed to be very picturesque."

"It is," says Marco, visibly impressed. "You never said he was clever **and** worldly."

Amy places her empty glass down on the table just as George appears with the next bottle, eager to provide us with refills. Mine is empty as well.

"Perhaps we could take some water, still," says the Italian, "a little calamari and antipasto misto for three. Cyrus, you like anchovies, yes?"

Even though there was a question,

clearly Marco never expected an answer. George pulls back the menus he was about to hand out and disappears to place the order.

I can feel the beginnings of a not-unpleasant buzz take hold. A sensible, less tipsy, but suitably humiliated Cyrus would swallow his pride and bolt, but this looser, slightly shocking version plows on, asking, "How'd you two meet?"

"In Burlington, at UVM," says Marco. "But work took me out west. Advertising."

Without asking, he tops off my glass.

"Would you prefer a pinot grigio with the appetizers?"

I think about Paul Giamatti in **Sideways**, and I'm tempted to order a merlot.

"I'm good," I say, thinking I'd best maintain at least some of my inhibitions.

Either Marco must place the same order every night or George is clairvoyant, because the man in black appears out of my peripheral vision with a steaming plate of crispy rubber bands and an assortment of cold meats, cheeses, olives, and sparkly silver fish. He's kind enough not to say "**buon appetito**" as he lays it on the table and backs off.

I unfurl my napkin and place it on my lap.

"Forgive me . . . but you live in different states and uh, neither of you wears a ring?"

This earns me the full force of her blue and brown lasers like I've said too much. I bow out by munching on a little salami and what I believe to be a sweet pickle. Naturally it turns out to be the hot variety and, in the absence of the water (still not delivered), I'm forced to consume a deep draught of bubbly mind-sapping fluid.

"You okay?" asks Marco, quick to refill my glass with more prosecco, just in case.

I nod and notice how my head moves, but my eyes and brain take a split second to catch up. I sense the languid blink, the smile threatening to contort my lips even though there's nothing funny inside my head. Not drunk, but definitely woozy. I'm going to need to call a cab.

Liberated by my lowered inhibitions, I finally feel myself beginning to man up. After all, I'm the one who's been duped. Amy's the one with the explaining to do. Time to ask the kind of questions I will later regret. They have begun to stack up in the back of my throat when Amy drops her napkin on the table, jumps up, and rushes to greet someone over my shoulder.

"Charles," she exclaims.

I turn in my seat to see a tall, lean man in a black leather jacket and white cashmere scarf. Like the guy in the corner with Ms. Bun-Head (who appears to be hiding behind a menu) I've seen this man before, but it's not coming to me. Damn those bubbles!

More cheek kissing (I wish she'd stop pretending to be so European) and Amy, taking Charles by the arm, guides him to our table.

Marco remains seated, a serious look on his face. Is he jealous?

I put down my napkin and get to my feet as Charles comes over. Amy makes the introduction.

"Nice to meet you," I say, gesturing to the seat next to me, "perhaps George can set another place at the table."

"Thank you," says Charles, "but we're not staying long."

I'm not sure whom he means by "we."

"Kevin says you're good to go." He's addressing Marco. "He says it's going to cost you, him working a Sunday, but everything is in order. We should be able to sign the paperwork at nine o'clock tomorrow morning. George has let me use his office. It's being faxed over right now."

Marco and Amy look at one another, scream in unison, and hug. I'm totally confused.

The Italian, suddenly all teary eyed, turns to Charles. "I can't believe it's finally happening."

"Well, it won't if we don't get your John Hancock on these documents."

Marco knocks back his glass and stands. "This may take a while," he says.

"We can wait," I say.

"No, please, order your dinner. We want to get this done. Right, Charles?"

"Absolutely. Don't make me stay in this Podunk town any longer than necessary."

And in his flash of anger I recognize Charles. The man fighting with Marco in the Humvee parked at the gas station.

I stand again (this evening is more like a game of musical chairs), shake Charles's hand, and watch as Amy squeezes her husband in a tight embrace. No kiss, but she places her lips by his ears and whispers something out of earshot. Whatever she says, it causes Marco to burst into laughter. Am I about to get stuck with the bill? How much does this Prosecco cost?

Amy and I watch them go, letting the sensation that we are alone settle in before returning to our seats, our plates strewn with the flotsam of nibbled appetizers.

"Very nice man," I say.

"He is. He's wonderful."

George magically appears, though without glasses of water.

"Can I take your plates?"

Amy nods.

"And how about a menu for dinner?"

Amy looks at me as though she wonders if I might run out on her. Finally I have her alone in a quiet, intimate setting.

"Please," I say, "and a wine list."

I'm definitely going to need a cab.

George hands out his large leather binders. It's standard Italian fare, with a generous smattering of the usual phrases— shaved, glazed, infused, seared. Seems as though Chef needs to unload an awful lot of truffle oil. Amy's quick to blurt out "chicken piccata" as though she already knew what she wanted. Her haste is infectious, baiting me to say, "I'll have the same," but in keeping with my alcohol-induced theme of "dare to be different," I order a bottle of Vermentino and opt for a shrimp fettuccini, the choice causing Amy to flash me a questioning glance. What could be wrong with Sunday seafood hundreds of miles from the nearest coastline?

"What did you think?" she asks as soon as we are alone. "About Marco?"

Where to begin?

"Um . . . well . . . you're a lucky woman."

She hesitates, the wrinkle in her nose signaling her annoyance.

"Come on. I can practically see the wheels turning inside that brain of yours. Don't stop now. You've got to be curious."

"Oh, I'm curious. But I'm also . . ."

"What?"

"Sad. Yes, sad. Sad that we met each other when we did. Sad that my timing was off."

Her wrinkle vanishes, replaced by an earnest cant of her head.

"So when were you going to tell me?" I ask.

"I could ask you the same question," she replies without missing a beat.

My turn with a "you've lost me" crinkled

brow just as Ms. Bun-Head stands up, tosses a glass of ice water in the face of her fellow diner, leaves her table, and heads my way.

"Oh my God . . ."

This inner monologue gets away from me as none other than Mrs. Crystal Haggerty, wife of Ken Haggerty, headmaster of Eden Falls Academy, dressed to display her ample cleavage and thighs, totters past on ridiculously high heels. She appears to wipe a tear from her eye as she hurries out of the restaurant. I look back to the young man at her table, wiping a napkin down his face, watching her go and realize where I've seen him before—he was the owner of a Lab puppy from our free clinic last weekend.

"You'd think she'd have a little decorum," I whisper, once Crystal is out of earshot.

"Because she's married?" says Amy, and then, hand on chest, hamming up her best Scarlett O'Hara accent, "Unlike certain ladies, I have a reputation to uphold."

I don't want to laugh, but I can't help myself, as the Lab owner asks for the check, drops a wad of cash, and leaves with his tail between his legs.

"Looks like someone made an improper advance."

Amy rolls her eyes.

"You have a lot to learn about women. Crystal has been hiding since we walked in. She knew she was busted. I guarantee that was all show to save face. No doubt she's headed to meet him right now back at the room she's already paid for."

I ease back in my seat and sigh.

"You got all that just from, what, female intuition and body language?"

"You bet," she says. "Oh, and that shocked expression earlier, when I said 'husband'—it might have won over your high school drama teacher, but not me. When were you going to tell me about computer boy?"

"You spoke to Gabe?"

"Of course not. But Charlie Brown did. I stuck around after you left the K of C yesterday. Thanked Doc Honey for her informative lecture and took her daughter out for a sundae. Hey, you want facts, you've got to play to people's weaknesses. You'll be pleased to know she's switched to low-fat, apparently she wants to squeeze into a bikini."

Hands clasped together (to stop them twitching), elbows on the table, I say, "Okay, it was wrong, but if you were me, wouldn't you have tried to find out who he was?"

"Yes," says Amy without hesitation.

"And would you have told me?"

"Course not."

I take a deep breath and reach for another drink. Here's the fork in the road, the turning point, old life or new? These past few days I've given up the first canine love of my life (yes, I admit it—love), cured a certifiable collie, and saved an Eden Falls institution. Put this way, it sounds like the stuff of Clark Kent. In fact all I've done is my job, my new job, a job whose best reward is the chance to give people and animals second chances. If this is my second chance, my only hope is that she'll cut me off before things get too awkward.

"Well . . . maybe this is easier knowing that you're a happily married woman. Being unattainable makes me realize how foolish I've been." My laugh is pure innocence. "I mean, I really thought there was something . . . I don't know . . . like when I was around you, something clicked inside me. Oh, not warm or fuzzy, no, it was more physiological, the way you switched on my sympathetic nervous system—increased heart rate, dilated pupils, dry mouth—totally beyond my control. I'm embarrassed to say you created these changes in me like no other woman I have ever met, and, not knowing you were spoken for, I enjoyed the way they made me feel. If that's the mark of someone who . . ." I catch myself just in time to avoid the next word—**fell**. "If trying to discover your mystery man came across as jealousy, then I'm sorry. But the truth is, I was . . . am . . . well . . . jealous."

Without saying a word we take a moment, staring at one another, before Amy pours me another drink. I take it, thinking, why not crawl into a drunken stupor and blame an alcoholic haze? Strange the way our silence is comfortable, easy, like with Stash when we had no expectations of each other, simply happy to share space and time.

Amy puts her lips to the glass, takes a sip, and says, "Charlie Brown thought as much. I mean, her mom's a great catch, especially for you, but the daughter sensed you were smitten—"

"Smitten. That's exactly the right word."

Just then, George appears with our meals and our new bottle of wine. My request for water sparks another bout of humble apologies and a promise that it will be right over. Despite the foreboding, the food is good, and thankfully, George has sufficient confidence in his chef that he knows better than to circle back and discover if everything is to our satisfaction.

"So I guess this will be our first and last supper," I say, spearing a shrimp.

Amy dabs the corners of her lips with her napkin and puts down her knife and fork.

"Okay, my turn. This was not how I planned to tell you about Marco. He is my husband, but I haven't been entirely honest with you."

My fork fumbles with a spool of fettuccine.

"Yes, we met when I was an undergrad at UVM, but what Marco didn't say was that he was a foreign exchange student over for a year abroad. During that year we became good friends, and ultimately he fell in love."

"Yes, I already got that, and it was incredibly uncomfortable the first—"

"Shut up, Cyrus."

This time I take a decent swig.

"He didn't fall in love with me. He fell in love with someone else."

"O-kay." I split the syllables, having no idea where this is going.

"They wanted to be together, and, for that reason, he wanted to stay in the country."

"Hold on. Where do you come into this?"

"Because the person he wanted to be with was another man."

"Um . . . so . . . Marco isn't—"

"He's gay. Always has been. We were best friends at college. I wanted to help him out, and he needed a green card to stay in the country. It's what friends do. Or so I thought at the time. I wasn't tied to another man, and Marco needed my help."

"Wait, so married in name only?"

"It's not rocket science. The truth is I haven't seen Marco for years. It didn't work out with his boyfriend. He moved to California, we tried to keep in touch, but it wasn't long before he vanished off the face of the earth. When you and I went out for that date, it was the first I'd heard from him since forever. He called me because he met someone, Charles, and they want to get married because it's legal in Vermont, but first he needed a divorce from me."

The muscles contorting my lips into a smile are way ahead of the pleasure swirling in my brain. Where's that bottle of Vermentino?

"So the faxing back and forth tonight is all the paperwork and . . . and . . . why the hell—"

I'm shouting, and the raccoons are suddenly more like meerkats—alert, erect, and attentive to my outburst.

I lean in and lower my voice. "Why didn't you tell me this sooner?"

"Because it was going away in a couple of days. What I did was stupid, but more importantly, totally illegal. I'm talking five years in federal prison and a quarter of a million in fines. I couldn't implicate you or anyone else, including my grandfather, in an illegal transaction to keep a foreign national in the country. I knew you were in the middle of this fight with Dorkin, and Dorkin's exactly the kind of person who might sniff around, find out what I did, and use me as leverage against Bedside Manor. Marco swore it would be quick and you and I would be able to pick up where we left off. And I didn't want you to think less of me. It was embarrassing. I hadn't reckoned on Sherlock Holmes not being able to let this go, nosing around, even hiring a hacker to investigate my computer records."

The air gets sucked from my lungs as I rock back in my seat, reach for another drink, catch myself, get to my feet, and scream across the room, "Can someone please get me a glass of water?"

Finally George scampers over with two glasses of ice water. I wait until he leaves to ask, "How could you be so sure you wouldn't lose me?"

Amy interrupts her eating, smiles, and says, "I wasn't. But I wanted to protect you. I figured I'd rather lose you by keeping you out than lose you by letting you in. Besides," she says, devilry dancing across her features, "I had to pay you back for snooping in my life. It was disturbing, though apparently, given the intensity of your feelings toward me, quite understandable."

"Hold on, that information was obtained under duress."

"Please, it was given of your own free will."

I drain my water, and this time George is there with a refill. As he pours, he slides a padded leather envelope in my direction as though I'm about to get the bill. Maybe he wants to let me know how much I've already spent.

I open the binder to find two items. Instead of a receipt there's a handwritten note.

**Dr. Mills,**

**Just wanted to let you know this dinner has been entirely paid for by Mr. Tellucci. He's insisted I put this on his bill. Also, in appreciation of your expert care of my cat Henry, I would like to offer you my finest suite, should you not wish to drive home this evening.**

**P.S. I recommend you take me up on this complimentary night's stay. Chief Devito loves to catch drunk drivers!**

**Warmest regards,**
**George**

The other object is a key attached to a small plastic fob bearing the number nine.

"What was that about?"

"Um . . . just business," I mumble, as an extraordinary—no, outrageous—idea begins to form inside my unchecked brain. In a dreamlike trance, I let it fly.

"Amy, this has been an evening of revelations, and in keeping with this theme, I have a proposal. It's totally out of character. It may be totally inappropriate, but I'm going to put it out there."

I push the padded envelope across the table, my chin inviting Amy to take a look inside. She takes it and opens it up on her lap in the manner of a book.

I clear my throat and ask, "How do you feel about a little adultery?"

The question hangs in the air between us like an echo, and for the longest moment nothing happens, Amy unable or unwilling to take her stunned heterochromic eyes off of George's note.

Suddenly she explodes, snapping the envelope shut, throwing her napkin down on the table, and getting to her feet as she takes my full glass of ice water and tosses it into my face. She storms off before I can mumble an apology.

Unbelievable. I will never understand this woman—no, make that women in general. I pick up Amy's napkin and wipe it down my face. That's when I feel the buzz in my pants and pull out my cell phone.

It's a text.

I look over my shoulder. I read the text again, then I notice the envelope, open it up, and begin to laugh.

George's note is still there, but the key to room nine has disappeared.

I place my knife and fork on my plate, push it away from me, get to my feet, and read the text one more time.

What R U waiting 4!

# « ACKNOWLEDGMENTS »

Trying to write about a general practice veterinarian certainly proves that **real** animal doctors know a whole lot more than a specialist like me. Any mistakes or erroneous remarks regarding disease, diagnosis, and treatment are mine alone, fallibility my relentless impetus to learn.

I must thank Jennifer Fisher for her insightful suggestions on the early drafts and the wonderful team at Hyperion including Martha Levin, Betsy Hulsebosch, Tareth Mitch, Cassie Mandel, and Jill Amack. After five books together, you'd think I might have run out of superlatives for my editor,

Christine Pride. Not so. Sharp, savvy, and spot-on, Christine's edits always manage to make me look far better than I deserve.

Jeff Kleinman, my agent, is the coach who knows how to get the most out of his players, inspiring you to try to deliver your best. Cheers, Jeff, I'm blessed to have you in my corner.

Now that my daughters, Whitney and Emily, have flown the coop, my wife, Kathy, bears the brunt of my desire to write, putting up with a husband prone to vapid looks, lost in thought, searching for the right way to tell a story. Her tolerance, patience, and unwavering support make these books possible.

Finally a big thank-you to Cathy Zemaitis and the folks at National Education for Assistance Dog Services (NEADS). What these incredible animals can do for those they serve is nothing short of amazing and I am thrilled to have adopted one of their so-called "Furloughed Favorites." Our labradoodle, Thai, has stolen my heart, making me a besotted, doting father all over again.

# « ABOUT THE AUTHOR »

Nick Trout graduated from veterinary school at the University of Cambridge in 1989. He is a staff surgeon at the prestigious Angell Animal Medical Center in Boston; the author of five books, including the **New York Times** bestseller **Tell Me Where It Hurts, Love Is the Best Medicine, Ever By My Side**, and **The Patron Saint of Lost Dogs**; and he is a contributing columnist for **The Bark** magazine. He lives in Massachusetts with his wife, Kathy, and their adopted labradoodle, Thai.